WHAM

Jim Brouwer

To all of the teachers who inspired me. To all of the authors of the great books that made me laugh and cry and think. To those people who care about others and the planet. Thank you, for all you have given.

Acknowledgements

First on this list are the proud, strong people from Western North Carolina that inspired the language used in this book. Of course, some of the language is just southern. And I'm sure I have butchered some of it.

"Back in the day" and "If'n a man" are great examples from folks that still believe in right and wrong and stopping in the middle of the road to chat with neighbors. And churches and parades and apple festivals and barn dances. Good folks.

Thank You so much for all the memories.

My daughter, Ariana, was an immense help with the killer book cover, editing, and making me raisin pie.

My good friend, Don Lewis, who kept pushing me to finish this book.

My uncle, Johanness, who lived on a farm all his life and painted his barn when he was 95 years young. Incredible!

These are the marvelous folks who read the proof and helped polish the book.

Ariana Brouwer

Alex Ellis

Mike Gipson

From Google Maps I see the low water bridge just outside of Boone, NC has washed away. I am sad. My hope is that the rumble of the cars crossing the wooden low water bridge in Wham will last as long as the Rump River flows.

Scarecrow

Wham Wooster knelt in the weeds of the large field.

"What's he a doin?" said Sludge

"Looks like he's a prayin," said Jeb.

"Mebbe he's hurt?"

"Nah, he's prayin," repeated Jeb.

Wham raised his arms to the sky and beckoned to the heavens. Jeb and Sludge could barely hear the pleas for help. They stood off and gave WW his time with God. Wham stopped and bowed his head to the ground.

"It looks like he's a kissin the ground," said Jeb quietly.

WW rose with the difficulty of an older man.

Jeb called out, "Dubya Dubya, how's it a goin?"

WW faced the two men and waved them closer. Jeb and Sludge smiled and came across the field of stubble and weeds.

"I's doin alright I guess."

"We's a lookin for someone ta give these fish to," said Jeb, holding up the wet burlap sack, "We's kind a tired a eatin fish."

WW looked at the two, "I ain't a lookin for no handout."

"Dadgum, WW this ain't no handout. We's just sick and tired of eatin fresh catfish all the time."

"Whal, I could see how that could happen, beins how you'uns fish all the time."

"Sometimes we hunts," said Sludge.

Jeb handed the sack to WW. Wham's arm dropped under the weight.

"Whoa, there's a bunch a fish in here."

"Yep, I think we got near twenty."

"Bout time for ya ta plant," said Sludge.

"Yeah, but the driveshaft on my tractor is broke and I ain't got no money ta fix it," said WW, "Even if'n my tractor id run I ain't got no money for fuel and even if'n I had money for fuel, I ain't got no money for seed this year."

"How old is that tractor?" said Jeb.

"It's a 48 Farmall."

The three men looked off across the field, down the road next to the Rump River. Turkey vultures hopped about in a circle and picked at a deer carcass. The windmill on the top of the hill groaned as the vane moved away from the breeze, the blades spun slowly, flicking sunlight, the pump arm raised and lowered with a rhythmic "reek....reek."

Sludge tried to look for the good, "Ya gots the biggest maple tree in Spasum County. In the fall people drive up here and stop in the middle of the road just ta look at her and take pictures."

Wham wore a sad smile, "The trees a dyin. Ever year its gots less branches. It used ta shade the shed real good in the summer...but not so much no more."

"Ya might could get a loan ta get a goin again," offered Jeb.

"I ain't a borrowin. Ya starts borrowin and ya just end up a sliden further backerds."

"Well, what's the worst that could happen," said Sludge.

Jeb raised one eyebrow and looked at Sludge.

"Whal," said WW, "I guess the house could burn down and Red and the kids could leave me. I could get a stroke and be paralyzed on one side like ol man Harper or I could..."

"Ya house ain't got no lectric problems, does it?"

"Nope."

"Ya kids don't play with matches, does they?"

"Nope."

"Ya got lightnin rods on the house, don'tcha?

"Yep."

"Whal, why in devil would ya house burn down?" said Sludge.

"You's the one that asked what's the worst that could happen."

"Dadgum, you's a gloomy Gus. Ya needs ta quit thinkin bad and start thinkin good. Ya needs ta smile."

"I ain't got nothin ta smile bout."

"Whata ya talkin bout? Is ya family healthy?" said Sludge.

"Yeah, we's been blessed with good health."

"And ya got enuf ta eat?"

"Yup, we got a pantry full a food."

"And ya got a sack a fish."

"Yup."

"And ya kids is smart."

"Yep, both Willie and Willis is real smart. They knows all bout usin a computer."

"And ya got a whole valley full a folks that care bout ya."

Wham swallowed, "Yup, the best folks in the whole world."

"Whal then," said Sludge, "Sounds like things is purty good."

"Dadgum," said WW, "Dadgum, dadgum. Ya just don't know, do ya? I ain't got money for taxes this year. I could lose the farm. My kids ain't had no new shoes in two years. I buys em extra big so they can grows into em."

Sludge looked at WW with his head bent low. "When Gramma Staggers was a girl bout ten or twelve, her daddy, Stanley, had a big ol bull and that ol bull started a lookin at the neighbors cows and gettin ide'ers. Whal after a while he found his way through the fence."

WW lifted his head and listened intently.

Sludge continued, "Whal the neighbor man got all upset and sent one a the help over and told Stanley to come get his bull. Gramma Staggers was the only one at home so Stanley told her she had ta go along and help get the bull. Gramma said she felt real important. Whal they jumped in the Model T pickup and off they went ta get the bull. Gramma Staggers said the ol pickup rattled so loud ya had ta yell ta get heard."

WW smiled, "My granddaddy had one of them pickups."

"Now where was I," said Sludge, "Oh yeah, Stanley chased the bull around the pasture and finally lassoed him. He led the bull to the truck and jumped in the back and told Gramma to drive. Gramma hadn't driven but a couple a times in her life but she said she felt big bein asked to drive. She ground the truck into gear and took off. The ol bull trotted faster and faster to keep up. He started bawlin and Stanley started yellin ta slow down. Gramma shifted gears and the bull's feet barely touched the ground. Stanley thought of lettin the bull go but didn't want ta chase him down again so he hung on. The bulls tongue hung off ta one side and his eyes got bigger with each step. By now Stanley was a screamin. The bulls sides heaved in and out and his nose blew snot. When they pulled into the yard Stanley kept a screamin, 'Slow down, stop, slow down, gull darnet,' even after the truck come ta a stop."

WW and Jeb were chuckling.

"The bull weaved side ta side a lookin like he was a gonna fall over. When Stanley saw they was stopped he yelled at Gramma a askin why she didn't slow down. She tolt him she dint hear him," Sludge grinned, "Gramma said that bull never went a courtin again."

Jeb laughed and crinkles appeared at the corners of Wham's eyes and then his snicker grew into a hearty laugh.

"I gots ta sit down," said WW. He sat and continued to chuckle."Thad make me quit jumpin the fence."

The three men sat down in the weeds and could no longer see the vultures.

"Lookee here," said Sludge, "A jonquil."

Sludge reached out and pulled the weeds out from around the yellow flower.

"That's a daffodil," said Jeb.

"Gramma Staggers says they's jonquils."

"They's daffodils."

"Jonquils."

"Daffodils."

A hint of a smile came on WW's weathered face. "I love flowers," said WW.

"Yep," said Sludge, "Flowers is real nice. Ain't a woman round that won't give ya some sugar when ya bring em some flowers."

"Theys a bunch a daffodils up on top a the hill," said Jeb.

"Jonquils," said Sludge.

"Yep, that's where the old homestead was," said WW, "Great gramma Wooster planted em up there. If'n somethin don't turn around I ain't gonna get ta see em next year.

Wham spotted another jonquil, pulled the weeds and let the sun get to it.

"Spring's the worst," said Wham, "Then again mebbe summer's the worst. Come ta think a it, mebbe fall's the worst. Hard ta say. The birds come eat the seed in the spring. It's like they can smell the seed and they peck it outta the ground. Then what's left ta come up the hoppers and mice eats. Then fall comes and the coons and deer and possums and ever other critter eats at night and then I ain't got nothin ta sell at my produce stand." The three gazed at the produce shack near the road. "Then ya sits around all winter, broke, a waiting for spring. I ain't never got no money for Christmas presents." WW looked away.

"Sludge and I been a talkin in the River Chairs and the ways we sees it ya needs ta work less."

Fire came into WW's eyes, "What the hell ya talkin bout. I's close ta losin the farm and you'uns tellin me I needs ta work less." Wham shook his head in disgust. "I ought ta stomp a mud hole in ya and walk it dry."

"Whoa down now. Let's not get are panties in a wad," said Jeb, "If'n what you's a doin ain't a workin ya needs ta do somethin else. Ya needs ta go the other way…It's like fishin in the same fishin hole and never catchin no fish. Ya needs ta change fishin holes."

"Yep," said Sludge, "And sometimes a man needs ta change bait. A man oughta use nightcrawlers sometimes, maggots sometimes, grasshoppers sometimes, minners sometimes. Ya needs ta keep the fish a guessin."

"Sometimes a man has too much sweat in his eyes ta see anything," said Jeb.

"I hate when sweat gets in my eyes," said Sludge, "It stings real bad."

"Yep," said Jeb, "God don't want ya eyes ta sting."

Wham's jaw was hard and he looked at the dirt. "I sweats most ever day. All you's a doin is makin me mad. Ya ain't got a family ta feed and bills ta pay."

"Ya's right bout that," said Jeb, "But we gots what most people don't got. We gots time ta think bout things. Most people is so caught up in the race they don't have time ta stop and think bout what could be." Jeb paused, "Wham, what's ya dream?"

"I ain't had a dream in a long time. Red used ta call me the big dreamer and loved me for it. But my dreams don't never come ta nothin and now...I's....I's fraid ta dream."

"A man's gots ta have a dream," said Sludge.

"What's my dream?" said Wham, "All I want is enuf money ta keep my farm."

"That ain't no dream," said Jeb, "A dream is who ya really wants ta be. It's the best thing ya ever thought bout doin."

"I love bein a farmer," said WW, "I just ain't no good at it. I love workin with my hands, makin stuff grow and buildin stuff. I built all them thar birdhouses up and down the road. Sometimes I wish I had a woodshop and could make stuff."

A smallish breeze rippled the grass, the windmill "reeked" a bit faster, and the men could smell the Big Bog.

"Ya seen the track of the super possum?" said Sludge.

"Not since last fall. The night afore I was gonna harvest my goobers he come and tore up half my field. People don't believe he's real, so I quit talkin bout him."

"How big ya reckon he is?" said Sludge.

"He's gots ta be at least four or five foot tall."

"I's thinkin he's bigger, mebbe seven or eight foot tall," said Sludge.

"Dadgumit, there ain't no super possum," said Jeb.

"Splain them tracks we saw," said Sludge.

Jeb was silent for a while. "Me and Sludge is been dreamin bout buildin the worlds biggest scarecrow and we just never seem ta get round ta it. Now, if'n ya'd put up the largest scarecrow people id come from miles around ta see it. Ya could charge, say, fifty cents a head."

"Twenty five cents," said Sludge.

"Fifty cents."

"Twenty five cents."

WW interrupted, "I ain't got nothin ta build no scarecrow outta."

"Stays here a second," said Jeb. He ran to the top of the knoll, close to the windmill. "Rightcher is where it needs ta be."

"What needs ta be?" said Wham.

"The scarecrow." Jeb stretched his arms to the sides and smiled.

"Majin the biggest scarecrow in the whole world," said Sludge, "Hoooweee, makes a man want some ambition ta just up and build im."

Jeb came back down the hill. "What if...what if," said Jeb and then he let the, what if ,linger, "What if'n we built the worlds biggest possum scarecrow."

"How big?" said Sludge.

"Ten foot," said Jeb.

"Twelve foot," said Sludge.

"Twenty foot," said Wham.

Jeb and Sludge looked at Wham. "If'n youuns gonna talk nonsense I might as well make the possum bigger."

"If'n the possum was twenty foot big ya might could see it from one a them planes a goin into the Myrtle Beach airport," said Jeb.

"I ain't got nothin ta make no scarecrow outta," repeated WW.

"Mebbe he could have a lucky hat," said Sludge.

"And mebbe he'd wave his lucky hat at folks," said Wham.

"Hoowee, now ya talking," said Sludge.

"Dadgum, and how in the devil is a man gonna make him wave his lucky hat?" said Wham.

The windmill "reeked" as the pump arm stroked up and down. The three men turned their heads to the windmill.

"Ya ain't a thinkin what I's a thinkin, is ya?" said Jeb.

"Lookee thar," said Sludge, "We could just hook up his arm a holdin his hat ta the windmill."

"Id be like a giant whirligig," said Jeb.

"I still ain't got nothin ta make a twenty foot possum outta," said Wham.

"Whal, two minutes ago we dint have a lucky hat or a way ta wave it and now we do. We just needs ta think bout it some more," said Sludge, "It'll come."

The three sat in the weeds a few more minutes.

"I's got fish ta clean," said Wham as he stood up, "I needs ta go ta the house."

"WW, we'uns gonna figger this thin out."

"Yep," said Sludge, "I sees a super possum a wavin his hat with one arm and holdin a fishin pole with the other."

"And he's a smilin," said Jeb.

Wham stood for a moment and listened to the windmill, "He could be a standin in a big ol' field a flowers."

Jeb and Sludge smiled.

"Thanks for the fish," said WW.

"Thars plenty more where that came from," said Jeb.

"Ya tell Red and the kids, hey," said Sludge.

WW walked down the hill towards the road with the sack of fish. When he got to where the rusted wire fence sagged, he stepped over and then looked back. Jeb and Sludge were gone; the windmill faced the wind and creaked merrily.

Δ

"Somethin's up," said Red, "Whatcha thinkin bout."

"Ain't nothin up," said Wham.

"Ya ain't a tellin me thar ain't nothin up, I heard ya hummin while ya was cleanin them fish."

"Can't a man hum without somethin bein up?"

"Ya ain't hummed in the last two years."

Wham stood still and looked at his wife. He studied her eyes. "Has it been that long?"

"Yep, I thought sometimes ya was dead."

"I's been worried and I couldn't see the good."

"What's changed?"

"Jeb and Sludge gots me ta thinkin, that's all."

"Oh garsh, ya been a talkin ta them two. That can't be good."

Wham smiled broadly, "Ya got that right. Ya member them big ol' possum tracks we saw last fall?"

Red hesitated and looked hard at her husband, "Yep."

"Whal, them boys was talkin bout the super possum and sayin how I needs ta build a super possum and people id come for miles ta see the super possum. They was a sayin the super possum id need ta be twenty foot tall."

The screen door banged and Willis and Willie came into the kitchen. "What's for supper?" said Willis.

"Fish," said Red.

"It's been forever since we had fish," said Willie.

"Jeb and Sludge gave us a whole sack full a catfish."

Red put the first filets in the hot grease and they spattered loudly.

Δ

An owl hooted and Red snuggled up against her husband's back.

"Ya still awake," she whispered.

"Yep."

"Wham, ya knows I loves ya."

"Yep, ain't too many women id put up with the likes a me."

Red reached for his hand and squeezed it. "I's thought and thought and then it kind a came ta me. I wantcha ta have ya dream. I wantcha ta hum some more.

If'n buildin a super possum il make ya happy then I say we build him."

Wham sobbed and Red rubbed his back. "Sides, what's the worst that could happen."

Wham sniffled, "Whal, we could go broke."

"We's already broke."

"Yep."

"Tell me agin bout the flowers."

"We'd plant flowers all the way from the road, up the hill ta the super possum. They'd be crocuses early and then jonquils and daylilies and irises and forsythia bushes and mebbe lilac bushes for smell. We could plant blueberries sos folks id have something ta munch on. We might even give em little baskets ta put the blueberries in."

Red kissed his back and Wham pulled her hand to his lips and kissed her fingers.

Mebbe Someday

Red signed the permission slips, and the two red headed kids ran out the door to the school bus. The screen door banged shut.

"Where they a headed this time?" said Wham.

"They's a goin ta Myrtle Beach to the aquarium."

Wham shook his head and smiled. "We ain't never been ta the aquarium, you and me. Mebbe someday..."

Red smiled, went over and kissed Wham on the forehead. "That's what I like ta hear. I got my dreamer back."

Wham smiled and got up from the kitchen table. He put his coffee cup on the counter and hugged his wife hard. Then he picked her up and swung her around the kitchen. When he set her lightly down they looked into each other's eyes. Wham's eyes glistened. "I need ta git."

"Where ya a goin?"

"To the fields and mebbe ta see Jeb and Sludge."

Red handed Wham a paper bag. "Ain't much in there."

He smiled, "I don't need much...I got you and the kids."

She hugged him with her red hair against his chest. "You'ins mine," she said softly.

"And you'ins mine."

Wham reached for the screen door handle and stopped. "Good luck at the doctor's office."

Red smiled, "All they's a gonna do is clamp my boobs in a vice and shoot pictures of em."

"Can I get copies of the pictures?"

Red grinned and pushed Wham out the screen door. "And don't come back, ya hear me."

"Wild horses couldn't drag me back in there."

They looked at each other one more time. Wham turned and walked down the dirt road. When he got to the bend he looked back over his shoulder and waved. Red waved back. She stood a few moments, then raised her right hand and touched her left breast.

Δ

Wham found Jeb and Sludge and Happy at the wood bridge just as the last of the river wisp disappeared and the sun touched the rocks on the west edge of the river. Wagging his tail Happy ran to Wham. "How's it goin Happy?" The red dog with one eye and one ear responded with a wuff and more intense tail wagging.

Jeb and Sludge took turns lifting their bobbers and bait from the water and placing the bait upstream again.

"Come set a spell," said Jeb.

Wham looked up the river and took a deep breath. "It don't seem right ta not be workin."

"We's workin," said Sludge with a smile, "we's fishin."

"Most people don't call that work."

"Well, somebody's gots ta catch the fish," said Jeb.

Sludge's bobber dipped below the surface, and he set the hook. The cane pole bent deep and then danced with the weight of the runaway catfish. Sludge maneuvered the catfish to the bridge and lifted him from the water. The catfish flipped off.

"Dadgumit," said Sludge.

Wham and Jeb smiled.

"Sometimes the catfish wins," said Jeb.

"He's probably a purty happy catfish," said Wham.

Happy wuffed at Wham.

"Here," said Sludge. "Ya need ta fish a while." Sludge stood up and handed the cane pole to Wham.

Wham's nose wrinkled up. "When's the last time you'uns took a bath?"

"Why?" said Sludge looking at Wham.

"Whal, you'uns smell just a bit gamey, like somethin died."

"That's dead possum smell," said Jeb. "We been a gettin our maggots from that there dead possum on River Road."

"Maggots?"

"Yep, that's what we been using for bait," said Sludge. "Ain't nothin better for catchin bream and they's purty good for catfish too."

Sludge reached down, grabbed a plastic soda bottle and shook out a couple of off-white wigglers and threaded them on the hook. Wham gulped.

"Set down and fish," said Sludge. "I'll go get me another pole. Hold it." He stuck his index finger in his mouth and then held it up to test the wind. "Ya need ta set on that side a Jeb."

"I might hafta stick ta farmin." Wham sat down upwind of Jeb and plopped the bobber in the water.

"We'll be right back," said Sludge. Happy and Sludge took off down the bridge, Happy peeing on each bridge post as they went.

"How's the wife and kids?" asked Jeb.

"They's good. The kids went ta the aquarium in Myrtle Beach today."

"I always wanted ta see them big ol sharks."

"Yep, mebbe someday me and Red'll take a day and do that."

A bullfrog "onk"ed. "That thars a big ol bullfrog," said Jeb.

"Ya can tell the size a the bullfrog from the way he croaks?"

"Yep, the bigger ones gots real low voices, kinda like Tennessee Ernie Ford."

Wham chuckled. An egret of stark white, trailing its legs, flew over the bridge.

"Them's the whitest birds," said Jeb. "They's so white, they's outta place, kinda like a patch a snow in the summertime."

"It don't snow much here," said WW.

"We had snow back three, four years ago. Man, it was a purty snow, big ol flakes. I come down and sat rightcher and watched it till my butt got cold. All them rocks got white, and the mistletoe looked like white blankets hangin in the trees."

Quiet descended on the bridge, and the two men listened to the stream talk. Doves cooed on the power lines along River Road. A train whistle came from the direction of the town of Bump. Sunlight inched across the bridge, touched the men and worked its way down their worn blue overalls.

Wham glanced over and saw that Jeb slept. Wham smiled, closed his eyes and thought of Red and the field of yellow flowers.

Her cheeks were full of color and her red hair cascaded down across the front of her egret white sun dress. Children ran on the paths and splashed in the river. The grinning possum waved his cap merrily.

"Wha...what the...what the heck." The cane pole jerked out of WW's hands, hit the water and headed downstream.

"Now ya gots ta run down to the shallers and get it back," said Jeb.

Wham got up and watched the cane pole being pulled this way and that and occasionally the handle end would rise up off the water as the fish tried to pull deeper.

"He'll get tired in a bit and then the pole il pull him downstream."

Wham trotted to the end of the bridge and then down River Road till he found an opening through the bushes to the river. He rolled up his overalls, waded into the shallow water and waited. The cane pole traveled back and forth across the water.

Jeb yelled, "That's a pretty good fish. He don't want ta give up."

The pole drew close and Wham grabbed the end. The pole throbbed and dipped with each surge. Wham would draw the fish near and the fish would run again. Each time the pull was less, and finally, Wham led the fish into the shallows. The catfish's gills flared but the fish had no fight left. Wham grabbed the fish behind the gills and hefted him for Jeb.

"Oooweee, he's gotta be three, mebbe four pounds. That's a dandy," yelled Jeb.

Wham put the fish down, picked up a rock and bashed it on the head. The fish shuddered and was still.

As Wham walked back to the bridge, he noticed a patch of daffodils amongst the weeds and then another small group of the yellow flowers across the road.

WW set the cane pole down on the bridge. "I best be gettin home with this fish."

"Yep, that thars a real nice one. Feed ya whole family, mebbe two meals."

Wham grinned. "That was fun. Say, whatever happened to Sludge?"

"No tellin. He probably sat down somewhere and took a nap."

"What time is it?" said Wham.

"I ain't got no watch," said Jeb. Both men looked at the location of the sun and guessed it was one o'clock, give or take.

"How long did I sleep?" asked Wham.

"You'uns was out a good while. Two cars come by and you didn't even move."

"That ain't right. I woulda woke up."

"Yep, Pastor Momar come by and then Pudge come by," said Jeb.

"Pastor Momar saw me a sleepin on the bridge?"

"Yep, said he was gonna do a sermon on slothfulness."

"Oh, criminetlies." Wham shook his head. "I gotta git. Thanks, thanks for everthin."

"C'mon back tomorrah night, we's goin frog giggin."

"I think I got some work ta do on the place tomorrow. But thanks. Sides, I gots ta figger how ta build the giant possum scarecrow outta nothing."

Jeb beamed and watched as Wham walked proudly down the bridge with his fish. When Wham was out of sight, Jeb yelled down through the bridge's wood boards. "OK, ya can come out now."

Sludge climbed up on the bridge. "Dadgum, my feets bout ta freeze off."

"Ya shoulda seen how proud he was a that fish. Ya ain't much for ide'ers but that was a good one."

"Yep, he'll be talkin bout that fish for a week. Ya don't think Uncle Seizure il miss that fish from his pond, do ya?"

"He might. What say we catch a big ol carp and put it in his catfish pond?"

Sludge grinned, "We ain't really stealin his fish if'n we put one back."

"Ya got that right." Jeb continued, "How bout one night we catch all his big catfish and swap em with little catfish?"

"There'd be a lot a screamin and cussing with our names in there...pretty good ide'er though."

"What's that bag a settin there?"

"Oh heck, Wham forgot his lunch."

Sludge peered in the sack. "It ain't but one slice a bread with some jelly.

Innernational Space Station

The fire had burned down to coals when Happy barked at the darkness.

"Who's thar," said Sludge.

"Willie Wooster."

"C'mon, join us," said Jeb. The lanky young man's shadow got large as he approached the fire. "Pull up a chair."

"We gots fila munyawn hot dogs," said Sludge.

Willie smiled, "I'd like a fila munyawn hot dog."

Sludge skewered a hot dog on a forked stick while Jeb blew on the coals and added some wood. Sparks floated into the night sky.

Sludge handed Willie the hot dog on a stick and sat back down. "Whatcha gonna look for tonight?"

The fire reflected in Willie's eyes, "The International Space Station."

"The innernational space station?"

"Yes sir. The website said it would be visible between ten and eleven in the north quadrant if the sky was clear."

Jeb, Sludge, and Happy lifted their faces upwards. "Good night for seeing stars," said Jeb.

Willie took a bite of his hot dog.

"Do ya really think you'uns gonna see it?"

"If it's clear I'll see it. Someday...."

"Someday, what?"

Willie looked away and the question hung heavy until a bullfrog croaked on the river. Happy looked toward the road and cocked his head. Jeb glanced in that direction and then back to the fire.

Sludge got up, "I'll be back in a minute," and he went inside the small school bus. Soon he came to the fire with a small cardboard box. "I found these a couple a years ago up near the Big Bog. Hunter probly lost em and I ain't never used em. They needs ta get some use," and Sludge handed the box to Willie.

Willie opened the box and pulled out a pair of binoculars. Willie swallowed hard, "I can't, I can't take these from you. My dad said I can't take something without giving something back and well..."

"He's right. Ya needs ta earn most a whatcha git in life. Let's see now."

"I knows," said Jeb, "Ya can pick blackberries and take em to Miss Chatty. Then she'll make us a pie and then we'll be all square."

"How many blackberries?"

"A five gallon bucket full. That way Miss Chatty can can some or put em in the freezer."

"It's a deal." Willie extended his hand to Sludge, "Thank you."

Willie put the binocular strap over his head. "I have to go meet the International Space Station."

"Happy, go with Willie, make sure he don't get lost up on the ridge." Happy wagged his tail and headed for the dirt road that switchbacked past the churches and led to the top of the hill and the stars.

Δ

A few minutes after Willie and Happy left, Jeb called out, "Is that Wham Wooster out there?"

"It might be and it might not be."

Jeb and Sludge smiled. Wham appeared at the edge of the clearing and joined the two men at the fire.

"That was mighty gracious of you'uns ta give Willie them binoculars."

"I's glad ta see them binoculars get used by a man that'll use em."

"Sometimes...sometimes I don't know what ta think of Willie. He's real smart." Wham paused and took a deep breath, "We'uns just don't see eye ta eye on a lotta thins."

"Wham, he's justa grown up."

"Yeah, but he wants thins and well..."

"What kinda thins?"

"He wants a computer, and a car...but the thin he wants most is a telescope."

Jeb poked at the fire with a stick, "Sounds like good thins for a young man ta want. He ain't inta drugs or drinkin or smoking or shootin out lights with a bb gun or smashin mailboxes."

Sludge added, "Or blowin up thins with dynermite."

"You'uns right. I just wisht they was a way he could earn some money...but they ain't no jobs here."

"Sounds like we needs ta go on a thinkin trip," said Sludge.

"Yep, sounds like thinkin trip time," said Jeb.

"Thinkin trip time?"

"Yep, like we's all been a thinkin bout how to build the Super Possom. The more we thinks and the more thinkers we gots the more thinkin power we has. Everbodies gots ide'ers, we just need em ta come ta the top of the water so's we can see em."

"So's ya thinks that a man can just think hisself where he wants ta go?" said Wham.

"Whal, I wanted Willie ta have them binoculars but I just couldn't give em to him, he had ta earn em. Sos we traded blackberries for binoculars. He went from not having binoculars ta having binoculars."

"I'll make sure he picks those blackberries."

Jeb looked at the poor farmer, "When you was his age did ya like ya ma and pa gettin on ya bout everthing?"

Wham looked deep into the embers, "I's just tryin ta get him ta do right."

Sludge said, "Willie's bout the best kid in the whole valley."

Wham smiled, "He is, ain't he."

"We only gots one smoked catfish hot dog left?"

"That sounds good."

The night was honking bullfrogs, cicadas, an owl, a campfire overlooking the Rump River, and ide'ers.

An "Eeeehaaaa" and a dog bark came down from the ridge.

The three men grinned. "Mebbe the aliens got him," said Sludge.

"Thar ain't no aliens," said Jeb.

"Is."

"Ain't."

"Is."

"Ain't."

"Mebbe," said Wham, "Willie thinks they might be."

The Start

"Wud the doctor say?" asked Wham.

"She won't know nothing for a couple a days. She'll call me If'n she wants me ta come back in."

"I got started," said Wham.

"Tell me about it."

"Dint know where ta start. Hard ta go from nothin," Wham scratched his head, "This ain't like farmin. And they's two thins goin on. I's feel real bad bout the farm. I feels like I's a quitter, like I's failed..."

"You ain't no quitter. That much I know. Ain't no one in this valley tries hardern you."

"I always thought if'n a man worked hard he'd make it. And that's what hurts the most. The soils wore out, the tractors wore out, and," Wham hesitated, "I's wore out and I ain't got a thin ta show for it."

Red could feel the man she loved falling away and she hurried to catch him. "What's the other thin that's a goin on?"

"I's scared...real scared this ain't a gonna work. Folks already talks bout me and the giant possum. Dadgum, I's feels like I's running down a rat hole."

"Ya said ya gots started. Wud ya do?"

"I started in by climbin the windmill."

Red's eyes widened, "You'uns afraid a heights."

"I tied a rope round me and worked my way up."

"Why'd ya climb the windmill?"

"I was a lookin for a good place ta commit sewercide."

Red slugged Wham in the arm.

Wham rubbed his arm, "Dang you'uns hit hard."

"You aint a leavin me till I tell ya ya can leave me."

"You'uns always was hard ta get along with."

"Why'd ya climb the windmill?"

"Just ta see what I could see from up there."

"And?"

"Nice view."

"Yep," said Red, "Ain't no need ta commit sewercide cuz I's gonna choke ya ta death."

"Lets see now. Crazy man that sees giant possum strangled by Red Rump River Valley strangler."

"Sos I's gots a red rump?"

"Uh, mebbe."

"I's glad ya ain't a writer. You'uns takes way too long a tellin a story."

Wham went to the stove and opened the oven door, pulled out his creation, and handed it to Red.

"It's a whirligig," she said.

"I used what I had," said Wham.

Red spun the blades on the windmill and the little hat on the end of the wire waved back and forth."

Red set the whirligig on the kitchen table and wrapped her arms around Wham.

"We's gonna be alright, ain't we?" asked Wham.

"Yup."

Aquarium

"I ain't ev," Willis stopped short and looked to see if Mrs. Michaels had heard her. She smiled at her.

"I'm never going in the ocean," said Willis.

A ten foot shark passed over the students. "What if the glass breaks?" said one of the seventh graders.

"It won't," said Mrs. Michaels, "The engineers have calculated how strong the glass needs to be."

"How did they make the glass bend like that?"

"That is an excellent question. I really don't know. When we get back we can do some research and find out."

"What do they feed the sharks?"

Willie whispered to Willis, "Scuba divers."

Mrs. Michael's eyes twinkled. "I don't know that either. I may not know the answer but I usually know where to find the answer. And where do we get our answers?"

"Books."

"The library."

"The internet."

"Google."

"Yes, those are all good places to look for answers. And do we always believe everything we read?"

"No," said Willis, "We need to check our facts."

"That's right," said Mrs. Michaels.

"What about the Bible, Mrs. Michaels? Everything in the Bible is true," said Chelsea.

"Uhm, I'm not...now we need to move along. There is another group behind us."

"I want to stay right here forever," said Willie, "it's like a place that could never be."

"You can come back some other time."

"I don't think that will happen."

A small wrinkle showed in Mrs. Michael's brow. She looked at Willie in the eyes. "You can make it happen. If you want it bad enough you can make it happen."

Δ

Whal, I knows what I wants it ta look like. Wham spent the early morning sitting on the hillside until the sun had taken the dew, listening to the windmill spin in the cool breeze. He closed his eyes and listened hard; the windmill, the Rump River gurgle-talk melded with the weeds moving and new bees in the patches of clover giving a soft buzz.

"Dear Lord, If'n I was a bee I'd know what I was ta do. But I ain't. And now, whal, I have a dream and I don't know if'n it's rights or wrong. But I can sees it. I knows I ain't much and I's a goin where I ain't never been." Wham took a deep breath. "My knees is a shakin Lord. I feels like when the Hood brothers threw me off Deep Gorge Bridge or when I was stuck in the suckhole and just went round and round and round or when I asked Red for are first date or when I grapt holt of that lectric fence and couldn't let go." Wham shook his right hand and flexed it. "And Lord, I knows I got it good compared ta some folks. So's please hep them first." Wham stopped praying and raised his head.

A hummingbird of iridescent green hovered in front of a small yellow flower, probed it and zipped off. A small smile and then puzzlement came to Whams face. The windmill noise was absent. Wham turned his head to the windmill. The rotor with the blades clanged down the side of the metal framing, smashed into the earth and exploded. Metal blades flew into the air, suspended in the sunlight and then fell to the field.

Wham got up and walked up the hill. He picked up the vane and looked at the manufacturer's name through the rust. *If'n only I could read...Someday.* He bent down, picked up one of the blades and sighted down the edge. *Not bad.*

Most of the blades were still connected to the main hub. He studied the blades and the short metal bars that held the blades and the nuts and bolts that had rusted and fused together long ago. Four of the blades were missing and after a short search he had all of the parts but one connector bar.

"Whatcha lookin for?"

Wham gave a start and then smiled wide, "I needs one more a the bars that holts the blades tagether."

Red asked, "What's it look like?"

Wham pointed at one of the connectors. "Like that un...The windmill flew apart while I was a prayin. I was gonna use the windmill ta wave the possums cap."

Red smiled, "Don'tcha see?"

"See what?"

"The possum mighta hurt somebody. The Lord's looking out for us."

"You'uns right." Wham looked toward the shed, "Whal, how bout the broke driveshaft on the tractor?"

"Whal, mebbe he don't wantcha farmin no more. Mebbe he's got somethin better for you'uns ta do."

"I swear you'uns the craziest woman alive. If'n I dropped dead rightchere you'uns id say it was a good thing cuz...cuz..."

"Cuz the Lord wanted you'uns up in heaven."

"I ain't ready ta go ta heaven."

"When ya gonna be ready?"

"I dunno. I gots a super possum ta build."

"And a hillside of flowers ta plant," said Red, "And forsythia bushes and lilac bushes and blueberry bushes and...and..."

"I wants ta build some benches for folks ta sit on and some more birdhouses for the bluebirds and we needs some a them bushes that the butterflies likes.

"Whatcha doin out here?"

"I's come ta hep."

They stood side by side over the damaged windmill for a moment and then Red brushed Wham's hand with hers. He looked at the woman with the fiery red hair and eyes the color of her faded blue overalls. She looked up into his eyes. The bees hummed. Red gently put her hand in his. "Let's git started. What's first?"

Wham shook his head slightly, "What am I a gonna do with you'uns?"

She smiled and moved close. Her blue overalls and his blue overalls came together.

Wham spoke, "The list in my heads gitten too long. When I gits too many things ta do I ends up doin nothin."

Red giggled. "Yep, I thinks that happens ta lots a folks."

Wham looked far off.

Red knew the gaze, "Whatcha thinking?"

"I wants ta learn ta read and write. Willie and Willis can find are house from outer space on the computer and I can't read nor write." Wham dropped his head and stared at the ground.

"Ya been too busy a workin. We'uns both been too busy a workin."

"Willie ain't said ten words ta me in the last month."

"Mebbe ya needs ta take him fishin."

"All he wants ta do is go ta the liberry and play on that damned computer."

"Computer folks makes good money."

"Yeah, I know. Seems like the whole worlds gone crazy for computers. Thangs is all walkyjawed. Used ta be where a man worked ta make a livin. Now folks sits and types stuff into a computer and makes money. It just don't seem right."

"I don't think we is gonna change how the world is. We just needs ta work on what we can."

"Whal, let's git started. First, I wants ta tear down that bobwire fence but leave the fencepost. I can put birdhouses or whirligigs on em later."

The grass slowly stood up where the two sets of footprints went down the hill.

Δ

"We gots ta touch stingrays and horseshoe crabs and see scuba divers and sharks and..."

"How in the world didja touch a stingray?" asked Wham.

"They was in a small pond and they flew round and round. We gots ta sit on the edge and put our hands in the water and evertime they'd come by we'd try to touch em. They was smooth, as smooth as glass. We'uns gonna write stories about the trip. I's gonna write about the stingrays."

"Whatcha mean they flew?" asked Red.

"They's gots wings and they use their wings ta fly through the water. They's graceful as I dunno what. We'uns gonna use the computers in the library ta do research. I's gonna look up how stingrays fly."

Wham shook his head. "No one got stung?"

"Nope, Mrs. Michaels says stingrays is harmless. Said yud hafta ag...agitate em afore they'd sting ya."

Willie shook his head and rolled his eyes.

"Yessiree, that's what she said," spouted Willis.

"She said that you would have to provoke them before they would become aggressive."

"That's what I said."

"That's not what you said."

"Same thang."

Red said, "Whoa down you two. We get the point."

Willis kicked Willie under the table.

Willie exploded from his seat and shook his finger at Willis, "If'n you kick me again I'll make you eat that shoe."

"Bring it on, little brother."

Wham pushed back his chair and rose. The wood chair fell back and clattered on the wood floor. Wham's jaw was tight and his eyes focused on his son. "Willie, go outside."

Willie's shoulders fell, he pushed back his chair, and went out the screen door. It slapped the jamb.

Wham pushed through the screen door and stood on the porch. *He's one of the best kids in the valley.* Wham sighed. *Dammit, this is hard. My dad woulda... I'm not him. I never want to be him.* The under-inflated football in the corner caught his attention.

"Willie, go out and cut right."

Willie took off and as he neared the road, cut right. The spiral was in the air before he made the turn and the timing was perfect. Willie reached for the ball and pulled it in.

Tuggin or Nudgin

"The earth is too close to the sun," said Willie.

Jeb and Sludge both raised their eyebrows. "I kinda like the sun where its at," said Jeb.

Happy, Jeb, Sludge, and Willie sat on the low water bridge as the sky reddened and darkness began to soak into the valley.

"Yes, but the sun is getting hotter and eventually the earth will burn up."

"I knew it felt hotter lately," said Sludge.

Willie pushed on, "If we could nudge the earth further from the sun we could place it in a more favorable spot in the habitable zone."

"Sos we needs ta nudge the earth inta a gooder spot?" asked Sludge.

"For life as we know it to continue we will have to leave earth or move the earth further from the sun."

"So you'uns sayin that God dint put the earth in the right spot?" said Jeb.

"Uh, it was in the right spot for life to get started but the sun is aging and as it does it becomes hotter. Right now the earth is just inside the edge of the habitable zone."

"Sounds like we's in trouble again," said Sludge.

"What happens If'n we gets outta the zone?"

"We'd start sizzling like bacon."

"Ooooweee, that don't sound no good."

"How we'uns gonna move the earth? We ain't got no Superman no more."

"Well, a couple of solutions have been proposed," said Willie, "They both involve redirecting an asteroid so that as it comes by earth it gives a gentle gravitational tug."

"Is'n we tuggin or nudging?" asked Sludge. "Tuggin's pullin and nudgin's pushing,"

Willie was patient, "As the asteroid zooms by it would be tugging on the earth."

"What if'n the asteroid ain't on target?" said Jeb.

Willie grinned, "If it hits earth, we all die."

"I don't think we needs ta be a messing with tuggin or nudging the earth around," said Jeb.

"How long we got afor we burn up?" asked Sludge.

"Oh, scientists estimate about a billion years."

Happy, Jeb, and Sludge looked at Willie. "I thought you'uns was talkin like next week."

Willie grinned, "We have some time to work out the solution."

"Well in that case, I's in favor of tugging," said Sludge.

"I say we ride'er till she burns up," said Jeb.

Happy got up from between Jeb and Sludge, shook his head, and trotted off down the bridge.

Slabs

Wham spotted the piece of paper under a box of eight penny galvanized nails on top of the pile of slab lumber. *Probly a bill. Dammit! I ain't never gonna get outta debt.* He folded up the piece of paper and stuffed it in his pocket.

Wham ran his hand over one of the twelve foot long slabs. *Its.* Wham searched for his thoughts. *It's the smell and the sawmarks and the knots and the colors and lines. Its bettern most pictures.*

A breeze caught in the trees along the river and he watched the tops of the trees move about. He drew the smell of the sawmill lumber deep into his nostrils. *Pine and some oak.* There in the pile was some greenish lumber, poplar. Wham scrutinized the pile. *Had ta be a purty good sized truck...or trailer.*

If I use it, I owe Fred. Wham went into the shed and sat on the tractor. *Dang it's cold. Spring ain't never gonna get here. Oughta set it a fire.* Wham got down and stood in the sunlight at the front of the shed. *Feels good rightcher. Well, what's it gonna be, benches or birdhouses? Or sawhorses. Huh, mebbe I could make em look like horses?*

Wham pulled the handsaw off the wall of the shed. It needed sharpening and the handle was loose. He hunted for the file and a screwdriver. *Dammit, I's goin backwards again. That lumber il rot before I get it sawed. Folks just don't know how much trouble they give a man when they give him a pile of warped up slabs.* There was a touch of warmth in the air when the saw bit into the pine.

Greenpeace

"Would ya shoot the giant possum?" asked Sludge.

"If'n he was attackin me, I'd have ta shoot him," said Jeb.

"No, I mean like If'n ya saw him in the bog a huntin frogs."

"Bog an frogs rhyme." Jeb paused, "Might be a good start ta a country song."

"Would ya shoot the giant possum?"

Jeb started in, "I was a huntin the giant possum in the bog.

And all I could hear was bull-frogs.

Happy, my dog, and I was lost in the fog.

And now we's possum fritters."

Happy put a paw over his one ear. "Happy gives ya a one outta ten." Sludge repeated his question, "Would ya shoot the giant poossum?"

"I dunno. Ain't spent a lot a time thinkn bout it."

Happy looked at Jeb and then Sludge and shook his head, flapping his one ear.

"I don't think I'd shoot him," said Sludge. "Now, if'n I had a camra I'd try ta get a videa of him."

"Man, would that be something."

"Id be as good as a bigfoot videa."

"They'd do a TV show bout you and the giant possum. Thar'd be a hunert folk down here a tryin ta get a picture of him."

"They'd be a whole bunch a folks lost in the bog. They'd send out hellercopters and drones a lookin for folks. Might send in the National Guard."

"Ya don't think the giant possum id kill somebody, do ya?"

"Hard ta say. If'n a reporter id be all crippled up from snakebites he might put him outta his misery."

"Would he eat him?"

Jeb hesitated and then frowned, "Dammit Sludge, they ain't no giant possum."

"They might be. We'uns just talkin hyperdermicly."

"Yep, I'd shoot the giant possum just so's yud shut up bout him."

"What If'n theys two of em?"

"I'd shoot em both."

"It ain't right ta go round killing innorcent giant possoms. They gots a right ta live just like we'uns."

"Ya needs ta join Greenpeace and go out on a rubber boat and get et by a whale."

"That's what I figgered. You'uns all bout killin whales and giant possoms. We'uns needs ta get the giant possum on the indangered speeches list."

"He ain't indangered cuz he ain't real."

"I hope he's awright out there in the bog."

"Since they ain't real, they might be a whole family of giant possoms."

"Ooohh, wouldn't that be cool. Mebbe we need ta get T-shirts with "Don't Shoot the Giant Possoms" on it and id have a picture of a giant possum on the front."

"I ain't a wearin no T-shirt with no possum on it. That damned dogs a smilin agin."

"Happy quit that."

"He's a smilin bigger."

"He does that when he knows you'uns wrong."

"I ain't wrong."

"Is."

"Ain't." Jeb got up and stomped off across Church Ridge Road without looking both ways.

Boobs

"What did the doctor say?"

"Well, do you want the good news or the bad news?"

Wham frowned, "Just tell me what's happenin."

"I have calcification clusters in my breast."

"And."

"And they needs to do a biopsy to see if'n I gots cancer."

Wham scrutinized the knot in the pine table,"You'uns can have one of my boobs. They can do a transplant."

Red smiled, "Your boobs have hair on em. I don't think I want no hairy boob."

"Whal, don't say I dint offer."

Red continued to smile. "What If'n I need a brain transplant, would ya give me ya brain?"

"I'd hafta think on that one."

Red punched Wham on the shoulder.

Quiet settled inside the four walls. Wham whispered, "My brain wouldn't fit in your head. It's too big."

"Just cuz you'uns head is big don't mean ya brain is big. There might be a lot of empty space inside that head."

"You'uns right bout that. Thins ain't always what they seem. I might have a little ol bird brain inside this big ol head."

"What other body parts is ya willing to give up if'n I need em?"

"I could give ya a couple a fingers or toes."

"It's just a biopsy," said Red.

"We won't know till we know."

"Most times we fret over thins that don't never happen."

"Yep."

The Scream

"Let's go hunt for the giant possum," said Sludge.

"I ain't a runnin around in the bog after no make believe giant possum. Sides we got fish ta catch," said Jeb.

"We can catch fish anytime."

Δ

Sludge and Happy angled off the road towards the Big Bog. "Now there ain't nothin ta be scared of."

Happy slowed his pace behind Sludge and went on full alert; his one ear, one eye, and his long nose magnified each sound, sight, and smell.

"Just stick close and make sure ya member how ta get us outta here."

Blah, blah, blah.

A pervasive stench surrounded the two and Happy curled up his nose.

"If'n I was a giant possum this is where I'd live. Gots plenty a food and ain't nobody gonna come in here and bother ya."

Happy shook his head. Does he ever hear himself talk?

There in the stench, the parts per million, were tiny bits of animal smells, most of them familiar and Happy tried to sort it out.

As Sludge started to wade into the muck he let Happy catch up. He whispered, "Now, ya gots ta be real quiet, lessen ya see the giant possum, then ya can bark."

Bark? Are you insane? If I see a giant possum I'm outta here.Way outta here. You'uns gonna see a dog with wings.

The swamp with its ancient trees held flits of movement and half-noises. Small birds crisscrossed in the branches. Frogs croaked, running together in a solid din, broken by small splashes of turtles dropping off logs. The far off scratching could be a bear or a giant possum sharpening his claws on a tree.

Sludge took a few quiet steps, stopped, and slowly turned his head from side to side. He became one with the trees and water and imperceptible movements. Time and progress slowed, a blending of man and dog and muck. Baby turtles barely able to tread water raced past Sludge.

Happy smelled and then spotted the deer. He nudged Sludge and pointed. One of the deer flicked its ear and Sludge pieced it together. He reached down and petted Happy.

Sludge wasn't sure how big the bog was; only that it seemed forever big when you were in it.

The muck was deeper here and a chill ran up Sludge's back. It was too quiet and Sludge stood still much longer. The frogs seemed very far away. The trees were empty.

Happy was concerned. He no longer heard the scratching.

The two waited, the three eyes searching for anything out of place or a slight movement.

A whiff of something heavy and nauseating filled Happy's nose.

Sludge whispered, "Sorry bout that."

Geez oh pete, I'm not going to be able to smell anything for a week. Happy's eye watered. Great, now I can't see or smell.

The sloshing of water came from two directions and then the scream shot through Sludge and Happy.

Sludge passed Happy as they neared the edge of the bog and then Happy passed Sludge as they broke out onto Rump River Road. Happy's legs cramped up, he listed to one side, and keeled over. Sludge involuntarily laughed.

He picked up the red dog and walked quickly up the hill to where Wham was working.

Sludge laid the dog down in the grass. "That had ta be one a the funniest things I ever seed," said Sludge.

"What's that?" asked Wham.

"We'uns was bein chased by the giant possum and his two right legs quit on him and he fell over."

Sludge massaged Happy's right legs.

"Did ya see the giant possum?"

"Whal, not exzactly. They might be two of em. We heard water splashing and then one of em screamed a gruesome scream." Happy nodded.

"The giant possum screamed?" asked Wham.

"Horriblest thin ya ever heard."

"That ain't good. Now we'uns gots ta add screaming ta the giant possum."

"A screamin giant possum waving a hat id sure make me stop the car. Be real good for bizness."

Sludge looked around, "How'd ya get the weeds cut?"

"There was a old scythe hanging in the shed, probly put thar by my grandpa."

"That's a lot of work," said Sludge.

"Felt good oncet I got a goin. I was swingin and thinkin...it was like I wasn't workin."

"Ya was in the zone. I gets in the zone when I fishes or sits on the bridge...or when I's drivin. It's like I's there but I ain't there. Jeb don't like my drivin."

"Yep, I was in the zone a cuttin them weeds but not cuttin them weeds. I cut them weeds for a long time. The next morning I couldn't get outta bed I hurt so bad."

"Ya gots ta be careful with the zone."

"What made ya go in the bog?"

"Happy and I was a lookin for the giant possum. We might wanna get him on the indangered speeches list sos folks don't shoot him. And I's gonna get a T-shirt that says, "Don't Shoot the Giant Possum" on it."

"That might be real good advertizin," said Wham. "Whoa down, if'n we get some t-shirts, Willis could do the art work."

"And we'd put a picture of a giant possum on the back with him a snarlin or screamin."

"Well, we might just put him a smilin sos folks id like him."

"That's a good ide'er."

"We don't really know where this is a goin, do we?" said Wham.

"It don't matter."

"It don't matter? It's scarin the hell outta me. Whatcha mean it don't matter? It matters ta me an my family. I gots ta make some money soon."

"Whoa down, let's not get all twisted up," said Sludge, "I's just a sayin that sometimes thins don't always walk a straight path."

"Happy's smilin."

"Are ya all better?"

Happy did a feeble shake "no."

Sludge smiled, "Dadgum you dog, you'uns ain't pullin that on me, you'uns fakin. Ya needs ta get up and walk it off."

Happy rolled his head back and let his tongue hang out of his mouth.

Sludge and Wham grinned. "Ya gots ta be the craziest dog ever," said Sludge. "Don't pay him no never mind."

Happy rolled on his back, put his legs in the air, closed his one eye, and continued to dangle his tongue off to one side.

"I hopes rigamortis sets in," said Sludge.

The red dog got a tiny grin at the end of his mouth. Wham shook his head, "I ain't never seen a dog play possum."

Sludge touched Wham on the elbow. "Oh my gawd, it's the giant possum."

Happy did a corkscrew and jumped up, head swiveling in all directions.

"Yep, now yas all better."

"It's a miracle," said Wham. Both men chuckled.

Sludge sat down, facing the river. Happy sat down next to him. "It's a startin ta look real nice. Takin down that bobwire fence was a real good ide'er. What's out thar on the fence post?"

"Whirligig that waves a little hat. It ain't the best but it works."

"And I likes the rocks round the jonquils. Where ya getting the rocks?"

Wham sat down. "From the pile a rocks that runs down the property line atween the Rumps and the Woosters."

"So is some of them Rump rocks?"

"Mebbe."

"So's you'uns a rock thief."

"Ya needs ta call the sheriff."

"So ya granddad took all the rocks outta the field and now you'uns puttin em back."

"Yep, thought bout that when I was a doin it. I could see granddaddy a lookin down on me and yelling from heaven, "What the hell are ya a doin?! You'uns gots ta be the dumbest clod a dirt in Spasum County."

Sludge stifled a laugh. "You'uns ain't your granddad. This is your life. Ya needs ta do it your way and if'n moving the rocks back is ya way then ya can't listen ta nobody else.

"Them rocks is gonna be wore out."

Sludge laughed.

A breeze came up the valley and the sun was warm. Bees worked on the flowers. "Whatcha gonna name you'uns new project?"

"I ain't thought bout a name. Uh, Disneylands taken."

"Ya need a name and a sign and something ta give ta folks."

"I needs ta make some money."

"Ya got it backerds. Ya needs ta ask what ya can give folks...something special."

"I ain't got much ta give."

"Dang. Ya got a start on a place that folks will want to come and spend the day. You'uns gonna give em a day they will talk about. Can't do no bettern that."

"I had a crazy ideer," said Wham. The words were stuck and didn't want to move forward. "What if'n city folks id do the plantin. Like make em farmers. We'd give em some majic pumpkin seeds and a little spot to plant and the folks could come back just afore Halloween and get their pumpkins."

Sludge shook his head in disbelief, "Oh my gawd, that's the best ideer I ever heard. That might be bettern the invisible dumpster."

"If'n I do this, it needs ta happen quick," said Wham, "plantin season il be here in two or three weeks."

"Ya needs a name for the farm ana sign."

"Whal, its gotta have possum in the name and mebbe farm," said Wham.

Happy woofed and went on point. Both men followed the point to the edge of the bog. "Theys somethin a movin around way, way out thar. It went back in the bog."

"I dint see it," said Wham.

Both men watched where the field met the bog but there was no more movement.

"Whal, Happy and I both saw something. Ain't no tellin what it was. It was too far away."

"Ya don't reckon the giant possum eats pumpkins, do ya?" said Wham.

"Ain't no tellin what a giant possum id eat."

Happy rolled in the grass.

"Let's go listen to the river," said Sludge.

"I'uns listenin ta a crazy man, a man without a job, a man that ain't got no bills ta pay, and now he wants ta listen ta the river."

"We'uns needs ta do some figgerin. We'uns needs ideers and thar ain't no place bettern ta figger than sittin on the bridge."

Wham sighed, "I's getting closer and closer ta goin crazy. At some point thins is gotta give."

Sludge looked at the worry in Wham's eyes. He'd seen that look before, the I ain't a gonna make it look. "We got three weeks. We can do this but we needs some sortin it out and some putting it together." Sludge looked at Happy. "Let's ask Happy."

"What the..."

"Happy, this here hand is stayin here and this hand is goin ta the bridge and a listenin ta the river." Sludge winked his right eye. Happy nudged Sludge's right hand.

Wham shook his head, "And now I's takin advice from a one eyed dog."

Happy woofed at Wham and then ran towards the dirt road. Wham and Sludge followed the red dog.

Tattoo

"I wants a giant possum tattoo," said Willis.

"Ya ain't a getting no tattoo," said Wham, "not now, not never."

Willis had listened intently and smiled at the double negatives. *English might be worth something after all.*

Wham picked up on the lack of resistance and scowled, "Don't get smart with me young lady."

"You want me to be smart, don'tcha?"

Wham replied, "They's smart and they's smart alecky and yas crossin the line inta smart alecky."

"I guess I'll just have to wait until I'm eighteen to get one."

Wham sighed, shook his head, and muttered, "Dadgum."

Red smiled as she put the last dish in the drainer, "Let's see your sketches."

Willis turned over the sheets of typing paper and spread them out on the table.

"Well, we ain't a doin that one," said Wham, "it looks like a giant devil possum."

"I kind of like it," said Red.

"That one's my favorite," said Willis. "I thought we'd let folks choose which one they wanted on their t-shirts."

Wham's eyes settled on a sketch on the second row and feebly pointed to it, "The giant possum ain't got wings."

Red said, "Are you sure? It was kind of late in the evening when you saw him. Sides a giant possum with wings is scarier."

Willis crossed her arms in front of her and smiled.

Wham sighed, "It's a real good drawing. Oh, what the heck."

Red said, "If'n I was ta get a tattoo that's what I'd get."

"Where would you put it?" asked Willis.

"Mebbe someplace where folks couldn't see it."

Willis giggled. Wham scrunched up his face, "Ya ain't gettin no tattoo."

"I's over eighteen and if'n I want a tattoo I'll get a tattoo."

"Ya ain't getting no tattoo."

"Is."

"Ain't"

Willis chimed in, "What do you think of this one?"

"He looks like a hobo giant possum."

"That's what he's supposed ta be. I gave him a tin cup. And this one is a street preacher giant possum, I gave him a bible and I made him fat like Pastor Momar."

"Ya might be crossin over the line with that one. Some folks is real touchy bout religious stuff," said Wham.

"If'n they don't like it, they don't have ta buy it."

"I's just sayin, ya needs ta be real careful. We don't want ta get chased outta the valley by folks with torches and pitchforks."

Willis and Red laughed.

Wham took another look at the sketches, "Why is it that you can draw most anythin real good and I can't draw stick people?"

"Mebbe cuz I's gifted."

Wham rolled his eyes and smiled.

"We're all gifted in some way," said Red.

"I's fifty years old and I still ain't figured out what I'm gifted at."

Red bit her tongue. She would tell him later.

Moxie

Mr. Darwin opened the large wood doors to the General Store at precisely 8:00. The light traveled through the screen doors and laid long on the wide knotty pine boards. The small bell on the screen door tinkled. Willis stood for a second and let her eyes adjust.

"Mr. Darwin, how ya doin?" said Willis.

"I's good. Whatcha up to?"

"Well, its kind of a long story but I want ta make giant possum t-shirts ta advertise my dad's new farm. Here are my sketches of the giant possum that I'll be puttin on the t-shirts."

Mr. Darwin spread the sketches out on the counter. "They's purty good. You'uns got some talent. I have a hard time drawin stick people."

"My dad said the same thing. Mebbe stick people are hard to draw."

Mr. Darwin smiled, "So, what is your proposal?"

"So, well, I uh, was thinkin..."

Mr. Darwin interrupted, "So you want me to give you some t-shirts so you can do the art work and then I could sell them and we split the profit."

"Uh...."

"Well, I think it's a good ide'er. I love it when young people show some moxie."

"Moxie?"

"Yeah, I read that word last week. It means spunk or spirit." Willis smiled. "What are you going to call your new business?"

"I hadn't really thought of it too much?"

"How about Moxie Enterprises? That way when you expand into other things you don't have to rename your business." Mr. Darwin moved from behind the counter and headed for the clothes section. "What color t-shirts do you need and what sizes?'"

Things were moving too fast. "Uh, mebbe we should do one of each design and see what sells."

"A test market. I like that idea. Are you going to screen print em or airbrush em?"

"Uh, well, I was going to use one of those black marker pens."

"Hmm, that might work. Then again it might bleed on the fabric. Let's do one. What color do you like?"

"My favorite color is sunshine yellow."

Mr. Darwin grabbed a medium yellow t-shirt and went to the next aisle and pulled a black permanent marker off a hook. "You'll need a piece of cardboard to put inside the shirt. Go out on the back porch and get us a box."

Willis hurried out the back door and returned with a flattened box. Mr. Darwin pulled a box cutter knife from his pocket and cut the cardboard to size. "OK, let's see what we got."

Willis hesitated, "What if I mess it up?"

"The Wright Brothers tried lots of different wing designs before they got off the ground. Failure is good."

"They sure don't teach that in school."

"Yeah, there's a lot of things they don't teach in school."

"Go for it. Hold it, just a sec. I'm going to time you." Mr. Darwin laid his pocket watch on the counter and watched the second hand. "OK, go."

Willis steadied her hand, glanced at the sketch, and touched the marker to the shirt. A black dot appeared and then grew. Willis moved tentatively and the lines were too thick. She frowned but kept the pen moving; there was a flow and then she found her rhythm and touch. "Done."

"You'uns not done. Ya need ta sign it."

Willis smiled and put WW in very small letters on the possums cap. "Done."

"Four minutes, thirteen seconds."

Mr. Darwin propped up the t-shirt against the cash register. Then they both stood back.

Willis waited for Mr. Darwin to comment.

"What did we learn?" asked Mr. Darwin.

"The lines aren't crisp. I can't get any sharp details. The teeth and eyes aren't right. I can't do any shading to give depth."

"So, if you were giving it a grade, what would you give it?"

"A C minus maybe."

"Willis, this isn't school. You don't get a C just for trying. This is business. Would you buy this shirt?"

Willis was silent and her eyes began to water.

Mr. Darwin propped up the sketch next to the t-shirt. "You have the talent but we don't have the right tools. Also, it took too long. Time is money. You need to do a lot more research on how to put designs on t-shirts."

Mr. Darwin pulled out a yellow legal pad and a pencil. "Google or YouTube screen printing and airbrush...uh, and making stencils." He tapped the pencil on the counter and looked at the ceiling. Then he wrote some more. "Also, look up cartoon drawing or caricatures." He tore off the sheet of paper and handed it to Willis.

You have the talent.

Failure is Good.

This is business.

Moxie.

Willis swallowed, "Thanks Mr. Darwin."

"So what did I tell you to do research on?"

"Screen printing and airbrush and cartoon drawing."

"And stencils. You need to pay better attention."

"I thought you were writing these things down."

"Why should I? You just need to listen better." His eyes smiled in his oak colored face. "Do your research and then tell me what you need to get started. I want to make some money on this."

"Me too," said Willis.

"Shake." Mr. Darwin extended his hand. Willis shook his hand and headed for the door. "Take your t-shirt with you and hang it up where you can look at it."

Where's Willie?

"Where's Willie?" asked Wham.

Willis stared at her plate, "He's not coming home." Tears ran down her face, "I kicked him too many times."

Wham and Red exchanged glances. Red reached over and pulled Willis' chin up and said, "It's not your fault. Willie's just...," and she paused for a few moments, "he's just growing up. He needs some space to think about thins. He'll be alright."

Wham got up from the table and went out onto the porch. He listened to Red asking Willis about her day at school. *I gots ta be the dumbest clod a dirt that ever was. Giant possum. What the hell's wrong with me? No, not just a possum. Hell no, I'm goin ta build a twenty foot possum. Thar ain't nobody that stupid. On a scale of one ta ten you'uns a hunert and fifty.*

Red came out onto the porch. "It's gonna be alright."

"How in the hell can you say that?"

"Ya gots ta look at the good."

"Thar ain't no good."

Red touched her man, "We needs ta go for a walk."

Wham looked into the eyes of the woman he had always loved, "It ain't right. You'uns deserve bettern this, a lot better."

"I'm right where I needs ta be. Ain't no place I'd rather be."

Tears rolled down Wham's weathered face. "Dammit, dammit, dammit, dammit."

Red spoke through the screen door, "Willis, c'mon out here, we's goin for a walk."

"Are we gonna go find Willie?"

"Nope, we's just goin for a walk."

Wham wiped the tears away and stepped off the porch. Red grabbed his hand and the hand of her daughter. At first the steps were disjointed but soon they found the rhythm and walked in sync down River Road.

"I got an "A" on my paper bout the stingrays."

Red squeezed both hands, "Excellent. You need to read it to us when we get back."

Willis smiled, "We ain't...we haven't been for a walk in a long time."

As they approached the place where the fence posts held the bird houses Red remarked, "It, it looks so green...hey, theys a rock on the post where the whirligig was."

Wham shook his head, "Somebody stole my whirligig."

The three stood for a moment. "Pick up the rock," said Willis.

Wham lifted the rock and dollar bills floated to the ground. Red and Willis retrieved the money. "Somebody bought ya whirligig," said Red.

"How much we get?" asked Wham.

"Twenty two dollars."

"Ain't nobody gonna pay tweny two dollars for a whirligig made outta twigs and wire."

"Some folks likes the old timey lookin stuff. One thins for sure, ya needs ta make another one."

"The next one I'll make a lot better," said Wham.

"No ya won't. You'uns needs ta make it the same way. Somebody liked it just like it was."

Wham grinned, "That's why I ain't got rid a ya. I needs someone with good sense."

"You'uns ain't ever getting rid a me," Red raised her voice, "ya hear me."

"Ya sure is a pesky thin."

"You're not getting rid of me either," said Willis.

"You'uns both pesky thins. Worser than ticks on a dog's ear."

Red and Willis smiled and then the happiness drained away. Willis asked, "Do ya think Willie's gonna be OK?"

The Cigarette

Wham checked the fence posts along Rump River Road to see if any more whirligigs had been purchased. The dew was on the grass and his feet were cold and wet inside his boots. He could hear it and then not hear it. The mix of tire and muffler noise came and went with the corners. Uncle Seizure's old Chevy pickup slowed and stopped in the road alongside Wham. He rolled down the window with the handle. Cigarette smoke exited into the crisp morning air.

"Mornin," said Wham.

Uncle Seizure coughed and then said, "Mornin. How's it goin?"

"Well, it could be better."

"And it probly could be worse."

"I don't think so."

"Ya ain't a pushin up daisies."

"Might as well be."

Uncle Seizure didn't want to ask and yet it felt good to know that others suffered just as bad as he did, "Ya seem a bit down."

"Ain't nothin goin right. My well pump gave up on me this mornin. I knew it was gonna go, it wasn't doin right and now we ain't got water and I ain't got no money at fix it."

"I heard Red might have cancer and Willie ran off and ya truck don't run and ya tractor don't run."

"Ya ain't makin me feel better."

"Ya needs ta get a job or two or three," said Uncle Seizure.

"They ain't no jobs in the valley and my truck don't run and I ain't got money for gas."

"I might could ask if'n they needs hep at the sock factry. Then we could ride tagether and we could split the cost a gas."

"I don't know nothin bout makin socks."

"Well, it ain't easy. Ya gots ta be real pricise. Ain't nobody better at sewin up the end of a sock than I is."

"All I know is farmin."

"You'uns probly hafta go through the prenticeship program where they teach ya stuff bout runnin the machines."

"How much does it pay?"

"Minimum wage. They tolt me three fifty an hour but I think its more than that now."

"Don't seem like a whole lotta money," said Wham.

"That's why a man's got ta have two or three jobs."

"Do ya get cash?"

"Nah, they give ya a check that's got the taxes taken out and then ya take it ta the check cashin place and they charge ya ta cash it."

Wham frowned and kicked a rock on the ground.

"And they hold back the first week's pay and if'n ya gets hired at the wrong time in the schedule it might be clost ta a month for ya get ya first check for the first two weeks."

"Months a long time."

"And they makes ya sign a paper sayin ya won't join a union. If'n ya don't sign it they don't give ya the job." Uncle Seizure flicked his ash out the window. "And they don't hire just any ol body. A man's gots ta have a bunch goin on upstairs.

"And ya don't never want ta be late. They dock ya half an hour if'n ya come in late. I makes sure I's there twenty, thirty minutes early. I ain't been late in fifteen years. One mornin I had a flat tar and ya ain't never seen a man change a flat so fast. I looked like Nascar. I still got there ten minutes early."

"I's been tryin ta think a other ways ta make some money. Sludge was sayin ide'ers is the way ta make thins work when ya don't have no money."

"Sludge ain't worked a day in his life. He and Jeb don't know work from apple butter. They's gots ta be the most worthless knots on a log there ever was."

"They seem ta get by without a job."

"They'll be a day a reckonin. Someday they's gonna need a doctor real bad and they won't have no money ta pay him."

"I ain't got no money ta pay for Red's doctor bills."

"That's what I's a sayin. A man needs two, three jobs so he can pay doctor bills." Uncle Seizure coughed a ragged deep lung cough. "The factry is kinda dusty and they's a bunch a noise. We gots a stamper machine that makes a bangin noise and about eleven o'clock my eye starts ta twitch in time with the bangin. Smack Johnson lost his hand in the stamper machine. They let him take the rest of the day off with pay.

"Sometimes we get's busy and we works moren forty hours one week and then the next week we work less'n forty hours so they don't hafta pay overtime. I likes them short weeks. It lets me git caught up with the work at the house.

"For a while I had tinnitis. It's a ringin noise in ya ears. But I can't hear it no more. The wife says I talk too loud cuz I can't hear nothin. Most men couldn't do what I do. Fact is, I's lasted longer than anybody in the factry," said Uncle Seizure proudly. "A man's gots ta take care a hisself if'n he's gonna make it ta the finish line."

"Finish line?"

"That's a metterfore for gittin old and dyin." Uncle Seizure grunted, cleared his throat and hawked a brown luggie onto the road.

"I's been thinkin real hard on makin money and I ain't got it figured out."

"Ya can't think yaself inta money," said Uncle Seizure. "It ain't possible. A man's gots ta face the music and just do what needs ta be done."

"What kinda music?"

"Music's a metterfore. Music ain't music. Music is life and life is hard as nails."

"I'll give ya that."

"And when I ain't a workin, I's workin on my book, "Life is Hard and Then Ya Die.""

"Purty good name for a book."

"A man's gots ta learn how ta suffer. Ya don't whine, ya just keep er all locked up inside ya. My ol man beat me if'n I whined. He said, "I'll give ya somethin ta whine about, and he did.""

Wham kicked a small rock with his boot, "Yep."

"These kids is spoiled, bad spoiled. They ain't got no respect. They don't listen ta nobody. They's had it way too easy."

Wham was quiet and then spoke up, "My kids is purty good."

"Willie ain't gonna stay here. He's gonna run off ta college and he ain't never comin back."

"Ya might be right on that one."

"He's gonna sit in front of one a them damned computers and try ta make money. Ya can't have everbody in front of a computer and nobody workin. Somebody's gots ta do the work."

Wham sighed, "It sure ain't like it was when we was brought up."

"Mark my word, they's gonna be a day a reckoning."

"Didja get the belt or a switch?"

"Switch."

"Yep."

Uncle Seizure eyed the gold ring on Whams left hand, "Mebbe I could hep ya out. I knows well pumps kinda expensive and ya needs the money now. Why don't I just give ya thirty dollars now and you can pay me back thirty-five dollars a month from today and If'n ya don't have the money I get your weddin band."

"Nope, I ain't a riskin my weddin band, not now, not never."

"Suit yaself. Tell ya what, I'll check ta see if'n they got any jobs at work." Uncle Seizure dropped his cigarette butt onto the ground. "Good luck with the well pump."

Wham nodded. Uncle Seizure put the Chevy in gear and drove off. Wham reached down and picked up the cigarette butt. *Damn him.*

Uncle Seizure looked in the rearview mirror. *Nice wedding band.*

Wham climbed the hill, up past the windmill, to a spot near the charred rock foundation. He knew exactly where it was. When he was done he pulled up his overalls. *I hope ya die again and again and again.*

Grasshopper

"What about the twenty-three pound grasshopper?" said Sludge.

"I think they doctored up that picture," said Jeb.

"And what about the aliens a shakin hands with the President?"

"Same thin. Them pictures is all fake."

"They canst be putting fake stuff on the front page of a newspaper."

"They can too. They can put any ol thin that pops in thar heads. Sides, folks likes readin and lookin at fake stuff."

Jeb and Sludge sat in the River Chairs, looked off to the horizon, and waited. The breeze was from the north, a place of cold. "Wisht the sun id come up. Its sure a takin its time this morning."

"Funny how it does that sometimes."

"Them possum tracks in the mud down at the bog ain't fake pictures and me and Happy heard the giant possum scream. Ain't that right Happy?" Happy woofed an affirmative.

"That dog il bark at anythin you'uns tell it ta bark at."

"Will not. Happy tells the truth. Don'tcha buddy?" Happy nodded his head up and down. "See thar. Happy needs ta be on the front page of the newspaper; world's smartest dog."

"Dadgummit, he's smiling again."

"Why does you'uns have such a hard time complimentin folks and dogs?" Happy turned his head sideways and looked at Jeb.

"Most folks ain't done nothin ta compliment."

"Sounds like somebody needs a hug. Happy give Jeb a hug." Happy jumped up on Jeb and licked him in the face."

"Phht, phht, get offn me. Git off." Happy backed down.

"Now, don'tcha feels better?"

"He done spilt my coffee and I gots slobber all over my face."

"Happy, give Jeb another hug."

Happy jumped up on Jeb and licked him again. Jeb dropped his coffee cup off to the side and petted the red dog. "Aright, aright, that's enuf. Yeah, you'uns a purty good dog."

"What If'n the giant possums smarter than the president?"

"That might not be all that hard."

"Oooh, Willie says possums have maripossum thumbs just like humans got. What if'n we came from possums?"

"We dint come from no possum. Mebbe ya did, but I dint."

"What if'n they get disguises and suits and run for congress?"

"I'd vote for em."

"What If'n the giant possums are from another planet and their spaceship crashed in the Big Bog and just afore they crashed they sent out a distress signal and another spaceship with hunerts more giant possums is on the way here?"

"You'uns had too much coffee. Ya needs ta settle down."

The three sat in silence as the red sky lightened. "Ya think the giant possum sits at the edge of the Big Bog and watches the sun come up?"

"Yep, he probly sits thar and drinks his coffee and talks to the wife and then makes sure all the little possums git on the school bus."

"I hope he knows enuf ta not look straight at the sun and hurt his eyes," said Sludge.

"Mebbe we needs ta git him some sunglasses."

"Now, thars an ide'er for the Save the Giant Possum t-shirts; have him a wearin sunglasses."

Jeb chuckled. "I already tolt cha, I ain't a wearin no t-shirt with no possum on it."

"It's for a good cause."

"What the hell cause you'uns talkin bout?"

"Whal, they's two causes. We gots ta save the giant possum from distinction and it's good advertizin for Wham's new farm."

Jeb paused in thought, "I don't think Wham's gonna make it."

Sludge's eyes narrowed, "He's gonna make it."

"He ain't got nothin ta sell."

"Ya member long time ago when ya said that If'n ya don't have nothin ya needs ta come up with ide'ers."

"I said that?"

"Yep."

A sliver of orange broke the horizen. Two wood ducks whistled down the river, opened their wings, and sat down in an opening in the fog.

Gettin Wet

"OK," said Sludge, "we needs ta figger out whatcha gots ta give ta folks?"

Happy sat between Sludge and WW on the edge of the bridge facing upstream and watched the water curl around the smooth rocks.

"Lemme see," said Wham,"I gots bills ta pay, Red might have cancer, and Willie ain't come home in two days."

"Ya gots a bunch a folks that cares bout cha and Willie."

Wham pondered the "and Willie."

"Most folks gots their own problems. They don't have time ta be messin with my problems."

"Let's backer up. We'uns here ta figger out whatcha gots ta give."

"I gots a piece a ground that won't grow nothing cept weeds and the weeds is havin a hard time of it."

"That ain't right. What bout all them jonquils. Ya needs ta think good stuff."

"I gots a windmill that just fell apart."

"If'n ya says one more negatory thin I's gonna throw ya in the river."

"Ya ain't man enuf ta throw me in the river."

Sludge reached over and shoved Wham off the bridge. The water rushed around Wham and took him under. Sludge and Happy jumped up and ran to the other side of the bridge and watched as Wham was flushed down the river. Wham faced upstream and bounced off a rock and then spun around into calmer water. He tried to stand but slipped on the slick rocks. Wham turned over, crawled into shallow water, and then stood up.

Sludge said, "Happy, go get his cap." Happy took off to the end of the bridge and then raced down the road.

WW yelled, "Now, I's gonna come up thar and kill ya."

"No, ya ain't."

"I is." Wham struggled to walk to the riverbank.

Gravel crunched on the road and Pastor Momar's Escalade rumbled onto the bridge. The window rolled down, "How's it going?"

"Whal, purty good I guess. I had ta throw Wham in the river."

"Uh, may I ask why you threw him in the river?"

"He was being negatory."

"I see."

Wham, with his fists clenched, got to the road, and screamed, "I's gonna kill you, Sludge," just as the school bus came by.

Pastor Momar said, "He looks pretty upset."

"He just needs ta dry out."

"Are you aware that you need a preacher's license to do baptisms?"

Sludge grinned. Pastor Momar shut off the car and got out. "Care if I join you?"

"They's always plenty a room on the bridge."

As Wham stormed down the bridge, Sludge laughed at the water soaked man. "He's so mad he's a walkin like a robot."

Pastor Momar stayed standing and greeted Wham, "In the name of the Father, Son, and Holy Ghost I pronounce you baptized."

"Lemme at him," yelled Wham.

Pastor Momar stood between the two, "Sludge said you were being negatory."

"I's gonna negatory him like he ain't never been negatoried."

Pastor Momar smiled, "I have to agree with Sludge. You do seem in a negative state of mind."

"Tolt ya," said Sludge.

Pastor Momar pointed back beyond Wham, "Happy's brought your cap."

Wham half turned toward the dog. Pastor Momar grabbed Wham by the overalls and threw him off the bridge.

"I git ta do him next." said Jeb. "I heard a bunch a yelling and thought I otta come down and save ya."

Jeb and Pastor Momar sat down on the edge of the bridge. Happy gave the cap to Sludge.

Sludge inspected the cap. "I ain't never seen a worser looking cap. Happy, go up ta the bus and get him that new green cap I found last week." Happy took off down the bridge. Sludge tossed the old cap into the river. The cap sank as it flowed with the current.

"If'n I had a gun I'd shoot all a ya," screamed WW.

"Whal, we'uns glad ya don't have a gun," said Jeb.

"Why don'tcha come up here sos we can do some bridge thinkin?" said Sludge.

"We're here to help you, Wham," said Pastor Momar.

Wham watched the half submerged cap enter the riffles, gain speed, and float downstream. "Why'd ya throw my cap away?"

"Ya needs a new one. Ya needs a new attertude, "said Sludge.

"We'uns gonna keep a throwin ya in the river till ya straighten up," said Jeb. "I gits ta throw ya in next."

"We're gonna have a contest ta see who can throw you the furthest," said Pastor Momar.

"We needs ta mark it on the calendar that this is Wham Throwin Day."

"If'n we had a cannon we could see how far we could shoot him," said Sludge.

"If'n we'd make a giant slingshot we might could shoot him all the way ta Miss Chatty's house."

WW sighed and then waded to shore. *It ain't no use. They ain't got a clue how bad it is.*

Wham came from one end of the bridge and Happy came from the other with the green cap. "Happy, go give Wham the new cap."

Happy ran forward with his prize and gave the cap to WW. Wham put it on, took it off and adjusted the strap.

"Now ya can sit with us on one condition," said Sludge, "ya gots ta think good thins."

"I ain't got nothing good ta think bout."

"Happy, didja hear that?"

Happy sprang into the air and caught Wham on the side, pushing WW into the river.

The three men laughed. Happy jumped in, retrieved the green cap, and took it to Wham who was sitting in the shallows.

"Dadgummit, I ain't had my turn," said Jeb. "Wham, c'mon back up here sos I can toss ya in."

WW put on the green hat and sat for a while with the Rump River. He stood up and worked his way through the weeds toward the road. There in his path was a small patch of yellow jonquils. He stomped and kicked at the flowers until they were no more. WW reached the road and then turned away from the bridge.

"We hurt him," said Sludge. In an instant, Sludge was up and running with Happy at his side.

Before the first turn, Sludge pulled alongside Wham. The three walked in silence, connected by the presence of the others. When they reached the gate to Wham's yard, WW spoke, "Is Willie OK?"

"Yep and he's eatin good."

Wham closed his eyes for a second and then a look of understanding came to his face. "Thanks. Ya best be goin."

Sludge and Happy walked back down River Road.

Boxing

Red asked, "How'd it go today?"

Wham's jaw hardened, "Sludge threw me off the bridge."

"What?"

"Ya heard me. Then Pastor Momar threw me off the bridge."

Red raised her eyebrows.

"Then Happy pushed me into the river."

Red giggled.

"It ain't funny."

"Whal, it is," said Red. "Ain't never heard a nobody getting tossed in the river by a preacher or a dog."

"Pastor Momar said I was baptized."

Red grinned, "Can I ask why they kept throwin ya in the river?"

"Said I was bein negatory."

"Well, were ya?"

"Mebbe."

"Ya thoughts is hurtin ya," said Red.

"I canst help it. Thins just keep gettin worser and worser. Only thin to the good is that Sludge said Willie's awright and he's eatin good."

"That sounds like he's stayin at Miss Chatty's."

"I think so."

"Whal, Willis sees him at school. But he ain't a gettin on the bus."

"But if'n he's at Miss Chatty's why ain't he a gittin on the bus?"

"Ya think mebbe he's a stayin after ta use the computers?"

"Dadgum, ya is smart. I just ain't got it figured how we can be this smart and this poor. Makes me mad thinkin bout it."

"Ya knows why they threw ya in the river don'tcha?"

Wham looked into Red's blue eyes, "Why's that?"

"Its cuz they love ya?"

"Whal, I's gonna love em back by thrown em in the river in January."

"How bout we walk down ta the bridge sos I can throw ya in?"

"Ya ain't woman enuf ta throw me in."

"Put em up." Red clenched her fists and bounced around the room.

"Ya got ya fists wrong. You'uns gonna break ya thumbs that way. If'n ya gonna box somebody ya needs ta do it right."

Red held her hands out, "Fix em."

Wham put Red's thumbs on the outside of her fists. "And ya ain't a standin right."

"Show me."

"Let's see. You'uns left handed so you'uns backerds from most folks. Ya needs ta lead with ya right." Wham put a chair in front of Red. "Make believe that chair is me a standin thar." WW set Red's arms in place close to her chest. "Now, ya stands at a angle." He kneeled down and placed her right foot forward and her left foot back. He then moved his hands to her knees. "Ya knees need ta be bent. I canst see what's goin on. Ya needs ta take off ya overalls."

Red's breathing came faster. She reached up and pulled the suspenders from her shoulders and stepped out of the overalls.

Wham pushed the overalls out of the way and realigned Red's feet. "Now, ya needs ta bend ya knees and hunker down just a little bit. Ya weights needs ta be on the balls a ya feet. Now, bounce around like ya was before."

Red bounced around in front of Wham.

"OK, now let me set ya up again." He placed her feet and then ran his hands up her calves to her knees. "You'uns too tense. Ya needs ta be loose. Don't go nowheres, but bounce on the balls a ya feet."

Wham stood up.

"When do I get ta hitcha?"

"Soon."

"Now, this arm is ya jabber. It's out front and ain't got far ta go. It's ya fast punch." Wham held his hand out in front of Red. "Jab at my hand."

Red jabbed three times.

WW's eyes widened. "That was...really fast. Do it again."

Red jabbed five times.

"That was smoking. Now, do a jab real slow and stop when ya gets ta my hand."

She did a slow motion jab and stopped.

"Ya needs ya fist in a straight line with ya arm." Wham bent her hand so it all lined up. "Now, jab slow, makin sure ya fist is straight with ya arm."

Red smacked his hand three times.

"OK, now go fast."

Red flicked her fist three times just grazing his hand each time.

"That's all I's learnin ya today." Wham pushed the kitchen table up against the wall and took off his overalls. They stood looking at each other in their long t-shirts.

"You'uns the best lookin boxer I ever did see," said Wham.

"Put em up."

"Now, member ta stay loose."

"I's loose."

The List

"I's gitting all bumfuzzled," said Sludge.

"Yep, they's too much ta think bout."

"We just need to make up a list and then concentrate on the most important items first," said Willie.

Jeb and Sludge glanced at each other across the campfire.

Willie zipped open his backpack and got out a spiral notebook and a pencil.

"OK, what's the most important thing?"

"Majic pumpkin seeds," said Sludge.

"Nah, that ain't right. Ya needs some money ta buy hoes and shovels for everbody."

"We ain't got no money ta buy nothing," said Sludge. "We needs ta use ide'ers. Yas thinkin backerds agin."

"I ain't."

"Is."

"Ain't."

"Whoa down. We're getting off track," said Willie.

"We does that a lot cuz Sludge don't think right."

"I think right. You don't think right."

"Stop!"

Jeb and Sludge looked at Willie. Sludge said, "Ain't no need ta get riled up."

Willie sighed, "How the hell do you two get anything done?"

"Whal, we ain't gots too much we gots ta do and what we gots ta do we'uns pretty good at."

"We's real good at fishin," said Sludge.

"And huntin," said Jeb.

"OK, OK." Willie looked at the empty sheet of paper and wrote down, magic pumpkin seeds.

"Wud ya write down?" asked Sludge.

"Magic pumpkin seeds."

Sludge smiled.

"What bout money for the hoes and shovels?"

Willie wrote that down.

"We need to do brainstorming," said Willie. "We're going to take turns."

"I's first," said Sludge.

"No, I's first," said Jeb.

Happy woofed.

"Ya don't get a turn," said Sludge.

Happy turned his head sideways and looked at Sludge with his sad eye.

"Oh, awright, ya gits a turn."

"No, I's first." Wham walked in and sat down across the campfire from Willie.

Everyone stared at Wham and waited.

Sludge offered, "Ya want some coffee?"

"Yeah, that'd be good."

Sludge got up and retrieved a cup hanging from a short broken limb on the nearest pine tree. He wiped out the bottom of the cup with his t-shirt and handed it to Wham

"Ya looks kinda beat up," said Jeb.

"Red hit me."

"Did she tie ya down in the bed and then beat on ya?" asked Sludge.

"Nope, it was a fair fight. One minute I put up my fists and the next minute I was on the floor." Wham poured himself a cup of coffee. "Red's gots ta be the best wife a man ever had."

Willie looked puzzled but Jeb and Sludge smiled.

"OK," said Sludge, "ya can go first but ya canst be negatory or we's a gonna throw ya in the river."

Wham smiled, "I's tired a bein tossed in the river."

"I dint get my turn," said Jeb.

"Ya scared a lot a fish," said Sludge.

"We need ta...to get back to brainstorming."

WW said, "We needs a name for the farm."

Willie pointed at Sludge "Its gots ta have possum in the name."

Willie wrote quickly and suggested, "We need customers."

"A twenty foot possum with a fishin pole and waving a straw hat," said Jeb.

Happy woofed and then showed his teeth.

Sludge said, "Happy says the possums gots ta be smiling."

Willie shook his head as he wrote.

"And we needs t-shirts with "Save the Giant Possum" on one side and a picture of the giant possum on the other."

Jeb added, "And he's gots ta be wearin sunglasses."

"Willis is already working on those. Keep going," said Willie.

"Mebbe the kids could paint the t-shirts," said Wham.

"And we could show em how ta make whirlygigs and birdhouses."

"That thars two thins. Yas hogging the ide'ers."

"I ain't."

"It's my turn," said Willie. "We need innertubes so people can float the river."

"And cane fishing poles."

"And we could sell maggots and night crawlers," said Jeb.

Willie was writing at a feverish pace, "We need a telescope so folks could come and look at the stars at night."

"We could learn em how ta use a slingshot," said Sludge.

"And how ta skip stones on the river."

"We needs a outhouse."

"We needs a bunch a food and drinks for folks whilst theys a farmin."

"We needs a place inside during bad weather," said Willie.

"We needs a pile a money," said Wham.

"Yas on the edge a bein negatory," warned Sludge. "Wes goin ta get thar but we needs ta give folks somethin first."

"How about selling memberships?" said Willie. The three men stopped poking at the fire with their sticks.

"Whatcha talkin bout?" asked Wham.

"When we were at the aquarium in Myrtle Beach they were selling memberships for the whole year. They were expensive but if you had a membership you could go see the fish anytime, all year long."

"We ain't got nothin like a aquarium," said Wham.

Sludge said, "We do so. We gots a purty piece a land that needs farmin by folks that needs farmin lessons. A membership id give em a chance ta farm."

"So we's gonna sell memberships ta folks so they can work from sunup ta sundown. Thar ain't nobody gonna pay good money ta work their asses off in the hot sun."

"Did ya hear that Happy?"

Happy ran forward and grabbed Wham by the pant leg. Jeb and Sludge each grabbed an arm and a leg and headed for the cliff overlooking the Rump River.

"Alright, on three," said Sludge. "One..."

"Don't," screamed Willie.

"We gots ta," said Jeb. "Two."

"Please don't," pleaded Willie.

"Whatd ya think Jeb."

"I ain't had my turn ta throw him in the river."

"Ya gots a point."

Sludge yelled, "Three."

Jeb and Sludge hoisted Wham back and then forward. Jeb let go and Sludge swung Wham out over the edge, then pulled him back, and set him down. "Next time you'uns negatory I's lettin go."

Willie put his hand on his dad's shoulder, "Are you alright."

"Yeah, but now I needs ta buy a gun."

Willie smiled, "When we sell enough memberships you can buy a gun to shoot Jeb and Sludge."

"I'd like that."

Jeb and Sludge grinned big. "Come over here and set down sos we can hammer this thin tagether."

Jeb added some wood to the fire. "A membership farm sounds like it might work."

When Wham and Willie sat down Sludge asked, "Did Red give you that black eye?"

"Yep, best black eye I ever got."

Willie picked up his notebook and pencil, "What kind a farm is it going to be? What are you going to grow?"

It was quiet for a few moments and then Wham asked, "What if'n the farmers figger it out. Like have a meetin where they talks bout what they wants ta grow. If'n they buys a membership they gets a say so."

"That'd make em real farmers," said Jeb.

"I like that idea," said Willie.

"They might argue," said Wham.

"And they might find a way ta git along and make some money," said Sludge.

"If'n they argues I'll just send Red in ta straighten em out," said Wham.

"How much are memberships and when are we going to have the membership meeting?" asked Willie.

"Ain't nothin ta go by," said Sludge. "Ain't never heard tell a no membership farm."

"I think the concept is viable," said Willie, "but we need to define the parameters and expedite the business strategy."

Happy turned his head sideways and looked at Willie.

"Ya ain't runnin for Congress, is ya?"

"I say we throw him in the river for talkin like that," said Jeb.

"Sludge, ya gots a bar a soap?" asked Wham.

"Nope."

Willie's blue eyes sparkled as he laughed. "What I meant to say was, I think the ide'er il work but we needs ta kick er in the ass."

"Now, yas talkin," said Wham.

"I love ide'ers," said Sludge.

"We need to priori...uh, we need ta line up our ducks in a row and shoot em one by one."

"I say we use my 10 gauge," said Jeb.

"Let's see," said Willie, "I could get on the internet and tell people about the membership farm meeting."

Jeb said, "We could get Miss Chatty ta put out the word here in the valley."

"OK, now we need to generate excitement about our product," said Willie.

"What product?" said Wham.

"The membership farm is our product. It's what we're selling."

"We needs ta get folks fired up," said Sludge. "I likes bein fired up."

Wham's face turned granite hard, "We still ain't made no money."

"Wow, you just don't get it," said Willie.

"You'uns don't get it. We's gonna lose the farm without money."

"And how do you make money?" asked Willie.

"If'n I knew that I'd be a making it."

"You give. You create something to give to people."

"I've give all my life and I ain't got nothin ta show for it. It's like all my works been for nothin."

"You can't compete with the big corporate farms," said Willie. "You have to move on. You have to create a new product. A writer can't write the same book over and over. He has to create some new characters, a new plot, a surprise ending."

"We can sit around and jaw all night but we still ain't made no money."

"Dadgum, ya gots ta have the hardest head in Spasum County," said Sludge. "All four a us is tryin ta hep ya."

"I needs ta make some money."

"You'uns runnin round and round that tree and ya ain't seein the birds."

Willie said, "If I wasn't your son, I'd throw you into the river."

Willie and Wham stared hard at each other across the campfire.

"Happy, give Wham a hug."

Happy jumped up on Wham and gave Wham a big slobber kiss.

Wham sputtered, "Git down, git down."

"Ya needs ta be like Happy and be givin folks somethin for free."

"Now, ya's real crazy. I needs money and ya wants me ta give something away for free?"

"How bout ya build a whirligig and raffle it off at the General Store when Willis does the t-shirts?" said Sludge.

"Ya could charge a dollar a ticket and then draw the ticket outta a pickle jar," said Jeb.

"What kinda whirligig?" said Wham.

Willie jumped in, "A giant possum whirligig."

"Where am I gonna get a giant possum?"

"I's real good at whittlin," said Jeb. "I'll do ya one when we's a fishing tamarra."

"I needs some copper wire," said Wham.

"Happy, go over ta Jeb's and get a couple of pieces of copper wire bout yaah long. It's under the camper."

Happy took off across the road.

"Ain't no way that dog is gonna bring back copper wire," said Wham.

Jeb and Sludge smiled. "We'uns recyclers," said Sludge. "Folks throws electric stuff away at the dumpsters and we get the wire and strip off the insulation."

"Be a lot easier a burnin it off."

"We ain't a burnin it off. Smells real bad and it can't be good for the envirement."

Happy came back to the campfire with two pieces of 12 guage electric wire and nudged Wham on the leg. "How'd he do that?" asked Wham.

"We ain't sure how Happy knows all he knows. I think its cuz he listens real good with his one ear and picks up on stuff."

"I think its cuz he only has one eye so he members stuff real good. Two eyed dogs ain't near as smart as Happy."

Wham reached down and petted Happy under his neck, "Ya the best." Happy smiled and wagged his tail.

Sludge said, "I can make him lick his nose. Come here, Happy." Sludge scratched Happy on his back just in front of his tail. Happy licked his nose and they all laughed.

"Willie, what do we need ta do first?" asked Jeb.

Willie looked at the list, "Jeb, you need to whittle a giant possum.

Δ

Wham and Willie walked side by side down Church Ridge Road and across the bridge.

"Ya comin home?" asked Wham.

"No, I'm working on some stuff."

"Thanks for helping with the farm."

"I really think this is going to work."

"Ya know we love ya."

"Yep, I love you too."

"Say a prayer for your mom."

Willie hesitated, "Tell her I love her."

Wham turned and went north and Willie went south.

Dancing Possum

"What do you think, Mr. Darwin?"

Mr. Darwin's eyes moved about the new sketch. "I think you just hit a home run. I love the movement and the energy. Mr. Darwin smiled, "A dancing giant possum will sell."

"Do you have a minute? I'd like to show you something."

"Sure."

Willis pushed through the screen door and Mr. Darwin followed. When Willis got to a large oak tree she stopped. "Look at the bark on this tree."

"It swirls around the tree."

"This tree dances at night beneath the full moon."

"That's, that's a beautiful way to look at it. Artists see such things. I will never again look at this oak as just a tree. It is the dancing oak. And now I have something to show you."

They walked back inside and Mr. Darwin took his place behind the counter. "Well, I made an executive decision." Willis waited. "I found a nice airbrush set on Craigslist for a hundred dollars and I bought it." Mr. Darwin pulled out the wood box and handed it to Willis. "You're an artist. I can see it. Airbrush gives you a lot of freedom."

"I don't have a hundred dollars."

Mr. Darwin smiled, "I need a new logo for my website and business cards. You don't know anyone that could design that for me, say for a hundred bucks."

"I'm all up in it. Do you have any ideas to get me started?"

"It has to be something old timey, maybe a line drawing of the front of the store and use an old timey looking font for the information."

"Uh, I'll need an air compressor for the airbrush."

"There's a small one in the shed out behind the store you can use." Mr. Darwin continued, "I thought we'd set you up on the porch."

The Connection

"Willie, what are you looking for?" asked Mrs. Halbert.

"I need to put an ad on Craigslist about, uh, selling something."

"What are you selling?"

"Memberships to the farm."

"Would you like to elaborate on that?"

"My family owns a farm and my dad has worked real hard for years and never made any money. So, this year we're trying a new business model. We are going to sell memberships to people who would like to be farmers."

Mrs. Halbert reached up and touched her chin, "Tell me more."

"I got the membership idea from when we visited the aquarium in Myrtle Beach."

"Well, let me make this perfectly clear. You can't use the schools library computers to run a business."

Willie sighed.

"How much are memberships?"

"We kicked around a lot of prices and we settled on $50 a year."

"How many memberships are you going to sell?"

"As many as we can."

"Willie, go see if Mr. Shoemaker is still here and ask him to come to the library."

"Yes, maam."

Δ

"I'll lock up if you want to go," said Mr. Shoemaker.

"I appreciate it. I still haven't done my taxes. I don't know why I wait so long."

"If you need some help, let me know. I'll check them and we can file them electronically."

"I'll work on them tonight. Thank you so much."

After Mrs. Halbert closed the library door Willie asked, "Is there a way to test business models before we choose one?"

Mr. Shoemaker looked at the ceiling, "We could make a prototype of each business model and put them on the internet to see which one gets the most traffic or is seen in the best light. Or you could do a survey on the internet. Or you could just build your website and do a leap of faith."

"Mrs. Halbert won't let me run a business using the libraries computers."

"She's a great person but she's wound up too tight. How long would it take you to put your website together?"

"I'm not sure. When I did the research some of the free website builders said you could build a website in minutes using a template. I don't know what's involved."

Mr. Shoemaker got a grin, "It has always seemed like a waste of taxpayer dollars not to have the library open on the weekend. If we put a website together on Saturday we would be optimizing the taxpayer's money."

Willie shook his head and grinned, "I believe you're right. I'm all for optimizing the counties resources."

Possum Patch

The rain rattled on the rusty tin roof of the shed and Wham sat on the large shiny metal seat of the 48 Farmall. He spent considerable time looking at his hands on the steering wheel, hands that were old, scared, with thin skin. It didn't seem right to have worked this hard and this long and have next to nothing. The thin gold wedding band brought tears to his eyes. *I have nothin and I have everthin. Why in the hell does everthin have ta be so damned hard?*

From the half darkness of the shed he could see his past; the twenty-one acres, the hillside, the broken windmill with the water tank beneath it, the stone foundation grown up with weeds, and the long rock pile that snaked its way up and over the hill. The rain ran down the hill in rivulets exposing the red clay. For a moment the sky lightened and the rain went from gravel thrown on the tin roof to a tinkling.

Damn the rain. If'n only there were a way to make some money from the rain. Three robins pecked and looked for worms. *It ain't never gonna get no better.*

Footsteps came around the side of the shed and Willie stepped into the shadows. "How's it going?"

WW didn't answer the question, "It's good to see you. We sure miss you."

Water dripped off the bill of Willie's red cap, "I miss you too."

"I's sorry thins is the way they is," said Wham.

Willie pulled off his backpack and pulled out the spiral notebook, "Mr. Shoemaker teaches math at school and he has a business degree. I told him about the membership farm and he was intrigued by the idea. He said there were a number of ways of possibly making it work. One, is that we sell a lot of memberships at a small price and have special rates for families. Or, two, we just sell tickets or wrist bands to people who come to the farm for the day. Or, three, we sell a small number of yearly memberships and ask a big price for each membership."

"He really thought this id work?"

"The more I talked about it, the more he seemed amenable to the idea. He embraced the idea of letting the membership owners decide how to run the farm and if they made a profit that they would split the money."

"The whole ide'er seems crazy. Folks a spending their money ta try farmin."

"People try things all the time knowing they won't make any money. People spend a bunch of money to learn to ski at Sugar Mountain knowing that they have an outside chance at breaking a leg or getting frostbite."

The sun shot through a few breaks in the clouds and rods of light came through the holes in the tin roof. The grass sparkled silver. Wham said, "Well, did Mr. Shoemaker give you his ide'er of the best way ta go?"

"Because of our circumstances, having negligible resources, he felt like the high priced membership plan would bring in enough capital to jump start the community farm."

"Community farm? I kind of like the sound of that."

"Have you decided on a name for the farm?"

"Possum Patch," said Wham.

"I like it," said Willie, "I like it a lot, very country. Now, I've got a name for the website." Willie wrote the name in his notebook.

"Website?"

"The Possum Patch Community Farm website will be up and running by Monday. How many whirligigs can we make by Sunday afternoon?"

Wham scrutinized his son, "Whoa down. Go back ta the website?"

"I'm building a website that will be on the internet. It's...um...it's a place where you advertise or share things with the rest of the world."

"The world's a purty big place."

"Not anymore it's not."

"You'uns losin me."

"Once the Possum Patch Community Farm website is up and running it will be visible to everyone in the world who has internet."

"Everbody in the world will see our farm?"

Willie smiled, "Yep."

"Well, it ain't much ta look at."

"It will be," said Willie.

"Everbody in the world?"

"That has internet, and that's most of the world."

"So you'uns a sayin that folks in Russia's gonna see our farm?"

"If someone in Russia does a search on the internet and puts in certain keywords like possum or farms in Spasum county our website will show up."

"How much is this website gonna cost us?"

"It's free."

"Ain't nothin free. They's gots ta be a gimmick."

Willie scowled. There it was. Willie screamed, "Fuck this farm!" He wheeled around, picked up his backpack, and was gone.

Wham sat on the tractor for an hour and then spoke to the tractor, the shed, the farm, "There ain't never gonna be no twenty foot possum." Sadness fell from the sky, grey, overpowering, deep, and the tears mixed with the rain dripping through the tin roof. *Uncle Seizure is right, life is hard and then you die.* Wham looked at the rope that he had used to tie himself to the windmill. *Would it be so bad? There would be quiet and peace. Thar ain't never gonna be no twenty foot possum. Damn the taxes. Ya don't own the land, the government does. Bastards. Ya fight with the land and in the end the government takes the land.*

Mebbe God wants me in heaven.

Happy ran into the shed and woofed at Wham.

Wham was despondent. He slowly turned his gaze to the red dog.

"Nothin makes no difference."

Happy woofed at Wham again. Wham set his head against his hands on the steering wheel, "I's too tired."

Happy barked at Wham but Wham didn't move.

The red dog spun around, dashed out of the shed, and sprinted down River Road.

Δ

Jeb shook WW awake. "Is you'uns OK?"

Wham sputtered, "Hep me down."

Jeb reached up and steadied Wham as he got off the tractor. Concern came to his face, "When's the last time you ate something?"

"I'll be alright."

WW swooned and Jeb caught him. "We needs ta get ya to the house." Jeb supported WW to the truck and helped him in. When Jeb opened the driver's side door Happy jumped in and sat next to WW.

The truck pulled out onto River Road.

"Where we a goin?"asked WW.

"We's gonna stop at Miss Chatty's. She'll fix ya up. Ya's blood sugar's too low."

The VW pickup pulled into the yard and Miss Chatty came out onto the porch with her walker. She watched Jeb rush around to the passenger side and help Wham out.

"He's not feelin good. I think his sugar's too low."

"I've got just the thing," said Miss Chatty, "raisin pie."

Heavenly Bodies

Willie paced at the school door that the custodians used on the weekends. Mr. Shoemaker pulled his Ford Focus into the nearest parking spot. As he got out he smiled at Willie, "Good day to break some rules."

"I don't know if the class Valedictorian should be doing this."

"We have high aspirations, don't we?"

"Yes, sir. I know where I'm going and I know how I'm going to get there."

Their footsteps echoed in the empty hall. "When I was your age I had no idea what I was going to do and all I had on my mind was girls."

"I like girls."

"That's a good thing." Mr. Shoemaker pulled out a key and opened the door to the library.

"I never realized that each classroom was locked after hours."

"It's just a precaution in case persons of dubious character would get in the building. I've already told the custodians we would be here."

Mr. Shoemaker turned on one of the computers. Willie pulled up a chair, "Um, we have a snafu." Mr. Shoemaker waited. "My dad and I had a, uh, difference of opinion and now I'm hesitant to do the farm website."

"My dad and I never saw eye to eye...on anything. So what are we doing here?"

"I want a website. I want to start an Astronomy Club."

"Excellent."

"I know this isn't what we had talked about but if we put together an Astronomy Club website I'll be ready to tackle my dad's website down the road."

Mr. Shoemaker turned on the next computer. Willie looked at him. "We can cover twice as much if both of us are working."

"It'll be like dueling computers."

"Yeah. First let's Google free website builders. What's the name of your astronomy club?"

"The Heavenly Bodies Club."

"Uh, please don't tell Mrs. Halbert I had anything to do with this. Uh, you might want to do a little more thinking on that website name. I don't know if it conveys....Oh, what the hell. It's your website...and I know that name isn't taken...uh, I hope it's not taken...uh, you need to check."

"And Willis can make the t-shirts with the giant possum looking up at the stars."

"And you can sell them on your website."

Outhouse

"There ain't no way that itty bitty smudge haa gots a name," said Jeb.

"Yessireebob," said Sludge. "Willie said that was the Onion Nebular."

"Willie don't know everthin."

"He knows a lot. He's always got his head in a book and Wham said he's doin real good with computers."

"Willie ain't got no computer."

"They gots em at school and lets the kids use em."

The sounds of night, cicadas and bullfrogs spoke loud along the river below. A large fish splashed.

Sludge looked into the heavens, "Ya ever think sometimes we's got left behind."

Jeb took a long time to answer, "Sometimes."

"Sometimes what?"

"Sometimes I wonder what id be like ta be all book smart and all caught up in the human race."

"The human race?" said Sludge.

"Yeah, you know, runnin around like ya had six cups a coffee, drivin fast ta a job ya hates ta get a paycheck that gots half the money gone a fore ya cash it and the only time ya gots ta fish or hunt is on the weekends."

"Don't make no sense, does it?" said Sludge.

"Most folks that's book smart is crazy."

An owl hooted.

"Most folks ain't never heard a real owl?" said Jeb.

"Owls and doves sound a lot alike," said Sludge.

"Yep, ya gots ta listen close. Doves run outta wind at the end. They gets three notes just right and then they stumble on the fourth note."

Bats zigzagged in the moonlight over the river.

"Most folks ain't never gone ta the bathroom in the woods."

"Toilets don't seem right," said Jeb.

"Whatcha mean?"

"Don't seem natural. Yas like sittin in a chair instead a squatin. Its easier ta go in the woods."

Sludge looked up, "Oh heckfire, Wham's gonna need a bathroom for folks."

"Dadgum, I never gave it a thought."

"They won't letcha build a outhouse no more."

"Thins is too reglated," said Jeb.

"City folk ain't gonna use the woods or an outhouse."

"Wham might could get one of them Porta-Pottys."

"Wonder how much thad cost?"

The wheels of thought turned until Jeb broke the silence, "Sure is hard ta do thins nowadays. Why's thins gots ta be so hard?"

Willie's World

"Willie, can you get me some more tea?"

"Sure." Willie got up from the porch steps, took Miss Chatty's cup, and went inside. He returned with the steaming cup and placed it on the porch rail next to Miss Chatty's Bible.

"Do you want to play Scrabble tonight?" asked Miss Chatty.

"No, I've got too much homework." Willies sat back down on the porch steps with his back against the post.

"You just don't like losing to an old lady."

"I looked it up online. Verily is an archaic adverb. So, uh, I guess you were right."

"Of course I was right. Verily is in the Bible."

Willie grinned, "I need to start using scientific terms."

"Use whatever words you want, as long as they're not cuss words."

"Most cuss words don't give you a lot of points."

Miss Chatty giggled.

Willie watched the bats zig zag against the darkening sky. He sighed audibly, "I hate the valley and sometimes, I hate my dad. This is not where I want to live. The people here are too," and Willie knew he had to choose his words, "too backwards. It's like they're lost in the past. I can't stand it anymore. I can't stand being poor, never having any money. There's no internet. This is not my life. I have to escape this place."

"So you don't plan on spending the rest of your life living in the shed?" quipped Miss Chatty.

"Don't get me wrong, I appreciate you letting me stay in the shed until...I don't know."

"I appreciate you chopping the wood and bringing me blackberries." Miss Chatty looked at the young man, "You're right about us being poor."

"I want things, "said Willie. "Damn, I hate being poor. I want to see the stars. I get excited when I think of the Hubble telescope sending back pictures of distant galaxies at the furthest reaches of our universe.

"Some people fit here. They love the valley, the river, the quiet, the slowness. It drives me crazy. No, no, it makes me mad. I'm mad right now just thinking about how stupid this damn place is."

"We're not stupid."

"I know that. And sometimes I think it's just me. I'm sorry I'm ambitious. I'm sorry I want things. I'm sorry I'm a straight A student. I'm sorry I don't have patience with people who seem clueless. I'm going to get scholarships to go to college. I'm going to be an astrophysicist." Willie reached for his wallet, pulled out a tattered piece of paper, and handed it to Miss Chatty.

Miss Chatty lifted her glasses and read the child's handwriting.

"That was seven years ago. I knew then what I wanted to be."

"Have you ever shown this to your mom and dad?"

"They can't read."

Miss Chatty handed the piece of paper back to Willie. She poked at her mashed potatoes. "Your parents are good people."

"My father is dead. He's been knocked down too many times. The land killed him. He wears this pall of death. He is encased in negativity. I can't stand to be around him. He brings me down. I can't stand listening to him. We'uns, they'uns, ain't, if'n. What the hell kind of language is that? When I hear a person talk like that I know they're poor."

Miss Chatty could feel the rage and knew it was best to listen.

"I have to remove all the toxic people from my life. Those people bring me down and make me less than I could be."

"Lots of folks have problems and those problems affect how they think."

"Yes, and they will try to bring you down with them."

"We need to have compassion for those that are less fortunate."

"Everyone in this friggin valley is less fortunate...and poor. The lack of education and poverty are endemic in this valley. I'm sorry they have problems, but I'm not going to make them my problems. I can't change people. My dad won't change, he won't listen, he won't give up that damned tractor, he won't try anything new, or learn anything new. He hurts everyone around him with his negativity."

"Someday you will be old and feeble and have aches and pains."

"By the time I am old we will be able to replace body parts and have chips in our brains to do thousands of calculations in a second and regulate and optimize bodily functions. We will be stronger and faster and smarter and we will live a very long time."

"Willie, do you believe in God?"

Willie took a long breath and sighed. Then he clenched his teeth and did not answer.

The evening was leaving the valley and Venus was just downriver above the trees, but Willie did not look up. "I want a pair of blue jeans."

Miss Chatty glanced down at Willie and saw the tears fall on the rock steps.

Willie set his empty plate on the porch, walked out to the woodpile, and set up a chuck of wood. He lifted the maul and slammed it into the wood with all his strength. Again and again and again he slammed the maul into the wood.

Miss Chatty murmured, "We're going to fix some of this shit around here." And then she whispered, "Gawd dammit."

Onward Christian Soldiers

Pastor Momar spoke, "Miss Chatty has an announcement to make before we have our final hymn."

Miss Chatty stood erect and steadied herself with her right hand on the piano. She looked at the eyes, going from one to another. When she had finished looking at every person in the pews her face hardened, "We need to fix some things in the valley. And we need to start now. Now, dammit. Not tomorrow, not next week, or next year. Now!!

We are going to do two things. We are going to have classes for adults to learn to read and write. The classes will start immediately after the last hymn. The kids can play outside. The adults will stay after church. Those that can read and write will help teach those that can't." Miss Chatty took a couple of deep breaths to catch up, "And before I die, we are going to build a library. We are going to have books and we are going to have internet. Our kids need better. This is a different world. They need a place to study and learn so they can compete. We are not standing still anymore. We can't. We must not shut out the world. Our kids have to have a chance. We need to give them that chance. And we need to do it *now*."

Miss Chatty sat back down on the piano seat. "The last hymn is not found in the new hymnals. Some pantywaist thought that it was too militaristic. I'm tired of someone trying to tell me what songs I can sing. Please use the old hymnals found on the back of the pews and turn to page 134."

Miss Chatty waited until the church was quiet. She closed her eyes and her fingers went to war against the devil.

Mean Mr. Darwin

"Mr. Darwin's mean," said Willis.

"No, he's not," said Willie, "he's demanding. He expects more from you."

"I tried to do my best and..."

Willie cut her off, "You're lazy. You don't want to do the work. You don't want to put in the time and effort it takes to become the best."

"I'm a good artist."

"Yeah, and that's the problem. You think you can get by on talent. Good is not good enough."

Willis poked out her lower lip and looked hard at Willie."

The school bus was loading.

"Work on what you can work on. Do more sketches. Come up with more ideas. Push the envelope. Go harder, go faster, go smarter."

"Hard work never got Dad anything."

Willie sighed, "He's stuck...in a rut, a really bad rut. You need to move forward. You need to help him by making the best giant possum t-shirts ever. Then again, maybe you don't have what it takes to be an artist."

Willis lashed out, "Fuck you!"

"I see you've enlarged your vocabulary to four letter words. Is that all you've got?"

Willie sidestepped the kick, the second kick, and the third kick. The two faced each other.

"Willis, get on the bus," shouted the bus driver. "Let's go."

Willis picked up her backpack and got on the bus.

Willie, with a smirk on his face, headed for the library. *That was fun.*

Johanness

Wham walked down Rump River Road to do...he didn't know what. He knew he needed to work. Work was a part of him, as much as breathing and work took some of the worry away. The road was damp from the nights light rain.

As the road followed the river and moved down the valley he could begin to see the windmill on the hill and then the water tank. A man and a small dog walked the hillside of his farm. He heard the yip of the small dog. An RV was parked just off the road between two of the birdhouse posts.

WW waved at the man and he waved back. *Friendly. Probably lost.*

They met with a handshake. The white haired man with glasses said, "I got lost last night and rather than wandering around in the dark I pulled over. I'm Johanness Dittbrenner and this is my dog Elliott." The black dog, about one hand high, investigated every leaf and twig and blade of grass. "I was trying to get to the campground near Bump."

"I'm Wham Wooster. You'uns missed the turnoff at the metal bridge. They was a sign there but someone ran it down and it's still layin in the weeds."

"I was admiring your flowers and you have a real nice view from the top of the hill."

Wham smiled. He was glad he had his new green cap on. "Johanness, I ain't never heard that name before."

"It's German. I'm from Nebraska. Would you like a cup of coffee?"

"Tha'd be real nice."

Johanness opened the RV door and the little dog bounded inside. The heavy smell of brewed coffee filled the camper. Johanness motioned to a seat at the table and then pulled two cups from the cupboard.

"I ain't never been in a camper ya drive."

"What do you think?"

"It's, it's real nice. Little bit tight but looks comfy. Be nice ta just get up and go."

"I'm going to fix some eggs and toast. Would you like some?"

"Uh, well, just ta be honest I'd be much abliged."

Johanness handed the steaming cup to Wham and then began breakfast; putting the pan on the stove and getting the butter, eggs, and bread from the fridge.

Elliott jumped into Wham's lap. "Right friendly dog ya got here." Wham stroked the dogs back and watched the tiny tail fly back and forth.

"Elliott and I've been on the road for about six months. I always wanted to travel and see America with my wife when I retired...but I waited too long."

Wham was slow to answer, "Sorry ta hear that."

"She died last year from breast cancer."

"My wife, Red, might or might not have breast cancer. She's got calcification clusters."

Johanness held the eggs. "One thing I learned was that you need to get a second opinion. There are too many doctors who will operate and prescribe things just to make money."

Wham's eyes widened. "I wouldn't think a doctor that's sposed ta hep ya would do that."

"A lot of doctors work for big companies that have only one thing in mind, and that's making money."

Wham was quiet and enjoying petting the mini-dog.

"How do you like your eggs?"

"Scrambled."

Johanness stopped. "Do you like omelets?"

"I don't reckon I ever had one."

"It's omelet day!" Johanness reached up and buttoned the stereo. A hum began the "Flight of the Bumblebee." Onions and peppers hit the chopping block and Johanness diced and sliced to the tempo.

Wham said, "You'uns gonna make someone a good wife someday."

"I love cooking, but I don't like cooking just for myself."

Wham watched as Johanness folded the omelet. "I ain't never seen eggs smell and look so good. How much is I gonna owe ya?"

"If I was in the Bump campground, I'd be paying $35 a night. I still owe you for letting me park here last night."

"How many campers is in that campground?" said Wham.

"I don't know, but we can look at the campground website and it will tell us."

Johanness split the omelet, put half on each plate, and then sat down.

Wham folded his hands and bowed his head, "Dear Lord it's been a while since we talked. I guess you'uns knows how things is. Thank you for getting Johanness lost. Ya done good, real good. And now I's gonna eat a omelet. Amen."

"That was nice. I think getting lost might have been a good thing."

Wham took a bite. "Oh my goodness. It's like it's gonna float offn the plate."

Elliott yipped and Johanness let the dog out. "Now, stay close to the camper."

"Tell me Wham, it was late last night and there was a bit of fog, uh, I saw something pretty big cross the road. Do you have bears around here?"

Wham turned his mouth sideways, "Didja get a good look?"

"Well, what I saw didn't really look like a bear; it looked more like...I really don't know what I saw. I've got a video camera mounted on the dash but I turned it off when it got foggy."

"So you'uns didn't get a picture of it?"

"Nope, I only saw it for a second, but it looked like a giant rat."

"How big a giant rat?"

"Four, maybe five foot tall."

"Well, they's a giant possum that lives in the Big Bog. He was probably a movin round last night."

Johanness smiled, "You're having some fun with the city boy, right."

Wham looked directly into Johanness's eyes and sighed, "I seen what ya seen and I think others have seen him but they don't say nothing. He tore up my patch a goobers last fall just before I was gonna harvest. His tracks is as big as my hand."

Johanness flung open the camper door and yelled for Elliott. Shortly, Elliott jumped through the door and then onto the seat between Johanness and Wham.

"He ain't never hurt nobody but it's right worrisome ta walk around at night or in the fog."

"Did you report what you saw to, uh, I'm not sure who you would report it to."

"I told Sherriff Sprint but I think he just tore up the report. Then folks was given me a wide berth for a while."

"So I'm sitting across the table from a crazy person."

"Yep, they don't get no crazier. Right now I's tryin ta make somethin outta nothin."

Johanness smiled, "There's a lot of us like that."

Wham explained his failure as a farmer and how he was trying to do something different to make ends meet. He finished with, "And I ain't got nothin ta make a 20' giant possum outta."

"Would you like some more coffee?"

"Crazy farmers shouldn't have too much coffee. It sets em off."

"I'll take my chances."

Johanness filled Wham's cup then reached over, picked up his laptop and turned it on. After a few moments he reached for his cell phone and turned it on and stared at the screen. "Huh, I'm not getting a signal."

"This here's a dead spot. We ain't got no towers nearby and we's down in this hollar."

Johanness shook his head, "I've been on the road for six months and I could always get a signal."

"Yep, my son and daughter is all upset we ain't got no WiFi. They use the computers at school."

"So the valley has a giant possum and no outside communication."

"Well, we's gots reglar phones."

"I'm...I've never...Where the hell are we?"

"This here's the Rump River Valley. It ain't much but we like it. And we got some a the best folks that ever was."

Johanness' Ide'er

Wham said, "Lemme show ya round."

Wham and Johanness stepped out of the RV and into the morning. Elliott left trails in the dewy grass.

Johanness stood still and then closed his eyes, "Its quiet here."

"Yep, we gots a bunch a quiet."

"I mean, I hear birds and the river. I don't hear any cars."

"It's early, folks is just getting goin."

Elliott found a spot near the rock border between the properties and hunched up. Johanness said, "Let me get a plastic bag."

"You'uns ain't a pickin that up, is ya?"

"Well, yeah, I always clean up after Elliott."

"Ain't no need ta do that. This here's the country. Round here its called fertilizer."

Johanness hesitated and then gave it up.

"How old is Elliott?"

"Almost two," said Johanness. "A friend brought him over in a cardboard box after my wife passed away, thought I needed a friend."

"That was mighty nice."

Δ

As the water flowed under the low water bridge Wham described his predicament; no money and the ideas to save the farm. "And what really wears a man down is that everthin I own is broke. My truck ain't run in a year. My tractors driveshaft is broke. The roof leaks. I think I gots termites cuz late at night when its real quiet I can hear em chewin. My windmill's broke. My water pump just busted and now I's carryin water from the river. And I ain't got the money ta fix none of it. And now we's got doctor bills. It's insane what them people want."

Johanness was quiet for a long time, "This is a beautiful place. Reminds me of when I was growing up and the muddy little creek on our farm in Nebraska. I loved fishing for catfish, it was...I don't know."

"Restful," said Wham.

"Yes. We've lost the ability to know these places."

"My mind is all tied up in knots. It's hard for me ta sit still. I feel like I ain't gonna make it."

"We all have problems," said Johanness. "I went to prison for a while."

Wham's swallowed and his eye's got big. "So ya was a convict?"

"Yep, I could write you a bunch of country songs."

Wham smiled, "Hank Williams and Johnny Cash sure could make some good country songs."

"So maybe, for them, being in the big house was a good thing."

"I don't think I wants ta go ta prison ta write country songs."

"I went to prison because I'm a schemer. I was always trying to figure a way to make easy money without doing any work. I made fake ID's, mainly for illegal immigrants but also for young people who wanted to buy booze and cigarettes."

Wham listened intently, "What happened?"

"A young girl got drunk and ran into a bridge abutment. They traced the ID back to me."

Wham shook his head sadly, "My daughter, Willis, is sixteen. I worry a lot about my kids."

"That's because you love them. They are blessed to have you in their lives."

"My son don't think so."

Johanness changed the subject, "Let's just say you don't make it, that they take away your farm and you don't have anything. What would you do?"

"I don't know."

"Would you learn a new skill or trade or get a job?"

"I's old. I ain't for sure I could start over. It's harder to sop up learnin when ya's old...and I ain't never learned ta read nor write."

"Well now, think about it this way. You're a survivor. You somehow made it this far without reading or writing. That is a heck of an accomplishment."

"Ya make it sound like a good thin."

"Well, say there was a footrace and you didn't have any legs but you managed to use your arms and you finished the race. That would be incredible and that is basically what you've done. Without any education you've managed to stay afloat every single day."

"My wife and I've always worked hard."

"Would you mind if I camped on your property for a few days? I'll pay you $35 a night, if that would be OK?"

"That's a lot of money and sides ya fixed me the best eggs I ever had. It don't seem right ta take ya money."

"How about $20 a night and I'll fix you breakfast?"

Wham grinned, "It's a deal."

Johanness pulled out his wallet and handed Wham seven twenty dollar bills. Wham looked at the money in his wrinkled fingers, "This is more money than I seen in...a long time."

"Oh, one other thing. I need some help with a project I'm working on."

"I ain't gonna end up writin country songs, am I?"

"No, those days are long behind me. I need some help with shooting some video."

"I ain't a gitten naked."

Johanness looked at Wham and bit his lip, then he chuckled and then it rolled into laughter. "I don't do those kind of videos."

"I ain't never done no video shootin."

"It doesn't matter. You'll do great. In fact, let's get started." Johanness reached in his pocket and pulled out his cell phone.

Δ

"Is the water cold?"

Wham smiled, "The fish like it. A tad under warm. The other day Sludge threw me in the river, then Pastor Momar threw me in the river, and then Happy pushed me in the river."

"Uh, what exactly prompted this?"

"They said I was being negatory."

"Throwing you in the river is symbolic. Your friends want to cleanse you or move you to a better place."

"Ya ain't one a them brain readin people?"

Johanness said, "No, but I've made a lot of mistakes. One of the biggest mistakes in life is to get stuck. You're stuck."

"You'uns got that right. I ain't got no money and without the money I ain't a goin nowhere."

"When's the last time you sang a song or danced or acted a fool? When's the last time you thought about robbing a bank or being a hobo and jumping a freight car?"

"Yep, I's sittin on a bridge with a crazy person."

Johanness said, "Stand up. We're going to try something.

Wham looked at Johanness by pivoting his eyes and then stood up.

"We're going to skip to the end of the bridge and back."

"Skip."

"Yeah, skip, like when you were young, about seventy five years ago."

"I ain't a skippin."

"We'll both do it together."

"I ain't a skippin."

"I'll pay you five bucks to skip to the end of the bridge and back."

Wham scrunched up his face, "Five bucks?"

"Yep, five bucks. Hold my hand and we'll skip to the end and back."

"I ain't a holdin ya hand."

"Ten bucks if you hold my hand and skip."

"Ten bucks?"

"Ten bucks."

Wham looked like he had just smelled rotting possum. He listened for cars on Church Ridge Road and Rump River Road to make sure the coast was clear.

"OK, lets get this over with. No, no, no, I can'ts be holdin ya hand. I'll skip ta the end and back for five, no hand holdin."

"OK."

As the two men and Elliott made the turn at the end of the bridge Wham started to laugh. A few more skips and he stopped and bent over, shaking his head, and laughing hard.

Johanness came back to where Wham was.

Wham said, "Hard, heh, heh, heh, ta , heh, heh, skip, heh, heh, and laugh."

Johanness laughed with Wham. Wham fell to his knees and rolled over and lay down on the warm wood. His stomach jiggled from time to time. Johanness lay down on the bridge and smiled from ear to ear.

Wham heard the car coming down Church Ridge Road and had a notion who it was. "We needs ta get up. The preacherman's comin."

"OK, Skippy."

As Wham got up he told Johanness, "Don't ya ever call me Skippy."

Johanness got up, "OK, Skippy. We need to finish skipping to where we started."

Pastor Momar and Elizabeth watched the two men skip with the black dog as they came onto the bridge.

"I'm not going to ask them."

"Please," said Elizabeth.

"Nope, I don't want to know."

We Gots a Camper Man

Wham jumped over the step to the porch and flung open the screen door. Willis and Red both looked up. Wham grabbed his wife away from the stove and whirled her around. Willis smiled at her crazy parents. They waltzed around the table twice before Wham stopped. "We gots a camper man!"

"I saw the camper from the bus on the way home," said Willis.

"Yep, he got lost in the fog goin ta the campground in Bump and ended up stoppin at the farm."

Red grinned, "There's more to the story than a lost camper man."

"He wants ta camp for a week at the farm and he paid us $20 a day." Wham reached in his overall pocket and pulled out the money.

Red pursed his lips and hugged Wham tight. "Didja tell him he can camp for a year or two?"

Wham smiled large, "You'uns a Greedy Gus."

"Mebbe. Go wash up, dinners bout ready."

Brain Erasers For Sale

The fire alarm beeped loud and a second later the toaster popped up with the burnt toast. Johanness grinned, "I like mine burnt."

"Me too," said Wham, "just not that burnt."

Johanness turned off the smoke alarm and then scraped some of the black off the toast with a knife and put it on Wham's plate, "There you go."

"Ain't nothin bettern burnt toast with strawberry jelly."

"We're out of strawberry jelly. How about blackberry?"

"That'll work."

Elliott woofed to be let out. "I guess he doesn't like burnt toast."

Johanness let Elliott out, filled up the two coffee cups, and then sat down. "I'm not a psychiatrist or a psychologist. And I have problems. Everyone has problems. I have things in my past that haunt me, memories that won't let go. We all do. Somehow you have to get beyond that. It's hurting you and hurting those around you."

"I wisht I had a brain eraser where I could get rid of the bad stuff and keep the good stuff."

"I like that."

"What's that?"

"The brain eraser."

"Mebbe someday science 'ill invent the brain eraser."

"Why don't you invent it."

"I ain't much on inventin stuff."

"You just came up with the brain eraser. What's it look like?"

"A man could put a bunch of erasers in a box with Wham Wooster's Brain Erasers on the outside a the box. Id be like a matchbox. I like how ya slide em open."

"We have a new product to sell."

"Huh?"

"We'll add it to the product line."

"What the Sam Hill are you'uns talkin bout?"

"Your business product line."

"I ain't got no bizzness product line."

Johanness shook his head, "You'uns gonna be rich."

"You'uns gone off the deep end."

"This is top secret. You can't be telling people about Wham's Brain Erasers until we're ready to ship them."

"Shippin cost money and I still ain't got no money. And I ain't got no brain boxes."

"And you could sell them at the General Store. Have you got any matchboxes?"

"I got one and it's bout empty. We been a runnin the kerosene lantern since they turned off the lectricity. But we's bout outta kerosene so we won't be a need'n no matches."

"This is fun."

Wham raised an eyebrow, "It's fun that I ain't got no money or lectricity or kerosene or matches or bat-trees for the smoke alarm and I's afraid ta go to the bathroom cuz the septic tank might clog up?"

"No, it's fun coming up with new products."

"Ya think somebody id buy a box of erasers."

"Everyone has bad memories that they would like to get rid of. Let's see. There are over seven billion people in the world, that's seven billion customers. Say, we make one dollar a box, that's seven billion dollars. You're going to help seven billion people get rid of their bad memories. What are you going to do with your money?"

"Pay my taxes and then I think I'll run for President."

Johanness half-smiled, "Uh, you might want to do something worthwhile like building a hyperloop or solar panels or wind generators or electric cars."

"I'd like a lectric car. I could charge'r up with the solar panels."

"Then we've got two problems; you're not supporting the electric companies and you're not paying gasoline taxes."

"Bicycles is allowed on the road and they don't pay gasoline taxes."

"They might be liberal commies too."

"Ya think so?"

"No. Other countries use lots of electric cars and bicycles. How do they pay for their road system?"

"I ain't got a clue."

"And what happens when robots and computers take over most of the jobs? How are you going to pay people?"

Wham hesitated, "We'uns doomed."

"Just my opinion; we already pay lots of people, huge numbers of people who don't work. And how many people have jobs that do very little work? How many people are standing on a shovel right now and haven't moved a speck of dirt all day? And how many people are on disability and they're out there playing golf? How many people get welfare and food stamps? And how many young people are living with mom and dad and play video games all day? And how many people make money in the stock market and there is no value added?"

"Value added?"

Johanness wondered if he should open this can of worms, "Uh, OK, you take slabs and make whirligigs and birdhouses and benches. You have made a product and added value. Now, the stock market is different, real different. Companies put out stocks to raise money for expansion and research and paying bills and that helps them grow. But after the stock is out there the value of the stock is based on speculation. One person is selling thinking it is a good time to get out and one person is buying thinking it is a good time to get in. It's gambling. There is no further value added. It's kind of like if you go to a yard sale and buy a pair of scissors for a dollar and then you sell them at your yard sale for a dollar fifty. You've made money but the product, the scissors is still the scissors. It hasn't improved or had any value added."

"What if'n I sharpen the scissors?"

"Then you have added value."

"Seems like a man oughta sharpen the scissors."

"Yeah."

"Why are you in the stock market?"

Johanness closed his eyes, "Good question. I don't believe in the stock market and yet that is how most rich people got rich. Just because something doesn't make sense doesn't mean it doesn't work."

Wham closed his eyes, "What value added is bein a astrophysicist?"

Johanness smiled, "Whenever we seek to know more, we are adding value to our knowledge. Willie will be a part of the search of our universe. He will increase our knowledge and give us a better understanding of our world. Another thing that happens is that there are spin offs. When you build something that has never been built you run into problems and then you come up with solutions, solutions that have never been tried. Some work, some don't, but we learn, we move forward. The future will be made by people like Willie. He is the best value added."

"Damn, I gots ta go find Willie."

"He's in school."

"What's today?"

"Friday."

"Tomarra I gots ta have a talk with Willie."

Δ

At 3:22 a.m. one of Wham's eyes flung open. *What are we going to erase? We needs somethin ta use the eraser on.* "Red, wake up, wake up."

"This better be good."

"Has you got a bad memory you'uns want to erase?"

"Yep, and he's a layin right next to me."

Red Sets Things Right

Uncle Seizure rapped on the screen door, "Anybody home?"

"C'mon in"

"I can't stay long. They's a job opened up at the sock factry. Doctor said Miles Mercer can't work no more cuz a his COPD and emferzema."

Red looked over at Wham and could see the life run out of her husband. "What caused his lung problems?"

"Could be he smoked or could be he breathed too much dust."

"Is there a lot a dust in the factry?"

"Yeah, they's a lot a fiber dust but ya get used ta it. Ain't no worse'n if'n ya was in a dust storm. Ya could start next Monday."

Wham looked at the bottom of his coffee cup and sighed.

"I don't think we'uns gonna take that job," said Red.

"They said they'd pay ya a quarter over minimum wage. That's moren than I got when I got started."

"We appreciate the offer," said Red, "but we's got plans ta go another way."

"Wham, ya needs the money bad and ya gots a job offer. Ya truck don't run, ya tractor don't run, ya well pump is broke. What the hell ya a doin?"

Red spoke up, "We's got a dream and we's gonna make it work."

"You'uns just makin him lazy," said Uncle Seizure.

Fire came into Red's eyes, "You'uns gonna take that back."

"A man's got ta work. The more ya work the more ya gets. Ya ain't got nothing cuz he ain't worked hard enough."

Red's eyes squinted and stared hard at the ragged man, "Ya ain't gonna live long if'n ya don't take that back."

Uncle Seizure said, "And a woman's gots ta know her place. She needs ta back up her man and not tell him what ta do."

Red set her feet and balled up her fist with her thumbs on the outside. "I'll give ya one more chance ta take that back."

"Don't hit him," said Wham.

Uncle Seizure looked at Wham, "What, ya gonna have ya wife fight for ya? Ya, can'st even fight ya own fights? Now, that's a lazy man."

"OK."

Stars in a Jar

Wham sat down next to his son on the edge of the wooden bridge. "Where'dja get the computer?" asked Wham.

"I'm tutoring a student and he traded me tutoring for his old computer."

"Looks like a nice one."

"It's not great, but it works, and it's a whole lot better than having no computer."

"Whatcha workin on?"

"I'm writing a speech. Two years from now I'm going to give the Valedictorian speech."

Wham looked at his son for a moment, "What's a Valleydictator speech?"

"The best student gets to give a speech at graduation."

"I ain't never gave a speech. My knees id give way and I'd probly keel over."

Willie smiled, "I remember the first time, when I had to get up in front of the class and read a poem. My paper was shaking so bad that I couldn't read it and everyone in the class laughed. I went to sit down and Miss Peterson told me I wasn't done. She asked if I had the poem memorized and I said yes.

She said, "Put down the paper, visit every word, toy with the sentence, and linger before pushing on."

Willie got up from the bridge and took a few steps back. He pulled his shoulders back and looked slightly upward. He took a deep breath and spoke from his chest.

"Stars in a Jar

The night is cold
A cold that bites the skin
I climb the hill to see the stars

A train whistles beyond and beyond
The road ends at the last church
I take the trail on this moonless night
I climb to see the stars
My feet know the way
My breath is steam
The quiet is open ended
The distance is further yet
I've climbed the hill to see the stars
I throw down the tarp and sleeping bag
I've come to see the stars
The darkness is filled with suns
Thousands of suns, many with planets
Traveling, orbiting in the silent vastness
Satellites inch across the blackness
How big is the jar that holds the stars?
My breath is steam
And soon I dream"

Wham said, "That was mighty nice. It din't rhyme much but it went good places in the head."

Willie smiled, "Well the point was that I was scared to death, totally out of my comfort zone, and I did it. And the second speech went better. I've already started writing my Valedictorian speech."

Wham shook his head and smiled, "I can't read nor write and you'uns going to give the Valedictorian speech. I'm all proud inside for what yas doin. I can't tell ya how proud."

"I'm proud of you too."

"For what?"

"You never give up. Most men would have given up the farm a long time ago."

"Ya mom's the one that keeps me a going. She's the strongest woman I ever knowd

"Would you sell the tractor?" asked Willie.

"Ain't nobody gonna buy my tractor. The drive shaft is broke bad and ya can't get no parts no more."

"You didn't answer my question. Would you sell the tractor?"

"If only I could get the tractor fixed, I could go again."

"Go where?" said Willie.

The breeze was smooth and soft and the sun felt good.

"It's all I've got left."

"You're hanging onto the past."

Wham looked down into the swirling silver and blue water as it raced from under the bridge. "My granddad, died in the heat of late summer on that tractor. That tractor fed us and gave us what we needed."

Willie got up, walked across the bridge and sat down. Here he looked upriver and it seemed that everything was coming towards him. "I'm going to college in two years."

An oval of water cleared beneath Wham's worn out boots and he saw two catfish rocking back and forth in the current. "Have ya picked out a college?"

"Not yet. I'll probably go in state so it won't be so expensive."

"I wish I could hep ya out but I's a bit strapped for cash."

Willie sighed. "I'll be alright. I'll get scholarships and most colleges have jobs for students that need to work."

"You'uns got er all figgered out."

"No one has it all figured out."

"Stay away from the girls."

Willie smiled. "We've never had the talk about the birds and the bees."

Wham smiled, "Hard ta talk bout."

"How did you pick out mom?"

"Whal, let me see. It was Sadie Hawkins Day and she ran me down and kissed me."

Willie shook his head with a big grin. "How did that happen? You were one of the fastest runners in the valley."

"Sometimes a man wants ta get caught."

"So that's all you have as far as the birds and bees?"

"Yep, that's it."

Willie chuckled on his side of the bridge and Wham grinned on his side of the bridge.

"Oops, I forgot. Ya needs ta wear rain gear. Oh, one more thing, Saran Wrap doesn't work."

Willie laughed quietly. *Oh my gawd. Saran Wrap.* He knew it was one of those times, like when they threw the football.

"When ya go off ta college, ya gonna come visit us."

"Oh yeah, depends on how far away it is."

"I'm real proud of ya."

Willie sniffled and could no longer see the river.

"If'n ya want, I can sell the tractor ta hep ya go ta college."

Willie's shoulders sagged and he wiped his face with his shirtsleeve. "I was hoping that we might raise a little money so Willis could get what she needed to make up a bunch of possum t-shirts."

Wham was silent.

"We'll figure out another way to make the t-shirts."

Δ

As Willie walked the road to Miss Chatty's he pondered if he was a Saran Wrap baby.

No Lights

"Ya don't think that Social Services is gonna come and take the kids, do ya?"

Red hesitated, "Dadgum, now I ain't gonna sleep."

"We ain't got runnin water, we ain't got no phone, we ain't got a car, the..."

Red interrupted, "It's two in the morning and we can't fix any of these problems at two in the morning."

"And the roaches is getting bad again."

"Well, now I'm really not going to sleep." Red got up, went to the kitchen, flipped the light switch and the room remained dark. She listened and did not hear the refrigerator. She opened the door and the light didn't come on. She pulled open the junk drawer and found the box of matches. The third match flamed up and she lit the kerosene lantern. Shadows ran here and there. Red stomped on one with her barefoot.

At dawn the lantern sputtered and the light was gone. In the grayness Red swept up the victims and put them in the trash can. *We need something good to happen.*

Wham came in and sat down across from Red. They listened to the gravel crunch as Uncle Seizures truck went by. When the truck faded into the morning sounds Red spoke, "I'm going to Bump to pay the electric bill."

Wham grabbed the bucket and went across the road to get water.

Johanness Meets Willie

Johanness awoke with a start. He closed his eyes and listened. Nothing. He grabbed his phone from the bedside table. 3:14 am. Elliott wanted petting and Johanness obliged. "Ya ready to go look at the stars." Elliott bounded from the bed to the door. Johanness struggled from the bed, used the facilities, and put on his coat.

As Johanness stepped down from the camper a chill ran up his spine. He looked around. The deep darkness beneath his RV bothered him and he moved a few steps away. The landscape blinked hundreds of fireflies. A solitary bullfrog croaked. There was no breeze and the warm air hung humid. Johanness hesitated. *Maybe I should take the pistol.* "Stay close Elliott."

Johanness flicked on the cell phone flashlight and began his accent. Elliott visited every bunch of tall grass. The three quarter moon threw shadows. Half way to the top of the hill Johanness took a breather. Beyond the road the river was moonlit silver. The blackness of the shed was cavernous and the dying maple took on the look of sick hands.

Johanness quietly repeated, "Stay close, Elliott."

At the base of the windmill tower the light found the parts to the windmill. Johanness clicked a picture of the windmill in the grass beneath the moonlight. Elliott ran ahead and began barking.

"What the hell."

Johanness stood still and could hear muffled voices. He moved forward scanning with the phone. He stopped, smiled, and turned off the light. He had been young once and understood what the darkness held. Johanness summoned Elliott, "Come on Elliott, let's go." As he turned, his phone dinged and several text messages came in. *We have contact with the aliens.*

"Hey Mister, wait up."

The young man in overalls came forward in the moonlight.

"I didn't mean to interrupt you." Johanness smiled at the small innuendo.

"We were looking at the stars and we fell asleep."

"There's too much moon for seeing the stars," said Johanness.

Willie pondered the implications that someone besides himself would know that fact. "That's what I told her. I told her we should wait for the new moon phase."

Johanness smiled, "You must be Willie."

"Yes."

"I'm Johanness Dittbrenner. I'm renting a spot for my RV for a few days."

Willie looked puzzled. "Can I ask what you were doing up here?"

"Looking for the giant possum. You did tell your girlfriend about the giant possum?"

A young ladies voice asked, "What giant possum?"

Willie chuckled and then shook his head, "I'm glad you woke us. She needs to get home before her parents get up."

"You can thank Elliott."

"Uh, I'd appreciate it if you didn't say anything to my dad about this."

"It's just between you and me...and Elliott...and the giant possum."

"Thanks."

Aeromotor

Between bites of his quiche Wham asked, "What's a rig like this cost?"

Johanness was a bit embarrassed, "A lot, right at a hundred thousand."

Wham did a small whistle, was quiet, and then, "I ain't heard ah nobody spend that much on somethin."

"Well, I sold my house in Hebron and I had enough for the RV and some left over to put in the stock market. But I can't rely on the stock market. I lost money last year."

"What happens when ya run outta money?"

Johanness smiled, "Well, I hope that won't happen. I'm also making some money on my videos. Not much, but almost enough for groceries."

"Who buys your videos?"

"Advertisers. When we finish breakfast I'll show you what I do, on one condition."

"What's that?"

"You show me how to make a whirligig."

"Shucks, ain't nothin to it.

Δ

Johanness, Wham, and Elliott stopped at the inert windmill in the grass. Elliott peed on one of the blades. The men smiled.

Wham looked at the vane, "What's them letters say?"

Johanness was going to respond and then it hit him hard. He thought of all the great books he had read and how he treasured those in his little library and the beauty of the words and how this man had never cried or laughed or thought deeper because of those words. He sniffled and then tears came into his eyes. He sniffled again.

"What's wrong?"

"I take so much for granted. I've been very blessed."

"Me too."

"Damn." Johanness looked at the man with the weathered face under the green cap. "It says Aeromotor. We had one of these on the farm when I was growing up. There are still a lot of windmills out in Nebraska. I love windmills and red barns and small farms."

"Windmills is kinda magic," said Wham, "I likes seein the sun bounce offn the blades just when the sun climbs over the hills and the creakin of the pump and the free water."

Johanness sniffled again. "What do you need to fix it?"

"A miracle," said Wham, "It's mostly there but some a the bolts got gone when it banged down the tower and some a the blades needs straightenin and I got no ide'er why it came loose...and I hates gettin up there."

"Well, let's take the blades that need straightening and I've got a metal detector in the RV and we can find the rest of the bolts."

"I always wanted ta run a metal detector."

Johanness smiled, "Its fun looking for treasure."

"Treasure?"

"You never know what that next signal is going to be. It's the mystery. I've found a bunch of old coins and relics."

"You'uns gots a bunch a stuff."

"Well, I had to get rid of a lot of things when I decided to travel.

Wham pointed to the laptop, "You'uns said ya'd show me bout ya videos."

"Let's go to the very top of the hill."

Δ

When they reached the apex of the ridge Wham commented, "Somethin layed down up here last night."

Johanness noted where the grass was beat down. "Elliott and I were up here looking at the stars."

"Good place ta look at stars."

"I got a signal up here with my cell phone so I'm hoping we can get the internet."

"Ain't nobody gots internet in the valley cept Pastor Momar. Ain't sure how he got it."

The phone dinged in Johanness's pocket. "Yes, we have a phone signal."

Johanness sat down and opened the laptop. He moved around so the sun wasn't on the screen. Wham sat down. The little black dog ran and then rolled in the grass.

Boots

"Where's my boots?" asked Wham.

"Ya left em on the porch last night," said Red.

"Well, they ain't there." Wham walked out on the porch and scanned the yard. The fence was bent down and close by was one of the boots. "Red, come look at this."

Red pushed the screen door open and stood next to Wham. Wham pointed at the fence. "Ain't that strange."

"Looks like something climbed the fence ta get ya boots."

"If'n it was a man, he'd a come through the gate." Wham stepped off the porch and looked down one side of the house and then walked across the yard so he could see the other side of the house. "It had ta be somethin perty big ta bend down the fence like that." He picked up the boot. "It's chewed all ta pieces."

"It don't make no sense," said Red.

"Now, I don't have no boots."

"Them boots was wore out two years ago. The giant possum didja a favor."

Wham raised his eyebrows, "I never said the giant possum ate my boots."

"Well, what bent down the fence and ate ya boots?"

Wham frowned, then went back in the house and soon returned with a broomstick.

"What's that for?"

"Ta hep me walk."

"It ain't for fightin the giant possum is it?"

"I gotta go. I gots ta meet Johanness on the bridge before the sun comes up."

"What for?"

"Ta see nature."

Red chuckled softly, "Well good luck with that." As an afterthought she said, "Nature ate ya boots."

Wham hurried down River Road, avoiding the large sharp gravel with his bare feet.

Δ

"Who in the valley needs help, besides you?" asked Johanness.

"Ain't nobody needs more help than me."

"I know that isn't true."

"It ain't?"

"No, there are a lot of folks with a lot bigger problems than you have."

Wham was silent. The sun was taking away the red, easing into orange, and the dark blue of night softened. Two planets were still visible.

"That star there is Mars," said Wham, "and that one I ain't sure of."

"We can check later what planet that is," said Johanness. He put his phone on a selfie stick and continued filming. "Smile for the camera."

Wham forced a smile. "Whoever's a watchin this here videa might could hep me. The giant possum took my boots off'n the porch last night and ate em and now I ain't got no boots. If'n ya gots an extra pair a old boots that ain't a doin nothin, size ten and a half, I'd be real thankful if'n ya could get em to me."

Johanness aimed the camera at Wham's feet.

"My feet ain't much ta look at no more. I had good lookin feet when I was young, some a the best lookin feet in the Rump River Valley."

A tiny sliver of silver pierced the horizon. Johanness swung the phone behind them to capture the sunrise.

"Looks like half a shiny nickel," said Wham. Three doves sitting on the power line along the road cood. The

light worked among the trees. Swirls of fog drifted atop
the river. The planets were gone.

"Red wants ya ta come ta dinner. We gots an extra
chair since Willie left."

"I'll be there. What time?"

"Just afor it gets dark. It's the house up the road with
the bent down fence and the chimbly that's a missing
some rocks. They's a WW on the mailbox."

Supper

The two men sat across from each other. Willis and Red grabbed Johanness' hand.

"Willis, will you say the prayer?"

"Dear Lord, Everythin smells really good so I's gonna make this short. Please take care a Willie. He's the best brother ever. Hep us ta get a goin with the farm and the giant possum t-shirts. We needs all the hep we can get. Thanks for havin Johanness for supper. Amen."

Johanness squeezed Willis's hand and then let go.

I hopes you'uns likes spaghetti," said Red.

"I like almost all kinds of foods. I don't care for pickles and olives. They make me gag."

Everyone smiled. Wham said, "I don't see any pickles or olives so we's good ta go."

Johanness waited for Red to take the first bite before he cut his spaghetti.

Willis said, "I wants ta be a camper girl and drive around and see places."

Johanness replied, "Elliott and I've been on the road for six months and seen some wonderful places and met some wonderful people, you included. I brought my laptop to show you some of those places and people."

Red smiled, "I can't wait to see your adventures."

"Me too," said Willis.

"I feel very grateful to have gotten lost up here. I feel like I've made some new friends and your farm is beautiful."

"It ain't much. The soils all wore out. Last year was the worst crops I ever had and I ain't got money for..." Red kicked Wham. "I's sorry, I didn't mean ta get a goin again."

Johanness smiled at Red and then turned to Wham, "You are a lucky man, Wham Wooster. You have a beautiful wife and daughter. Your son is very bright and you live in a beautiful place. I will remember sitting on the bridge and watching the sun come up for the rest of my life. And you live in the valley of giant possums."

"Giant possums? I hope there ain't but one giant possum."

"They's gots ta be two giant possums," said Willis, "or soon there won't be any more giant possums. One giant possum would die from being lonely."

Red added, "I hope there is a whole family of happy giant possums."

"Me too," said Johanness.

"There ain't gonna be a boot left in Spasum County."

"That would be an opportunity for someone to open a boot store," said Johanness.

Wham said, "You'uns looks at thins different from most folks."

"Thank you."

"Johanness, what's Nebraska like?" asked Willis.

Δ

After dinner Johanness insisted on washing the dishes. Johanness washed and Wham dried.

Red said, "Willis, when you grow up, the most important thing ta look for in a husband is that they can do the dishes."

"Stop that," said Wham.

"Oh I forgot, this evening when I was walking the road on the way up here I passed a small house and watched an elderly lady with a walker, back down the steps on the porch and then reach up and get her walker. She needs a ramp before she falls down and hurts herself."

"That's Miss Chatty," said Willis.

"Why's she a goin down backerds?"

"She can hold onto the rail with both hands going backwards and I have a hunch she's afraid of going down forward. She's probably already taken a fall."

The room was quiet. "She's never said anything to anybody about taking a fall," said Red.

"Is she a proud woman, one that wouldn't ask for help?"

"That's Miss Chatty," said Wham.

"Tomorrow, we will build her a ramp."

"I ain't much of a carpenter," said Wham.

"It doesn't matter. I've done some carpentry."

"Who's gonna pay for it? I know Miss Chatty ain't got no money."

"The lumber yard will donate the materials."

Wham's eyes widened, "Huh?"

"It will be good advertising for them."

"This I gots ta see," said Wham.

"Remember, Wham, I'm a schemer."

Wham put the last dish on the shelf and hung up the dish towel. "I's ready ta see a video."

Johanness pulled out the laptop and a small projector. As he plugged in the laptop he looked at the ornate, paisley, 1920's wallpaper on the walls. "Uh, would you have a large white towel or bed sheet we could use for a screen."

"I'll get you one," said Red.

Johanness looked at the shelves with the plates and decided to use the plates and a cast iron skillet to hold up the sheet.

"OK, turn out the lights."

Δ

At three in the morning, Whams eyes flicked awake. *Did Johanness say he'd met Willie?*

Sunglasses

"Didja try ta make friends with the giant possum?" asked Sludge.

"What the hell are you'uns talkin bout? He ate my boots and bent down my fence."

"Didja see him do it?"

Wham shook his head, "And he tore up all my goobers. His tracks was everwhere."

"Well, he was hungry and ya didn't have no sign out there sayin don't eat the goobers."

Jeb cut in, "So you'uns sayin the giant possum can read?"

"Well, we don't know if'n he can't read or write."

"So now ya got him readin and writin?"

"He's got a maripossum thumb so he can hold a pencil."

Wham watched the trees reflection on the pools surface before the water ran beneath the bridge. "I wisht I could read and write."

"Jeb and I was a talkin bout that the other day. It might be nice ta write down a story or read a book."

Jeb said, "I'd read bout buyin stocks sos I could get rich."

"Might be a good thin ta do," said Wham, "Be nice ta sit back and just watch the money roll in."

"Now, there's an ide'er," said Jeb, "ya just needs ta sell some stock in ya new farm. Just get Willie ta print up some stock paper and sell em ta folks that wants ta invest."

"Ain't nobody stupid enuf ta buy pieces of paper that says Wham's Farm Stock."

"City folks might."

"It don't seem right, makin money and not doin no work," said Wham.

"They's lots a folks that make money and don't do nothing, leastwise no real work."

Sludge lifted his bobber from the water to check his bait, "Yep, a good days work id kill most folks."

"I gots ta get goin," said Wham, "I gots benches ta make."

"Benches is a real good ide'er. How bout ya build us a bench sos we don't have ta get up and down a sittin on the bridge?"

"I can'ts be a makin benches for folks and not gettin paid."

"Ya could put a sign advertisin your benches. Ever time a car id come across the bridge they'd see the sign and purty soon they'd want a bench."

Sludge said, "Ya needs ta make a bench for the giant possum ta sit on. Maybe put arm rests on it."

Wham stood up. "I ain't a buildin no bench for no possum."

Sludge took off his sunglasses, "Here, give these ta the giant possum. Just hang em on a branch out there at the Bog. He'll find em."

Wham looked Sludge in the eyes for a moment and could see the earnestness. "Where'd ya get em?"

"I found em when the stream was low."

"Wonder what that "O" means on the sides?"

"Might be a zero," said Jeb.

"I say it's a "O"."

"I say it's a zero."

"Why ya think they's a zera and a oh?" said Jeb.

"Yeah, I thought bout that one time. Why make two thins when one id do?"

"You'uns never thought no such a thing till I come up with the ide'er."

"I did so."

"Did not."

Wham said, "What if'n it's zimbolic?"

"Zimbolic. Ain't no such a word," said Jeb.

"Willie says zimbolic stuff. Sometimes some things mean somethin else. Might be a picture of the world."

"Willie likes them big words," said Jeb.

Wham took the sunglasses and put them on, "I'll...I'll put em on a branch."

"And make him a bench," said Sludge.

Wham took a few steps down the bridge, "I ain't a makin no possum bench."

Sprouts

Wham took in the sprouts under a grow light next to the sink, "Whatcha got a growin?"

"Uh, I've got quite a few different things started."

"It ain't none a that whacky weed, is it?"

Johanness smiled, "I've got some tomatoes, some peppers, and some herbs. These last three are camellia bushes that I can use for tea. It's an experiment."

Wham looked hard at the one inch tall sprigs under the clear plastic. "This ain't Colorado. I ain't havin my kids around no drug addict."

"I understand."

"Where ya gonna plant em when they get big?"

Johanness paused, "I don't need to plant them in the ground. They can grow inside my motor home using hydroponics."

"Where's the dirt? They's gots ta be dirt."

"Uh, plants need nutrients. Plants pull nutrients from the soil. Most farmers use fertilizer to improve the soil. I feed my plants using the same nutrients mixed with water."

"It ain't right. It's, it's, it's ..."

Johanness could hear the deep frustration.

"Willie was a tryin ta tell me about folks growing stuff inside buildings. It just don't seem right. It ain't right. It can'ts be right."

Johanness sighed. *This is going to be a tough sell.* "How about waffles this morning?"

"I ain't had a waffle in two, three years cuz our waffle iron broke. I like waffles real good."

Johanness plugged in the waffle iron and cracked the eggs on the side of the bowl. "After breakfast we'll go to the top of the hill and use the computer and I'll show you a few YouTube videos on hydroponics."

Wham inspected the lights over the sprouts, "What's a runnin the lights?"

"The lights run off a couple of deep cycle batteries and they can be charged by my generator or by my solar panels."

"Solar panels?"

"On sunny days the solar panels give me more than enough electricity to charge the batteries."

"You're gonna hafta show me them solar panels. I wisht I didn't have no lectric bill."

Johanness considered his friend, "Are you a prepper?"

"A what?"

"A prepper, somebody that is prepared in case...uh, in case things break down."

"I ain't no prepper. Everthin I gots is broke down. I ain't prepared for nothin. I lay awake at night and wonder what's gonna fly apart next."

Johanness' belly jiggled as he tried not to laugh, but his eyes betrayed him.

"Wham scowled, "It ain't funny."

"Sorry."

"And a man's gots ta have a boatload a money. Everthin takes money. Take like a truck. A man's gots ta have enuf money ta put gas in the tank, and get some retreads, and buy parts at the junk yard. And a man's gots ta have a hill ta jumpstart the truck."

"And then they want you to have a driver license."

"Yeah, who come up with that?"

"And insurance."

"How's a man spose ta keep up when the govement keeps throwin him under the railroad tracks?"

"And then they want to charge you taxes."

"Yeah, what's that all bout?"

"Life isn't fair."

"Tell me bout it."

"The rich get richer and the poor get poorer."

"Ya got that right."

"Desperate times call for desperate measures."

Wham got quiet. "Money's just too hard ta get. Makes a man full a hate. Ya can't just keep a farmin and get nothin back." Wham shook his head, "And everday I gets closer ta losin the farm. It's like that dream ya have where yas running as fast as ya can and the monster is takin one step at a time and he's catchin up. Now my stomachs all tied up in knots."

Johanness pulled the waffle off the waffle iron with a fork. "Maybe this will help."

"If'n ya wouldn't a got lost up here, I'd be eatin dirt."

Johanness watched Wham butter the waffle and then fill every hole with syrup.

No Nails

Elliott laid down in the grass.

Wham sat on the new slab bench while Johanness did a short video of the view from the top of the hill. "I'll use this to begin today's video and add some music to it."

"What kinda music?"

"Something soft and relaxing."

"Like funeral music."

"Probably not funeral music."

"How bout a church hymn song bout walking the fields with Jesus? I like that song."

"I remember that song from when I was growing up. Yeah, I liked that one too."

"Where ya gonna get that song?"

"I can probably Google it."

"You'uns sure do Google a lot."

Johanness put the camera on the tripod and sat down. "The world is YouTube and Amazon and Craigslist and Facebook and Google. Its about being connected with everyone in the world. Its power and knowledge and wealth."

"I needs ta be getting some of that wealth," said Wham.

"You need a brand. You need to stand up and shout to the world, "Look at me, look at what I have to offer."

"I ain't got nothin ta offer."

"Dammit Wham, what the hell are you talking about? You're rich. You just can't see it. You own this land. You have a pile of slabs to build with. You know how to make whirligigs and benches and birdhouses and...oh yeah, I forgot to tell you I saw a YouTube video about building carpenter bee traps."

"I run outta nails yesterday and the General Store ain't open on Sundays and I really can't afford nails right now."

"So you don't have enough money for nails?! Dammit Wham, you're driving me nuts."

"I don'ts have enuf money for nuts." Wham looked at the ground, "Yeah, I make everbody mad."

Johanness and Wham watched a hawk sail and bank and rise on a thermal. The hawk gained altitude and drifted out over the Piedmont.

"I want to rent for a month. How much will you charge me for a month?"

"I ain't real good with numbers."

"How about four hundred a month?"

"Do I still get breakfast?"

"Yes, you still get breakfast."

"Can Red come down for breakfast sometime?"

Johanness hesitated, "This isn't Waffle House."

Wham laughed, "I like Waffle House. I ain't been ta the Waffle House in three, mebbe four years."

"Bring Red tomorrow morning and we'll have waffles. She doesn't eat a lot, does she?"

Wham smiled, "She likes waffles real good."

"Oh Lord," Johanness reached for his wallet and handed Wham four, one hundred dollar bills. "Oh, would it be OK if I plant some of my plants up here so they can get a lot of sun?"

"I was a wonderin when ya was gonna stick em in the ground." Wham looked at the money, "This ain't money from sellin pot, is it?"

Johanness looked at Wham and decided this was not the time to broach the subject, "No, that is from my videos and from my stocks."

"Good, cuz I ain't a using no drug money."

"Well, we don't know where that money's been. Money changes hands a lot. It might have been drug money a month ago or a year ago or ten years ago."

"I ain't never thought bout where the money's been. I just wisht it would stop in here once in a while."

"What are you going to use the money for?"

"Nails."

"That's a lot of nails."

"Nails is first and then a new well pump and then I dunno. They's way too many thins that's broke and medical bills. Red just paid the lectric bill with her cookie jar money."

Johanness closed his eyes. I'll bet they charged her a bunch of money to turn the electricity back on. Man, it sucks being poor.

Johanness flipped open the laptop, "Lets see if we can find some YouTube videos on fixing a well pump. Maybe you won't have to buy a new one."

Breakfast

Elliott sat on the passenger's seat and wagged his tail excitedly as Wham and Red came through the door.

"Good morning. This is the first time I've had a lady in my RV."

Red eyed the plants under the grow light but didn't say anything. "It's sure enough fancy. I'd a never guessed it could be so nice."

"Thank you." Johanness spoke to Alexa and soft piano jazz came on.

"You'uns showin off," said Wham, "ya never did that before."

Johanness smiled, "I've had Alexa for a while, I just never got it set up until last night."

Red said, "Wham says you'uns a great cook."

"Yes maam, I am the greatest cook that ever lived."

"Miss Chatty might have somethin ta say about that."

"What kind of waffles would you like? I have blueberry, pecan, cinnamon, and regular."

"How bout one of each."

"Wham said you liked waffles."

"What else did Wham say about me?"

"He said you were a great boxer."

"I had a great coach," said Red.

Wham said, "Heckfire, you'uns only throwd two punches."

"I really didn't know how easy it was to knock somebody out."

"Go ahead, sit down."

Elliott jumped into Wham's lap and got petted. Then he jumped into Red's lap.

Red petted the bundle of energy with the hyper drive tail.

"Elliott, you need to go out for a while." Johanness opened the door and Elliott bounded out. "Stay close."

"OK, I'm going to start with the blueberry waffles. Did you want some eggs?"

"I wouldn't mind a scrambled egg or two."

"Thad be nice," said Red, "It don't feel right not doin the cookin."

"I've got it ready." Johanness poured the batter into the waffle iron. "Alexa play Eye of the Tiger." The radio went silent and then began the Rocky theme song. Johanness cupped his hands to his mouth and spoke above the music, "And in this corner we have the welterweight champion of the world, Reeeed Wooooooster."

Red's eyes sparkled, "That song makes me want to hit somebody."

Wham threw up his arms to defend himself. Red laughed.

Δ

After breakfast the three sat in lawn chairs in the sun.

"Wham told me that you have calcification clusters."

Red threw a glance at Wham, "Uh, yeah, that's what the doctors told me. They did a biopsy a couple of days ago but...well...they were sposed ta call but are phone ain't workin right now so I'll have ta catch a ride ta the clinic ta get the results."

"You can use my pho..." Johanness caught himself. "We can go to the top of the hill and then you can use my phone to call."

"Thad be real nice...I hate not knowin."

"I downloaded some information on calcification clusters."

Johanness started to get up. Red said, "Just tell us what it said."

Johanness sat back in the chair, "Well, calcification clusters can be a sign of cancer. However, most of the time...no I need to get this right. Let me go print it out."

Wham and Red sat quietly and watched Elliott run on the hillside.

"The sun feels good," said Wham.

"You'uns made a good friend."

Wham looked over at Red and saw the tears in her eyes."

"Yeah."

"God's lookin out for us."

Wham and Red could hear the printer.

Johanness sat back down and skimmed over the page. "There's two types of calcification clusters. The very small clusters are made ..."

Terrorist?

Jeb and Sludge and Happy walked down Church Ridge Road, headed for Miss Chatty's.

"Maybe he's a terrorist," said Jeb.

"What's he gonna blow up, the General Store?"

"Mebbe."

"Mebbe he'll blow up a barn or two. Mebbe he hates farmers."

"Mebbe."

"He ain't no terrorist."

"Well, splain ta me why he's s hangin around. And why's he videa tapin thins? He probly relayin the videas back to the main terrorist group."

"He likes it here."

"We can't have folks comin up here and likin it. We's talked bout this. That's why we took down the sign at the bridge, so's folks wouldn't come up here."

"You'uns a worry wart. Johanness ain't after are fish."

"Well, what's he after? He's after somethin. Everbodies after somethin."

"You'uns always lookin for the bad in folks."

"That's cuz most folks is bad."

"Most folks is good, real good."

Wham and Johanness sat on the bridge watching the river run. Elliott spotted Happy and ran to see his big dog friend. Jeb and Sludge got quiet as they came onto the bridge. Jeb sat down next to Wham and Sludge sat down next to Johanness, not too close, appropriately man spaced.

"Has ya gotter figured out?" said Sludge.

Wham responded, "They's a bunch ta think about, that's for sure. Where's ya's fishin poles?"

"We was headed to Miss Chatty's ta see if'n she made too many scrambled eggs and pancakes again."

"She does that a lot," said Jeb.

Sludge said, "Happy, go tell Miss Chatty we'uns comin for breakfast...and take Elliott with ya."

Happy and Elliott trotted down the bridge.

Wham pointed upstream, "Here they come."

Johanness hit the button on his phone and followed the flight of the two wood ducks.

"Didja get em?" asked Wham.

Johanness replayed the video, "It came out great. I can't believe how good the resolution is." He handed the phone to Wham, "Push the button on the bottom."

Wham and Jeb watched the two small ducks. "Why ya takin movies of everthin?" asked Jeb.

"So I can blow things up," said Johanness, "we terrorist like to do that sort of thing. I thought I'd start with the bridge."

Wham laughed, "We could hear ya coming down the hill."

"Lemme see the video," said Sludge. "Them's purty ducks alright."

"Wham, you need to build some wood duck nesting boxes," said Johanness.

"I ain't got time ta be a building boxes for wood ducks. Sides, I don't know nothing bout nesting boxes for wood ducks."

"We'll go on YouTube and watch how to put one together. It would be another product to sell. The slab wood would be perfect for making the boxes."

"Next, I'll be a buildin a house for the giant possum."

"That would be a good YouTube video," said Johanness.

"I hope the giant possum's gots a good dry place ta stay when it's a rainin," said Sludge.

Jeb got up, "There ain't no giant possum and I ain't hepin build no giant possum house and I ain't a wearin no giant possum t-shirt and, and, I's hungry."

"Oooo, I know," said Sludge, "We could get Save the Giant Possum caps."

"How bout underwear?" said Jeb.

"Now, you'uns talkin," said Sludge. "Most folks wears underwear."

The Knock

Wham knocked on the screen door.

"Who's there?"

"Wham and Johanness Dittbrenner and Elliott."

"C'mon in," said Miss Chatty.

"Miss Chatty, this is my friend, Johanness Dittbrenner."

Miss Chatty's and Johanness's eyes met and they both smiled.

"It's good to meet you," said Miss Chatty.

"Pleased to meet you."

"Well, don't just stand there. Grab yourself some coffee and set down.

"You'uns gots ta be the cookinest woman I ever seed."

"I like to cook," said Johanness.

"Johanness is a heck of a cook," said Wham, "Mebbe not as good as you, but clost. He made me an omelet and a quiche. Crazy what a man can do with an egg."

"Let me guess," said Johanness. He closed his eyes and breathed through his nose. "Chocolate chip cookies."

Miss Chatty grinned, "You'uns gets an extra cookie for that guess."

"I dint get ta guess," complained Wham.

"There's probably an extra cookie in there for you."

The piano caught Johanness's attention. "That's a beautiful old piano."

"It needs ta be tuned up."

"Would you mind?"

Miss Chatty nodded.

Johanness sat down on the stool and pushed open the key cover. "I'm a bit rusty. I haven't played in over six months." He looked at the sheet music, "What a Friend We Have in Jesus." "I know this one." His fingers touched the keys and he winced slightly but plowed ahead. When he finished the first verse he stopped. "Would you mind if I tune up your piano?"

Miss Chatty looked at Johanness, "You're a piano tuner?"

"I can be. I've done it before. I don't have what I need but I could get a hammer and mutes and the piano tuning software in a few days."

"You're not trying to get another chocolate chip cookie, are you?"

"I might be."

"What's your favorite cookie?"

"Oatmeal raisin."

"OK, here's the deal. One batch of oatmeal raisin cookies and a raisin pie."

"Dadgum," said Wham, "I gots ta learn ta tune pianas."

"I'll teach you how," said Johanness.

"How much ya gonna charge me ta learn?"

Johanness frowned, "Nothing."

"I gots ta pay ya somethin."

"OK, Skippy. I'll train you to tune a piano if you will skip out to the road and back."

"I tolt ya not ta call me Skippy."

"OK, Skippy."

"How much do piana tuners get for tunin?"

Miss Chatty spoke, "Pastor Momar pays a guy from Bump a hundred and twenty five dollars to do the church piano. Which reminds me; the church piano needs to be tuned again."

"OK, Skippy, I'll train you on Miss Chatty's piano and then we'll do the church piano together and split the money, but you have to skip out to the road and back waving your hands in the air while you skip. And I get to do a video."

Wham made his ugly face. Miss Chatty and Johanness laughed.

"If you help Johanness with the church piano, I'll make you a raisin pie."

"Dadgum, I hates bein poor."

The three filed outside and Miss Chatty sat down in her rocker. Johanness pulled out his cell phone and clicked on video. "OK, Miss Chatty, turn your rocker a little more toward the road. Now when Wham, uh, I mean Skippy and I get skipping just keep us on the screen. Just steady it on the rail." Johanness hit start. "Now we're ready to go."

Johanness and Wham stepped off the porch. "Are you ready, Elliott." The dog woofed. "OK, to the mailbox and back."

The two men skipped and waved their hands in the air while the little black dog ran alongside and jumped over the dandelions. Johanness skipped ahead and grabbed at the air like he was trying to catch lightning bugs. Wham mimed swatting flies.

Wham drew alongside and yelled, "Ya ain't right." Johanness gave Wham a shove. Wham, just a bit off balance, with his legs tangled up, fell into the newly plowed garden, adding some much need variety to the monotonous dirt lines.

Miss Chatty tried vainly to remain continent but each spasm of laughter jiggled away at her resolve. "Oh my."

Wham got up and reached for his green cap. Elliott grabbed the cap and chased Johanness. The cap posed a problem being the same size as the dog. Elliott stopped and regrouped, grabbing the adjuster strap between his teeth, looking out through the back of the cap. The green cap with black legs sprinted to catch up with Johanness.

"Oh my...Oh my."

Wham picked up a hoe at the edge of the garden and gave chase.

"Ya gots ta skip," screamed Miss Chatty.

Wham, shook his head, and then broke stride and went into fast skip mode.

At the mailbox, Johanness turned around to see the skipping farmer with the hoe chasing the running green cap. Miss Chatty's high pitched cackle laugh, "Aaahhh, haaa haaa," carried to the road and beyond. Johanness scooped up the running cap and skipped around the edge of the garden, still grabbing imaginary fireflies with his free hand. Wham slapped the mailbox and skipped in pursuit. Halfway around the garden Johanness slowed, his skipping faded to trudging. On an athletic good skip Wham's left calf tightened up and he used the hoe to remain upright. His tortured face turned sideways and he dragged his left leg. Miss Chatty's glasses fell off her nose but she kept the two blobs centered in the screen. At the porch Johanness fell to his kness releasing the cap with black legs. Moments later the gimp fell to the grass and kneaded his calf muscle.

"Oh my. You'uns tryin ta kill this old lady."

"It weren't worth it. I don't care nothin," Wham tried to catch his breath, "bout... tunin no piana."

"Oh my," Miss Chatty wiped away the tears and tried not to laugh, "my ribs hurt."

Johanness giggled between breaths.

"Ya ain't a hurtin as bad as I's a hurtin."

"Ya looked like crazies from the insane asylum."

Johanness laughed hard, "That's...that's what we were shooting for."

The black cap nudged Johanness and he lifted the cap and threw it at Wham. Elliott went back and woofed at Wham.

"Dadgum this leg."

"I think I broke a rib. How do you turn this damned thing off?"

"You...you...heh,heh...you hit the button at the bottom."

Miss Chatty pushed the botton. "My dependables weigh three pounds."

Johanness rolled over and laughed. Elliott licked Johanness in the face and then climbed on his chest and lay down.

"Well, Skippy, our work is done."

"My hates list just gots longer. I hates pianas."

Miss Chatty giggled and went inside to change.

Δ

"These gots ta be the best chocolate chip cookies in South America," said Wham.

"Uh, we're not in South America," said Johanness.

Wham looked puzzled, "We's in the south and we's in America, right."

"Yes, we are," said Miss Chatty, "Thank you very much for the compliment, but you don't get any more cookies. I need some for Jeb and Sludge and Willie."

Johanness pushed the cell phone at Miss Chatty's, "Here, watch the video again."

Miss Chatty spilled her tea, "Quit that," and giggled some more. "The green cap," she sputtered and shook, "Oh my."

"I sure hopes ya rib gets healt."

"Ok, you and Johanness can split one more cookie."

Wham jumped up and grabbed a cookie off the sheet.

"We need to get going," said Johanness.

"I thought we was here ta build a ramp."

"Oh yeah, I forgot." Johanness spun around on the stool and faced Miss Chatty. "We have something we would like to discuss with you. Many years ago, when I was young, we lived in a house in Nebraska that had a cellar. My mom used it for storing canned goods. She did a lot of canning. Well, as the years went by it was harder and harder for her to climb the steps. And one day I caught her going down the steps backwards. She was afraid of falling forward down the steps."

Miss Chatty's eyes narrowed. "And what's your point?"

"Well, Wham and I are tired of making whirligigs and birdhouses and skipping and we need a project. I happened to be walking down the road last evening and saw you back down the steps."

"I's getting by just fine."

"Yes, that's what Wham said. He said you were a strong woman with a lot of pride. And I admire that. I just thought it would be nice if you would allow us to build you a ramp. I know I'm being selfish, just trying to relive the days when I did carpentry."

"I don't think I want two mental patients building me a ramp."

"We'uns promise we'll behave," said Wham.

"I don't want ya coverin up the steps. Chet built those with the river rock and ever time I see them, I see him a carrying the rocks from the river."

"Well, we certainly wouldn't want to cover up the steps. Maybe you could help us with the design." Johanness went to the screen door and then walked out onto the porch.

Δ

"I's keepin an eye on you mister. I saw what you did. Ya got us a two jobs and extra cookies. You'uns could charm the whiskers off a catfish."

Fuses

"Ya don't know nothing bout lectricity, do ya."

"Yeah, why?"

"Well, I gots a couple a circuits that don't work."

Johanness rolled his eyes northward, "You really need to get an electrician to work on it."

"Ain't no way I can pay a man eighty dollars an hour for hookin whiress tagether."

"That's what electricians get today."

"I change my own fuses."

"Fuses?"

"Yeah, them little round things that burns out all the time and then ya stick a penny in there till ya can afford a new fuse."

"Oh, gawd no. Please don't tell me you did this."

"What's the problem?"

"The fuse burned out because there was an overload in the circuit. When you stick a penny in there you override the safety feature of the fuse, the wires get hot, and your house burns down."

"Everbody does it."

Johanness shook his head.

"Some a them pennies been in there three, four years, mebbe longer. Fact is, they was pennies in a couple of them slots when I got the fuse box from the old house. Might be wheat pennies in there...or Indian heads."

Jesus. "The inspectors should have caught that."

"Well, the truth is, the inspectors don't come up here no more ever since Rascal Rump used a nail gun and nailed the inspector to the wall with sixteen penny nails."

Johanness was silent.

"A man oughta be able ta build what he wants ta build."

Johanness sighed, "Inspections are there to keep people safe."

"Most folks don't like other folks tellin em what ta do and tellin em what's right. Who's side you'un on anyways?"

Johanness ignored the question, "We need to look at your fuse box after breakfast."

"Not ever man's got money ta buy fuses."

"Do you have house insurance?"

"What do you think? If'n I ain't got money for fuses or bug spray I sure as hell ain't got no money for insurance."

Business Cards

"Mr. Darwin, what if we make up business cards with a phone number for the Giant Possum Hotline and sell them at the cash register for fifty cents a piece."

"I like it. I like it a lot. OK, so you put a picture of the giant possum on one side and the phone number on the other side."

Willis handed Mr. Darwin the business card.

"Wow." Mr. Darwin examined the card, "We need to redo our business agreement."

"Uh, I..."

Mr. Darwin interrupted, "On this product you should get ninety percent of the profit. It was your ide'er."

Willis beamed and then did an impromptu fist pump followed by a happy dance."

"How did you do this business card?"

"They have a pretty good printer in the library at school and Mrs. Halbert gave me one sheet of card stock."

"Who's phone number is that?"

"Miss Chatty's. She runs the Giant Possum Hotline."

"You're kidding."

"Nope, she's been keeping track of all of the giant possum sightings."

"Naw."

"Yep, I haven't seen it but my dad says she has a map of the valley with pushpins marking the sightings. And she keeps a little notebook."

Mr. Darwin's head eased back and he looked into the rafters, "Hmmm. We need a copy of that map with the pushpins to display behind the cash register."

Willis smiled, "The giant possum keeps getting bigger and bigger."

The String

Willie spotted the pile of lumber from the road. Miss Chatty rocked in her rocker and read her Bible.

"Did the lumber yard drop the lumber at the wrong house?"

Miss Chatty smiled. "Nope, I's getting a ramp."

"Would you like to expand on that subject?"

"Your dad and Mr. Dittbrenner thought that because of my prominence in the community and because I'm over forty, that I should have a ramp."

Willie grinned, "You can't be over forty."

"Are you sure you don't have a girlfriend?"

Willie scratched his head and rubbed his eye, "Well, I might."

"What makes ya think ya might have a girlfriend?"

"Well, you remember I wanted a pair of blue jeans...so I wouldn't be the only student wearing overalls."

"I do recall something to that affect."

"Stephanie Hoffmeister, that sits next to me in algebra class wore overalls to school today."

Miss Chatty's eyes twinkled, "Well, you'uns as good as married. Have ya set a date?"

"It's kinda scary almost havin a girlfriend."

Miss Chatty giggled, "Do your hands sweat in algebra class?"

"Profusely."

"You have a girlfriend."

"It feels kinda goofy."

"That's what it's supposed to feel like."

"What's the string for?"

"The man that delivered the lumber explained to Mr. Dittbrenner and your dad that the ramp had to drop one inch in every twelve inches."

"How'd the man figure the angle?"

"He measured the height of the porch and then measured out that way twenty eight feet."

Willie's brow furrowed, then he walked out away from the porch and turned around. "I don't think he has the angle right."

"Who died and made you carpenter?"

Willie laughed. "If the land was perfectly flat, his calculations would be correct. But the hill slopes away from the porch, so the ramp is chasing the slope down the hill. Here let me show you." Willie opened his backpack and pulled out a sheet of paper and a pencil. Then he sketched a rough drawing of the porch, the ramp, and the hillside."

"I see what you're saying. The ramp will end up sixty feet long and it still might not be long enough. I'll have ta take a nap when I get to the end of the ramp."

Willie sketched another sheet of paper and then another. He stood for a moment and then walked to the other end of the porch. "This side looks very much like that side. There's very little difference in drop. So I see two options." He handed Miss Chatty the drawings. "You can either do a switchback to get the 1 in 12 angle or you can put the ramp at an angle so that it goes slightly uphill. Tomorrow morning give these sketches to Johanness and he can determine what he wants to do."

"I didn't know it was going to be such a big project."

"It's not. It just takes a little planning."

"Go wash up and we'll have some dinner and maybe some blackberry pie."

Δ

The valley was bathed in moonlight. Miss Chatty walked out onto the porch with her walker. The stack of lumber left the darkest of shadows. She moved to the end of the porch where the string was wrapped around a nail.

A woodnote came with the breeze as two trees rubbed each other.

"Dear Lord, I don't deserve this. I didn't work for it. I didn't earn it. Help us to put the string where it belongs. Help us to cut the boards right. Keep everyone safe. In Jesus name we pray. Amen."

As she pushed her walker to the door she looked at the rock steps. "I love you, Chet."

The Carpenter

Johanness and Wham stood off from the house and looked at Willie's drawings. "Your son is right."

Wham smiled, "He's pretty good at figgerin."

"Has he ever done any carpentry or construction?"

"Nope, nary a lick."

"Well, he certainly nailed this. He visualizes very well."

"He does a lot of things real good."

Miss Chatty spoke loudly, "Is it gonna work?"

"We're going to make it work."

"Did you need some more coffee and banana nut bread?"

"We might," said Wham. "A man's gots ta keep up his strength."

Johanness was not used to the pace. "We're burning daylight. We'll take a break in an hour or two."

Wham said, "Haste makes waste."

Johanness countered with, "He who hesitates is lost."

Wham shook his head, "They can't both be right."

Miss Chatty said, "There's carpentry tools in the shed. Willie cleaned up in there; it might be hard to find stuff."

Johanness opened the door. Three of the stud walls had workbenches with tools neatly hung above. A small woodstove was next to the fourth wall. The concrete floor was swept.

"Here's a tool belt," said Wham, "and its already gots a hammer and nails in the pouches. It's even gots a measuring stick. Wham handed it to Johanness.

Johanness put on the tool belt and hefted the straight claw hammer. He flipped it in the air and caught it.

"Ya was a carpenter, alright."

"Yeah." Johanness pulled the carpenter's square and a level off of their nails. "Grab those sawhorses."

"OK, the first thing we need to do is establish where the landing is going to be."

Miss Chatty overlooked the project. "Can the landing be big enough for a bench to sit on?"

"We'll make it happen," said Johanness.

Johanness went over to the wood pile, pulled his hammer, and cut the metal bands with the straight claw.

"You look like you've done this before," said Miss Chatty.

"Do you have a wheelbarrow?"

"There's one on the other side of the shed where the car is."

"Wham, can you grab that?"

"Yessir, boss man."

Wham returned with the wheelbarrow. "The tars flat."

"Miss Chatty said, "There's a tire pump in the shed. Wham, can I ask you a question?"

"Sure, Miss Chatty."

"Where's your shoes?"

"The giant possum ate em."

Miss Chatty tittered. "Oh, my rib still hurts." When she caught her breath she asked, "You weren't wearing them at the time, were you?"

"I left em out on the porch and when I got ta goin I couldn't find my boots. The giant possum bent down my fence and ate my boots."

"Oh my. Did you see him?"

"No maam."

"What size shoes do you wear?"

"The ones the possum ate were ten and a halfs."

Wham worried over the wheelbarrow tire; spinning the wheel, taking the air cap off, and finally hooking up the tire pump.

Johanness shook his head, "What are you doing?"

"Whatcha mean?"

"Let's go, lets go. Gramma was slow but she was old."

"A man don't want ta work hisself outta a job."

There it was. "This isn't a union job. We need to finish this by tomorrow evening."

Wham raised his eyebrows, "Tamarra evening? Is ya pants on fire?"

Johanness looked at the shoeless farmer. "We need to finish this so we can build some more whirligigs, put together some giant possum t-shirts, and do some metal detecting."

"You'uns all full a work ta do."

"We need to have the holes dug and concrete poured for the posts and the slab before we leave this evening."

"Might rain," said Wham.

Miss Chatty said, "Are you ready for a break yet?"

Johanness closed his eyes, took a deep breath and slowly let it out.

Wham asked, "Ya ain't takin a nap standin up, is ya?"

"No."

"Old man Harper could sleep standin up."

Δ

Johanness set up the sawhorses, plugged in the saw, and then looked for an outlet.

"You'll have to run the cord out the window," said Miss Chatty. "Chet said he was going to put a outlet outside but he never got around to it."

Johanness moved the string up the hill and then checked the angle using the level.

"How you'uns know when it's right?" said Wham.

Johanness moved over to the sawhorses and put the level on a 2x8. He pulled his tape out and began, "We don't have a transit or a string level, so we're going to use what we have. The level is four feet long and 2-1/4" wide. We need to be drop one inch for each foot." Johanness drew an outline around the level. "OK, if we go one foot down the level and one inch down we can put a dot here. If we go two feet down the level we can mark another dot at two inches. Now, if we draw a line from the corner of the level though the dots we have our angle. If I put a mark on the level at 2'-3-1/16" and then hold the level next to the line I can tell if the string is at the right angle."

"I's gonna hafta study on that one for a while."

Johanness walked over and held the top of the level even with the porch. "Now the level is level when the bubble is in the center of the lines. And see how the string goes straight through the mark I drew on the level."

"Well, I'll be dogged."

"When we get to nailing the ramp together we can check it again. This tells us the location of the landing for the ramp."

"So this ramp is a gonna go all that way out there?"

"Yep."

"Oooooweee, that's gonna be the longest ramp in Spasum County. Miss Chatty might end up in the Guinness Book a World Records."

"OK, next we need to figure out where the posts go."

At lunch, the three sat on the shaded porch and ate potato soup and turkey sandwiches.

"I wonder if'n the giant possum was around when the Indians were here and he ate their moccasins?" asked Wham.

"That reminds me. Wham," said Miss Chatty, "go in the house and look under the bed next to the wall. There's a pair of boots that might fit you."

"Are they Chet's boots?"

"Yep. Chet and I had a talk this morning I knew he would want you to have them."

"I gots ta pay ya for em," said Wham.

"You're building me a ramp. Oh yeah, there's a pair of socks in the bottom drawer of the chest of drawers."

Wham got up and went inside. In a few minutes he pushed open the screen door with the boots on. "They's just a hair big. Ta be honest they fits bettern the boots the giant possum ate. Red would say it was a good thing that the giant possum ate my boots and she'd a been right."

"How's Red doing?"

"Whal, the biopsy was good, but they want ta check her again in three months."

Johanness slapped a mosquito.

"Yep, sometimes the mosquitos get bad being close to the river," said Miss Chatty.

"You need some bat boxes."

Miss Chatty and Wham looked at Johanness. "Bat boxes are houses where bats nest. The bats eat...and I don't remember exactly, but each bat eats like a million mosquitoes per night."

"Ain't never heard a no bat houses."

"I saw the plans for building bat houses in Mother Earth News a long time ago. You just expanded your business from whirligigs and bird houses to include bat houses."

"I ain't got no plans for bat houses."

"I'm sure there are a bunch of free plans for bat houses on the internet."

"I ain't got no internet."

"Sure you do. I'll just take my tablet up to the top of the hill, download the plans, and then print it out on my printer."

"Then I's gonna owe ya."

"You need to quit worrying about who owes what."

"How bout I build ya a bat house?"

"You do realize that when you build Miss Chatty a bat house that everyone in the valley is going to want one."

Wham's eyes got big, "Holy chichen lips!!"

"And if you get a website you could sell your birdhouses and whirligigs and bat houses to the whole world."

Wham looked pale, "At this rate, I ain't gonna be able to keep up."

"And bats need a very warm place to live, that's why they like living in attics. And the bat house needs to be high off the ground, as high as twenty feet."

"I ain't a climbin no twenty feet tree ta put up no bat house."

"The bat house shouldn't be in the shade of a tree. It should be out in the open and facing south. I'll bet there are some YouTube videos on bat houses."

"And all this stuff is on the internet?"

"Yep."

"And its free?"

"Well, it is if you have a wifi connection."

"I see why my kids wants wifi."

"There's pornography on the internet," said Miss Chatty.

"Yes, there is." Johanness looked at the King James Bible on the porch rail.

"And there are ideas that run against the teachings of the Bible and God."

"Yes, there are."

"And I don't think Willie believes in God."

Wham bowed his head to the ground. Johanness looked at this strong, intelligent woman. "Miss Chatty, the world is a scary place, a place of good and evil. I'm not telling you anything you don't already know. How is it that you want to build a library and have the internet?"

"Willie, and all the young people in this valley need a chance to be the best they can be. Willie is going off to college to be an astrophysicist. He is going to do great things. He needs every advantage we can give him. And the reason he is going to do great things is that he was brought up right."

Wham looked at the ground, "Sometimes I feels like I's let him down."

"You and Red are two of the best parents I've ever seen."

The post holes were dug and Johannes nailed together a form for the landing. In the afternoon when the rain came the two men joined Miss Chatty on the porch.

"I love hearin the rain on the roof," said Wham.

"Makes me sleepy," said Johanness, as he lay down on the porch. Within a minute he was asleep. Elliott lay down next to Johanness and was soon running with his friend, Happy, on the forever grassy hillsides above the river.

Δ

Elliott nuzzled Johanness and his eyes flicked open. The shadows were long and Johanness murmured a "Dammit...Come on Wham, we got work to do."

Johanness moved quickly, throwing a bag of quick-set concrete into the wheelbarrow, adding water, and mixing with the hoe. "You don't want it too watery. When it looks like this, it's ready." Johanness pushed the wheelbarrow to the edge of the hole and dumped it.

"I ain't never seed a man pour cement down a hole like that. Most folks just put a rock in the bottom. Seems like a good waste a seament."

"We don't have time to discuss the merits of a rock footing. I'm used to doing it this way." Johanness grabbed another bag of cement, put it in the wheelbarrow, and ripped it open with the claw of his hammer. "Here you mix this one and I'll finish leveling the form for the slab."

Johanness screed off the top of the landing as Willie came up the driveway. "It looks good."

"It's dinner time. Come wash up."

"I gots ta go ta the house," said Wham.

"I have plenty. How about I call Red and she and Willis can come down and join us?"

Wham hesitated, "Uh, our phone don't work right now." He turned to Johanness, "I'll see ya on the bridge in the morning." He looked at his son, "I swear you'uns getting taller ever day. Love you.

"I love you too."

Wham headed for the road and turned back, "Hey, Miss Chatty, thanks for the readin lesson."

The farmer with his new boots and his green hat walked off into the darkness.

Kawack!! "I luuv mosquitos."

Δ

Deep in the night Johanness awoke and wondered why he had not thought of using a water level. Then worry slowly crept in. *Was the slab at the correct spot for the 1 in 12 pitch? Why did he think of the hose now?* He wished to go back to sleep but he ended up working on the videos until at last he yawned, said goodnight to Elliott, and lay down.

The Finger

Wham stood on the porch as soft light worked into the valley. He could hear the truck. He wondered how it had happened. *The man offers ya a job and ya end up beating him up.*

The truck with the headlights on came around the corner. Wham waved his howdy wave.

Uncle Seizure gave Wham the finger and screamed, "Asshole!"

At least he changes the cuss words every morning. Wonder how long its going to take afor he runs out of cuss words? Might be a while.

Red commented through the screen door. "He's bad to hold a grudge."

"Yep."

"He fell like a sack a taters."

"Yep."

"He shouldn't a said them things."

"Ya hurt his pride."

"What are we a gonna do?"

"I dunno. It ain't good the way things is."

"Mebbe ya could build him a bench or a whirligig."

Wham chuckled, "It could be a truck with a arm out the winder that gives the finger."

"Now that id be a funny whirligig. Ya need ta make it."

Willis said, "I'll bet you could sell a hundert of em."

"Hmmm, you'uns might be right."

"See there," said Red, "hitting him was a good thing. We'd a never thought a making a truck with a finger if it weren't for Uncle Seizure being such a dumbass."

Wham looked at the floor and shook his head, "We shouldn't be teaching our kids to hit folks."

Red looked at Willis, "Hittin folks ain't the right thin to do." Red couldn't hide her smile, "And sides, ya gots folks that's bad ta hold a grudge. Ain't no tellin what Uncle Seiizue 'il do."

Willis asked, "How ya gonna give the whirligig to Uncle Seizure?"

"I ain't the one that hit him," said Wham.

"You'uns said OK."

Wham sighed.

"We might could sneak over at night and set it up next to his pond."

"What's this "we?""

Willis said, "Just take it over when he's at work and ask Aunt Seizure where to set it up."

"Its gonna take a while ta whittle a truck and a hand."

"Have Jeb and Sludge hep ya."

Willis asked, "Can I paint the truck? I'll paint it green like Uncle Seizures truck."

"Heck yeah."

Rutabagas

It was early morning on the low water bridge. Elliott, Johanness, and Wham had arrived to say farewell to the last of the stars and planets. Happy, Jeb, and Sludge had joined them later with their cane poles. Willie stopped at the end of the bridge and listened.

"They's rutabagas."

"They's turnips."

"They ain't."

"They is."

"Ain't."

"Is."

"Rutabaga sounds funny, so rutabagas wins."

"Turnips sounds just as funny as rutabagas."

"Does not. Turnips ain't half as funny as rutabagas."

"Turnips sound like ya gots something up ya nose."

"If'n I had a horse I'd name it Rutabaga. Giddyup Rutabaga."

"If'n ya horse was Rutabaga they wouldn't letcha in a posse."

"Would so. They let anybody in that wants ta catch the bad guys."

"If'n I was the Marshall I'd tell ya ta go back ta the house."

"We needs ta vote on it," said Sludge.

"Git ya bobber away from my bobber."

"Ya git ya bobber away from my bobber."

"I was here first."

"No, I was."

"Go on now."

"Ya, go on now."

Willie decided that the message was more important than his sanity and approached the men.

Wham asked, "Why ain't you in school?"

"It's Saturday."

Johanness said, "You going to join us?"

"I don't think so. I just came by to say that the giant possum left footprints in your slab for the ramp."

"We got him now," said Sludge. "We'll get DNA evidence ta see if'n we evolved from possums."

Jeb and Sludge spun their lines around their cane poles and stood up.

Willie helped his dad up.

Wham said, "I'd name my horse Poverty."

Willie smiled and then pushed Wham off the bridge.

Δ

The troop, including the wet Wham Wooster, walked past the "Free Coffee" signs and up to the slab. Johanness already had his smart phone out and punched video.

"That's giant possum tracks If'n I ever seed giant possum tracks," said Jeb.

"Yep, got a mariposible thumb print. That's possum alright.

Sludge got down close to the slab, "I don't see no hair in the seament. We needs possum hair for the DNA."

"I don't think possums have hair on their feet."

"Ever one a my toes gots some hair."

"See, they's the proof we ain't from no possums."

"It don't prove nothin. We needs possum hair."

"When do we get are free blackberry muffins and coffee?" asked Jeb.

Miss Chatty smiled, "When I see some posts in the ground and some framin on those posts."

"You heard the lady," said Johanness, "Let's get to it."

Miss Chatty's Ramp

Miss Chatty walked down the ramp with her walker. The crowd got quiet. All eyes watched in anticipation. When she reached the slab at the bottom she turned around and walked up the slight incline. From the porch she faced the crowd.

Her eyes glistened and the sun erased her age. "I want to thank everyone that made this happen. It's almost as good as my raisin pie."

The crowd clapped and whistled. When at last she could hear the river, she spoke, "My friends, we have come together and made this happen. We were meant for bigger things, much bigger things. This is our chance to move forward." Miss Chatty took a long breath, "This ramp will be here long after I'm gone. It was built with cement and nails and boards and love.

"We are not going to stand still. Just as we built this ramp we can build a library. We will build a library. We will not take no for an answer. We will do it as a community, a united community. Money will not hold us back. You will build this library," Miss Chatty pointed to Willie and waved him to come up on the porch.

He rushed to her side, "I need to sit down... Finish this." Miss Chatty sat down in her rocker.

Willie looked at the small crowd. *Linger. Eye contact. Honesty. This is not about you. Say thank you.* "Ideas, or as most of you would say, ide'ers, and strength and spirit will build this library. Miss Chatty has a vision that everyone in this valley will be able to read and write. Everyone. She is making it happen, one person, one letter, one word, one sentence at a time. And soon, the book will be read. Knowledge is power, power to shape your destiny. We all need that chance.

"The ramp is more than a ramp. Johanness Dittbrenner saw that Miss Chatty needed a ramp and moved forward.

"How do you build a library without money?" Willie smiled. "You take the strength of Miss Chatty and a phone and magical things happen. Rumps Lumber Yard, that supplied the material for this ramp, offered to do the plans and get the permits. They have some roof trusses that were made but not paid for and these will be where we start. The trusses will define the building. Jim's Concrete said that from time to time they have extra concrete left over and will help with the foundation. Fred's Sawmill said they will supply the feather edge siding...We can do this. We must do this.

"Do you see what I see? I see a library with books, books that take you places, and computers and the internet. The world is small and connected. We are all connected. Today we built a ramp, a ramp to the future. Tomorrow we will build a library. It will happen because you will make it happen." Willie turned to Miss Chatty, "Thank You Miss Chatty. You're an amazing woman."

Sludge yelled, "Eeeehaaa, we's gonna build a liberry!"

Cookie Jar

"Wud the doctor say?" asked Wham.

"I handed her the pages that Johanness printed out and I told her that I would get a second opinion before I did any surgery. I don't know if she liked that. Anyways, she said that we needed to do another mammogram in three months to see if'n they was any changes."

"Sos we knows and we don't knows," said Wham.

"Yeah, but I feel a lot better knowin she knows that we knows."

"Yep, it's good ta know stuff before ya get into it." Johanness looked up well pumps and we can get a renourished one for bout half price and its gots the same guarantee. Eighty nine bucks."

Red closed her eyes for a moment and then went to the cookie jar. "Ask Johanness to order it."

"They's shippin and handlin and taxes sos it's gonna be probly a hunert bucks."

Red handed Wham the money. "We's goin forward. We just gotta hang in there."

"I wouldn't be nothin without ya."

"Ya got that right."

"Someday we's goin on a date ta the aquarium."

"Ya sure knows how ta sweet talk a lady."

"How much time we gots before Willis gets home?"

Red glanced at the clock, "Hour and a half."

"What'd ya think we should do?"

"I dunno, what'd ya think we should do?"

"I dunno."

"Mebbe we should box."

"Hour and a half a boxin is a lot of boxin."

Sawin

The wind was broken, the dandelions reached for the sun. A flock of robins probed here and there in the green dew. Wham sawed the pieces for the bat house and Johanness hammered a jig together to hold the pieces. "We need a shaving horse."

"I ain't seen one a them in years. Old man Billy Jensen had one. It's like having a extra set a hands ta hold stuff. Where'd ya pick up on shaving horses?"

"I worked in a wood shop one winter making craft items and I saw it in a book. The one I made worked great. I took it to a craft show to work on stuff and a guy offered me two hundred bucks for it."

"Ooowee, we needs ta make shave horses."

Uncle Seizure drove by and screamed colorful epithets. Wham and Johanness waved and laughed. "He ain't never gonna get over that."

Johanness said, "He's just a miserable old man."

"He ain't as miserable as I am."

"I ain't heard ya complain all mornin."

"That's cuz I's workin and I slept good. Best night's sleep in two, three years."

"A good night's sleep il do that to ya."

Wham looked at Johanness, "You'uns ain't talkin right."

"I's just a tryin ta fit in."

"Takes a while ta get the hang a talkin right. I wernt gonna say nothing but ya looks like ya got ya goin ta church clothes on."

Johanness smiled, "It's been a long time since I wore overalls."

"Yep, them's high falutin clothes. Folks knows right off, you'uns rich."

"Whal, I don't want folks thinkin I's uppity. I'll have ta pick up a pair of overalls."

"The General Store's got a bunch a overalls.

"Ya need ta keep a sawin. You'uns fallin behind."

"Dadgum, how many bat houses we gonna make."

"If'n ya don't get ta sawin we ain't gonna make any."

"We needs some music ta saw by."

"Sawin music comin up." Johanness walked over to the computer and plugged his rock and roll memory stick into the USB port.

Wham muttered, "Damn, hippie music."

The fourth song was "Stayin Alive" by the Bee Gees.

"Quit that. Somebodies gonna see ya."

"I don't care. I like dancing."

"Ya ain't sposed ta have fun whilst ya's workin."

"Why not?"

"It ain't right."

Johanness spun around doing his best Saturday Night Fever. "I'll stop dancing when I got some boards ta nail tagether."

"That there's disco dancing. That ain't allowed in the valley."

"I'm breakin the law, breakin the law. Uh, uh, uh, uh, breakin the laa-ah-ah.

Saw, saw, saw, saw, saw me some boards, saw me some boards.

Uh, uh, uh, uh, saw me some boooards."

"I's goin ta the house if'n ya don't quit that."

Johanness picked up the saw, pointed it at the sky, and spun around.

"Dadgummit, I's a warnin ya."

Elliott woofed and jumped around.

"One more bat house and then we make a shave horse."

"Fine with me."

"Can ya gets a picture of a shave horse on YouTube?"

"Oh yeah, but we'll have to go to the top of the hill."

Wham hurried sawing the last slab for the last bat house of the day. As he handed the board to Johanness he asked, "Did ya serve in Vietnam?"

"No, I was in college at the time and by the time I graduated Nixon had brought the boys home."

"Was ya a hippie?"

"I had long hair and smoked pot."

"Rupert Rump and Cecil Grim died in Vietnam."

"Fifty five thousand young men died in Vietnam. Over two hundred thousand were wounded and a whole lot more had problems from Agent Orange and thousands have PTSD. That war will never end."

Both men were quiet, lost in thought.

"I don't want to talk about it anymore," said Johanness. He hammered the last nail into the batbox and set it aside. "We need more posts."

"Let's go see how ta build a shave horse."

A Yams a Yam

"What is your greatest achievement?" asked Johanness.

Wham didn't hesitate, "One year I grew a seven pound yam. Biggest yam ever. Wouldn't fit in the stove. Crazy lookin thing. We's got a picture of it on the shelf above the sink."

"Seven pounds is huge."

"Biggest one ever growed in the valley. Randy Rump tried ta beat my yam with a yam full a splitshot. Rumps is bad ta cheat."

Wham and Johanness sat on the new sawmill slab bench atop the hill overlooking the Rump River valley and the flat piedmont beyond. Johanness spoke to his phone, "Siri, what is the world's biggest sweet potato?"

"In 1998, in Brazil, Fernando Paco, harvested a sweet potato that weighed 14.5 kilograms."

Johanness closed his eyes for moment, "That's 32 pounds."

Wham's left eyebrow raised and his lip lifted on the right side, "Ain't no way that woman knows bout yams."

"Uh, I beg to differ," said Johanness, "She is only a voice connected to a search engine that has looked through millions of bits of information in nanoseconds and picked out the best answer."

"Ain't no yam that big. Show me a picture."

Johanness scrolled to the article, enlarged the picture, and handed the phone to Wham.

"That can't be real. It's as big as the biggest punkin I ever growed. Yams don't get that big. That man in the pictures gots ta be really small."

Johanness said, "It might be a special kind of sweet potato."

"Whatcha mean special kind?"

"There are probably a bunch of different varieties of sweet potatoes."

"A yams a yam." Wham handed back the phone.

"Siri, how many varieties of sweet potatoes are there?"

"There are over 400 varieties of sweet potatoes around the world."

"Ooooweee-doggie. We need ta get us some a them big growin yams. Sure be fun ta show up at the Yam Festival with a thirty pounder."

"Yam Festival?"

"Where ya been? We gots the biggest Yam Festival that I know of. Dint they grow yams in Nebraska?"

"I don't remember anyone growing yams. We grew corn, wheat, and soybeans."

"Ain't nothin bettern a yam slathered in butter with some brown sugar."

An updraft rolled across the knoll and began to take the dew off the grass.

"This is a very valuable piece of property."

"How ya figure? If'n its so valuable how come I gets poorer and poorer ever year?"

"The view from here is outstanding. I'm only guessing but I would say Indians and soldiers from the civil war camped on this spot."

"I got a whole bucket a arraheads in the shed. I use ta find em ever spring when I plowed."

Johanness surveyed Wham's property down to the river and then his attention moved back to the charred foundation. "How did the farmhouse burn down?"

Wham was quiet a long time, the seconds ticked into minutes.

Johanness glanced over at Wham and saw anger in his eyes. "Uh, it doesn't matter." Johanness quickly said, "Have you ever heard of Wall Drug, South Dakota?"

Wham took a long breath, "Nope. Thars a lot a places I ain't heard a or been to."

"Well, about eighty years ago, right in the middle of the depression, a couple was looking for a place to call home. Ted Hustead was a pharmacist and wanted to start a drug store. They found a little town named Wall out in the middle of nowhere and decided that was where they would start their business. Business was poor, very poor. After almost five years they decided they might have to give up their dream and move on."

Wham listened intently. Elliott appeared and lay down between the two men.

"One hot summer day the wife said, "You know what the people going down the highway want."

"What's that?"

"A free glass of ice water."

"Mr. Hustead made up some signs and posted them along the road with one word on each sign so people could read them as they drove by. The signs said, "Free Ice Water at Wall Drug." Mr. Hustead said he felt foolish putting up the signs. By the time Ted got back to the store there were already people waiting to get their free ice water. They ran out of cracked ice and Ted had to chip some more off a block. And the folks would buy ice cream and sodas. The next year they hired eight girls to help run the business. Today, on a good day, twenty thousand people will stop at Wall Drug, South Dakota. "

Wham's eyes got big. "I ain't never seen twenty thousand folks. Wham's mouth opened and worry came to his eyes, "We can't have no twenty thousand folks comin up the dirt road. We's gonna have ta pave'r. We's gonna have a traffic jam and folks gitten mad at each other."

Johanness smiled.

"We ain't got enuf food for twenty thousand folks. They's gonna starve ta death up here."

Johanness laughed a hearty laugh.

"We needs ta take them signs down afor this gets outa hand."

Elliott got up and woofed at Wham. "What's he a barkin at?"

"He can't laugh so he barks."

"Starvin ta death ain't funny."

Elliott wooffed some more and then rolled around in the grass.

"I ain't never seen a dog roll around and bark at the same time."

It's Un-American

"Jeb and Sludge's pickup runs on donut oil," said Wham.

Johanness raised his eyebrows, "They run their truck on biodiesel?"

"Yep, it's un-American. Man needs ta buy gas. It ain't right. They ain't paying gas taxes and they's running up and down these dirt roads for free."

"I wish I could run my RV on biodiesel."

Creases ran across Wham's forehead, "I's surrounded by a bunch of communist."

Johanness thought for a moment, "Years ago congress tried to pass a bill that would tax the vegetables from your garden. They were saying that the vegetables were income and technically they were correct."

"Damn, them congress people. How the hell is a man sposed ta get by?"

"Now, you sound like you don't want to pay taxes."

Wham pushed out his lower lip, "I ain't no communist tryin ta get something for nothin. I swear half the folks in this valley is commies. They's on food stamps and that wicked program and disability and they brags bout how much they's gettin ever month. And they gots Obama phones that ain't worth a shot a powder cuz we ain't got no tower. They's living like kings while my family starves ta death. I ain't lookin for no handouts. I wants ta work. I wants ta make it." Wham slowed down and looked at the ground. He kicked a small pebble. He turned away from Johanness, "I just ain't no good."

Johanness knew there were tears running down his friends face. "We live in a strange country and to be honest about it, I don't understand it anymore."

"So you feel it too, that things ain't what they should be?"

"Yeah," Johanness took his time, "everything's messed up, a giant cluster fuck, and yet somehow most people are getting by."

"I ain't a gettin by. I's so tired. I's so tired a goin backerds."

Clouds had dulled the morning and far across the sandhills rain moved from west to east.

"You are what you think about."

Wham ran the thought over a couple of times, "So's what ya sayin?"

"Are you thinking that this new direction is not going to work and you'll lose the farm or are you excited about the giant possum project?"

"Thins keep breakin faster'n I can fix em. All I's doin is puttin out forest fires."

"When was the last time you and Red went to Waffle House?"

"What the hell you'uns talkin bout? We ain't got money ta do what we needs to do much less go ta Waffle House. We ain't even got a truck thad get to the Waffle House."

"What if you stole an RV that had a full tank of gas and plenty of food in the pantry and had marijuana plants growing under grow lights that you could sell for a thousand dollars a plant; where would you go?"

Wham sucked on his teeth, "I ain't never thought about stealin a RV. Sounds like it might be fun. I guess we'd go see the aquarium in Myrtle Beach. Then again, we might end up writing country music in the big house."

"Why don't you go to Yellowstone, or the Grand Canyon, or Alaska?"

"I'd get couple hunert miles from the house and the RV id break down.'

Johanness shook his head, "OK, lets go the other direction. Let's bring the Grand Canyon to Wham." Johanness typed in Grand Canyon.

"Oooowee, that's a big hole and ain't nobody farmin it."

"OK, lets go to Alaska. I'm going to put in driving the Alaskan Highway."

"Them folks got a rig just like yas."

"Yep."

Wham sat immersed in the video that lasted forty minutes. "I feel like I been there."

"That video got over 300,000 views. I'm sure their videos paid for their vacation."

"Kinda like what you'uns a doin."

"Yep, and since I've been filming you and the people in the valley, my subscribers have been growing. That means more revenue. The internet is sharing, which is a new concept for most people. If you have something to share, you put it on the internet. If I want to find out how to tune a piano or make a whirligig or a bathouse I simply go to YouTube and put whirligig in the search box and you will get hundreds of videos about whirligigs."

"They'uns ruinnin my business. They'uns givin away all the secrets of how ta make a whirligig."

"They're helping your business. These videos make people aware that there are whirligigs. A lot of people have never seen a whirligig. And these videos inspire people to try things. And not everything works and some videos show how they have failed; what went wrong so you don't have to make the same mistakes."

"So if'n the perpeller flies off, folks id want ta see that."

"Oh yeah, that would be funny and people love funny stuff. Thousands of people would want to see the propeller fly off."

"What if'n if flies off in the dark? Ain't nobody gonna see it."

"Well, we could do a before and after and maybe show how to make it better."

"What if'n it flies apart again?"

Johanness raised one eyebrow, "Do your whirligigs fly apart a lot?"

"Sometimes. It's hard ta make a good whirligig. They's a bunch a thins that can go wrong."

"Well, that makes a great video. People can see that building a whirligig is challenging and they get involved mentally. If it's too easy, most people find it boring."

"Ya cants be giving all the secrets away."

Johanness typed.

"Is that word whirligig?" asked Wham.

"Yep."

"Slow down and let me look at it. That's a big word. So if'n I writes that word on a piece a paper and then gets a computer I could get all this stuff."

"Yep."

"It don't seem right. Looks like a man could learn bout anythin."

"Yep."

"Why would anyone go ta school?"

Johanness adjusted his glasses and then scratched behind his right ear. "That's complicated. Name me something you want to know."

"I want's ta know how ta make some money before June 1st."

"That's too...OK." Johanness typed. "I just typed in how to make money. Today, on YouTube there are 73 million videos on how to make money. Tomorrow, there will be more videos on making money."

"We'uns gonna be up here a while."

A breeze carried the smell of rain.

"Let's do the math. Just say the average video on making money is five minutes." Johanness pulled up the calculator on the screen. "That would mean that to watch 73 million videos it would take 365 million minutes. Divide by 60 would give us hours or over 6 million hours and divide by 24 to give us days...that would be 253,000 days and divide that by 365 days to give us years. It would take 694 years to watch all the videos about making money."

"A man's gots ta sleep sometime."

"You're right. If I divide by 66% I should get the number of years. 1051 years."

"I ain't gonna make no money by the 1st of June, am I?"

"Not if you watch YouTube videos all day. Let's watch a couple of videos on making whirligigs or bat houses or bird houses or wood duck nesting houses and then let's get to work. We need to make a workbench and a place to put tools."

"Id be nice if'n the workbench id go in and out of the shed so I could work outside or inside."

"We could put it on wheels and I could make a video and put it on YouTube."

"Jeb and Sludge fix up bicycles they gets outta the dumpsters. They might have a couple a wheels."

"I could do a video of Jeb and Sludge dumpster diving and then fixing up the bicycles. Do they sell the bicycles?"

"Nope, they gives em ta the kids at the Luthran Children's Home at Christmas."

"Oh my goodness, that would be a great video."

"And you get paid for doin these videos?"

"Yeah, and what is really neat is that I will get paid months and years from now for doing these videos."

"Sounds too good ta be true."

"It does, doesn't it? It's called passive income. Uh, let's just say you grew one tomato."

"The hornworms got the rest of em."

"Yeah, uh, OK, so now you have one tomato and you sell that tomato for a dollar."

"Thad be a big un."

Johanness sighed, "Yep. Now you have one dollar and that's all the money you will ever get for that one tomato."

"I done purty good a gettin a dollar."

"OK, now say you made a video about how you grew that tomato; a video how you started the seed and a video about when you planted and a video how you cut off the suckers and so on. People who wanted to learn to grow tomatoes would click on your video, today and tomorrow and next week and five years from now. You would still be getting income from that tomato video five years from now."

"How much?"

"I don't know. Depends on how many people click on the video and see the advertising."

"I needs ta know how much."

"OK, lets say you made one penny a day from one video. That would be $3.65 per year. In five years," Johanness tapped the calculator, "it would be $18.25. In ten years that one video would've made thirty six dollars and fifty cents."

"Ya dint type that in."

"I didn't need to."

"Ya done that in ya head?"

"Yeah."

Johanness sighed, "Wisht I could do that."

"You can. Most people can. It's pretty simple when you know how."

"Could I learn it on YouTube?"

Johanness typed in Basic Math. "There are almost three million videos on basic math." Johanness clicked on a three minute video of kids counting carrots.

Wham looked perturbed, "I knows how ta do that."

Johanness clicked on another short video showing elementary multiplication. "Down the road you can learn algebra, and geometry."

"And all these videos are free on YouTube?"

"Yep. It's all about sharing."

Pastor Momar Analyzes

"What do you think of my sermons?"

Elizabeth was caught off guard, "I think they are very good. Is something bothering you?"

"Well, the best speech in my church was the one given by Miss Chatty. I've played it over and over again and I'm still at a loss as to why its so good. I'm the educated one. I'm the one that is responsible for selling the most important product of all; salvation."

Elizabeth said, "Show me the video of Miss Chatty."

Pasto Momar clicked on the icon on his desktop.

When it was finished, Elizabeth said, "It makes me want to cry. You don't hear it, do you?"

"Hear what?"

"The sincerity, the pleading, the power of how she connects with her friends. It isn't in the delivery. It's in the words that reach into the soul and asks for the best in each of us, the best we have to give. It's the giving. She is giving everyone in this valley a chance to be a part of something bigger, something good, something meaningful."

Elizabeth walked out onto the deck, stood at the rail, and in a few minutes Pastor Momar joined her. He placed the smart phone on the rail and pressed the button. They listened to the speech together.

Pastor Momar shook his head, "She should be a pastor."

"Some churches have assistant pastors."

"Let me think on that one. She might have to be accredited...and the church might have to pay her."

"I don't think she cares anything about the money."

"I don't understand people who aren't motivated by money."

"Miss Chatty is about people. Her brain gets its endorphins when she makes others happy."

"That's quite a theory."

"And now she has a cause, a focus. She has a goal to build a library before she dies. And just to be honest, I think she is unstoppable."

"There has to be a sermon in there, somewhere."

Elizabeth smiled, "There might be."

"I really liked the ramp."

"It's the best ramp in the valley."

"It's the only ramp in the valley," said Pastor Momar.

"What were you thinking?"

Pastor Momar pointed to a rise, "If we parked the car over there..."

Elizabeth interrupted, "We don't have the money for a ramp."

"If I die from climbing those stairs then the Church is without a pastor.

"Miss Chatty knows how much money is in the church heat pump fund."

"Maybe, maybe not. We can borrow the money from the fund and pay it back before summer when we need the heat pump."

What's That Smell

"I's goin up ta the General Store ta see how Willis is a doing with them t-shirts," said Wham.

Red said, "Uh, uh, I'm sure she is doin just fine."

"Yeah, but I might be able ta give her some advice."

Red turned away, "You might want to see if'n any more of the whirligigs got bought."

"Yeah, you'uns probly right. I gots plenty ta do, that's for sure. I still gots enuf wood for fifty bird houses. I was thinkin bout buildin a turkey vulture bird house."

Red giggled, "I always knew you'd go off the deep end someday."

"Folks could see it from the road real easy and id make em stop in."

"It might just work. And when we get the Giant Possum done this place will be bigger than Wall Drug Store."

"One step at a time, my sweetie."

Red closed her eyes and breathed slow, "What's that smell?"

"I dunno, I thought I smelt something couple days ago. Eeww, I hope it ain't what I think it is." Wham went out onto the porch. "Oh gawd, no."

Red scrunched up her face. "Pretty rank alright."

"We ain't got money ta fix the septic tank."

Red reached for Wham's hand. "We need to do what we can do. You go to work on the whirligigs and I'll go up to the General Store. Ask Johanness if Siri knows how ta fix a overflowed septic tank."

"I don't deserve you." Wham stepped off the porch, and headed toward the road.

Red yelled after him, "Ya need anythin from the Store?"

"A million dollars in small bills. Uh yeah, I need some six and eight penny nails."

"I'll get em. Love you."

"I love you, too."

A zephyr came across the puddles of heavy rancid fluid. Red tried not to breathe but it was no use. She could feel it on her skin. Her stomach churned. She ran to the opposite porch rail and threw up.

Δ

Johanness opened the camper door and Elliott bounded out. He could see Wham with his head bent down making his way along Rump Road.

As Wham approached Johanness asked, "Are you OK?"

"My septic tank is overflowed."

"That's not good. Come on in. We're having eggs benedict this morning."

"Do my overalls smell bad?"

Johanness scratched his nose, "Uh, how about we eat outside this morning."

Wham sat down in one of the fold up chairs, "I'll just sit out here."

Johanness hesitated and then said, "It's a great morning to sit outside and have breakfast. Let me turn up the music and I'll have breakfast ready in a little bit."

Elliott wagged his tail feverishly at Wham and was ready to bound in his lap when he suddenly changed his mind. He switched directions, ran up the side of the hill and sneezed and then sneezed again. Elliott rubbed his nose in the grass.

"I smells so bad Elliott won't come sit with me." *Wonder if Willis smelt it.*

Johanness turned up the speakers.

Δ

Johanness stopped with his fork halfway to his mouth and got a faraway look. Then he closed his eyes.

Wham knew not to interrupt a man in thought.

Johanness stood up and went inside. In a moment he came back and opened up one of the side panels with a key. "Maybe this will work." He held up a bottle. "It's for when the black water tank gets clogged up." Johanness looked at the label, "It has probiotics in it. You flush it down the toilet."

"Probiotics?"

"Yeah, they eat up the...uh...uh...stuff that is clogging the system."

"They's something alive in that bottle and they eat shit?"

"Yep."

"And I thought I had it bad."

The Quiet

"I woke up this morning and..."

"And what?"

Johanness said, "You've got a gold mine here."

Wham looked at Johanness and saw the excitement in his eyes, "Go on."

"People want what you have."

"I ain't got nothing."

"OK, think about what you don't have."

"I ain't got a pot ta pee in. I ain't gonna have a farm come June. My truck and my tractor and my windmill and my water pump don't run. I ain't got enough money ta pay for telephone or lectricty. And I's worried sick about Red."

"Yeah, yeah, yeah. And you don't have noise. You have a lot of peace and quiet. You don't have traffic. You don't have wifi or cell phone reception. You have a river with catfish. You have a great family and great neighbors. You have a giant possum running loose and eating your boots."

Wham interrupted, "And tearin down my fence."

"Do you realize what you have?"

"Trouble, lots and lots a trouble."

"You're going to be rich!"

"You'uns been doin happy drugs."

Johanness chuckled, "You have what people want."

"I ain't run inta too many folks that want ta be homeless and hungry."

"No, they want peace and quiet, a place to sit on a bridge and listen to the river. A place where the pace is slow, where they can leave the city behind. A place where you can roast marshmellows over a fire and see the stars at night. They want to be where the road is dirt and folks stop in the middle of the road and chat. A place where kids can tube on the river. A place where a fugitive can hide out."

Wham's eyes got big.

"Just kidding, just kidding."

"This id be a purty good place ta hide out. The law don't come up here much."

"I noticed that."

Elliott jumped up on Johanness's lap.

"The reason it kind of hit me was Elliott and I would like to stay here for a while. And I'd like to help build the library."

I Hate Him

The shadows from the clouds rolled up the hill and down the other side. Wham and Johanness sat together on the new sawmill wood bench and Elliott rolled in the grass.

"I's all tied up in knots and it's hard ta breathe," said Wham.

"Is the land making you happy?"

Wham frowned and then opened his mouth slightly, hesitated, and then spoke, "I ain't never thought bout it. I was always proud a bein a farmer."

"Right now you're worried about paying the taxes and you have been for a long time. What if you didn't have the land?"

"If'n I dint have the farm I wouldn't have nothin, cept my family and the farmhouse, and the farmhouse is bout done in. Me and Red built the farmhouse. We carried rock from the river for the foundation and the chimbley and we used sawmill lumber ta put her tagether."

"What happened to the house on the hill?"

"When my dad died, we put him in the ground, and then I burned down the house."

Johanness flinched.

"We dint put him in a casket, just threw him in the hole, face down, and covered him up."

Johanness raised his eyebrows and then waited.

"Damn, I hate him so bad." Wham took a long audible breath, "He was always drunk and he'd beat up my ma when he wanted sex and when I ran away, he caught me and tied me to a tree and beat me with a ......cane......pole. A breeze made the tall grass move. "There's thins ya don't forgive."

Minutes ticked by and Johanness could feel his heartbeat. Clouds and sun, clouds and sun. "Yeah, the parents of the girl that was killed because I made the fake ID will never forgive me and I don't blame them."

"And now my boy hates me. Seems like the hate just keeps a goin."

"I don't think your boy hates you...at all. I think he just feels stifled by where he lives and he and you are in two very different places."

"He don't care nothin bout the farm."

"He's got his head in the stars. He's going to make a great astrophysicist."

"Hard ta figure how a man that looks at stars is gonna make a livin."

"Have you ever seen some of the pictures that have been taken by the Hubble Telescope?"

"Saw something on the TV bout that a while back, before the TV quit. They had ta fix the eyeball."

"Uh, yeah. The lens needed to be fixed. The Hubble Telescope is the best thing the space program has done in a long time."

"So Willie's gonna be a eyeball fixer?"

"Probably not. There's a lot of different jobs that an astrophysicist can work on. He's going to do fine."

"I just don't want him ta hate me."

The Run

"I'll race you to the windmill tank."

Wham smiled, "How bout a little wager?"

"I love gambling, but this wouldn't be much of a gamble."

"If'n I win, we'uns play country music and if'n you win, you can play that no good, hippie, disco crap."

"What if I want to play jazz or reggae or Beethoven or rap?"

"No reggae or rap. This is my farm and we ain't havin no reggae or rap on my farm. A man's gots ta draw a line."

"Let's make this bet interesting. If I win, we play reggae for the rest of the day and if you win we play country. This will be the first reggae versus country music race."

"We ain't got no startin gun."

"I'll have Elliott bark."

"Huh?"

"OK Elliott, we need you to start the race. You need to growl twice and then bark."

Elliott nodded.

"We'uns needs a start line."

Johanness threw down a slab from the pile. "OK Elliott."

Elliott growled once, then again, then woofed.

Wham came out fast, pumping hard. Johanness fell back. Halfway up the hill Wham felt a side stitch. Johanness' left calf start to tighten. Wham faltered, broken by pain. Johanness gasped for air as he drew alongside. Both dug deep. The little black dog passed the men. The pace slowed, the hill taking its toll. Johanness pulled ahead and glanced at the grimace on Wham's face. Wham, down to a walk, bent over clutching his side.

Johanness' calf knotted tight and he fell to the ground. Wham slogged past the downed man. Elliott ran back down the hill and grabbed Wham by the overalls. Johanness rose and cripple stepped toward the tank. Wham stopped bent over. Johanness fell forward and slapped the tank. Both men lay on the grassy hillside, chests heaving, hearts pounding. Elliott ran back and forth barking at the fallen men.

Sheer angel wing clouds drifted across the sky and the sun was warm.

Wham and Johanness listened to the river and the crows. A turkey buzzard soared above.

"We'uns better move soon or he'll start peckin at us."

"I don't care."

"It sure ain't like it used ta be."

Johanness waited.

"I used ta outrun any man in the valley."

"I'm ready for some reggae."

"Hard ta run with a dog hanging on."

"So you're going to tell people that ten inch tall dog named Elliott made you lose the race?"

"He seemed a lot bigger when he was a hangin on."

Summoning the...

The dimension of distance was lost in the morning fog. Clouds overnight had held the earth's heat. The men sat beneath the awning, not quite ready to attack the pile of slabs with saw and hammer.

"Property tax gots ta be the worst, hits like a bill ya never pay off. A hunert years from now it still ain't paid off. It ain't never gonna go away, always a knawin atcha." Wham took a breath. "It's like a tick latched on in the middle of ya back, where ya can't get at it, suckin the life outta ya."

"OK, OK, but you don't have any control over your taxes. You need to work on what you can control."

"I ain't controllin nothin. Everthins a fallin apart or broke down. I's fightin everythin. I canst sleep, a thinkin bout bills. I just want it ta stop and it keeps chasin me down."

Johanness said, "You still have to work on what you can work on. What can we work on right now, in the next five minutes, to move forward?"

"Five minutes? Ya gots ta be looney. I can't fix nothin in five minutes."

"I guess you're just not smart enough. You're not strong enough. You don't have what it takes. You let the farm beat you. You're not going to make it. The county's going to take your farm. You're not fast enough. You let a sixty five year old man beat you to the water tank. Uncle Seizure could beat you to the water tank."

Wham jumped from his chair, with his fist balled up. His lower lip quivered. Fire in his eyes became wet. "Get the hell off my land!"

Johanness sat calmly, "I paid my rent for the next three months. If you give me the money back, I'll leave."

Wham tried to stare through the wetness. "I'm going to kick your ass."

"No you're not. You don't have what it takes."

"I killed my old man and I'll kill you."

"Well now, maybe you do have what it takes. But killing me isn't going to pay your taxes. You're not mad at me, you're mad at yourself because you can't figure it out."

Δ

Johanness stared at the empty chair. "Come here, Elliott."

Elliott jumped up in his lap and licked Johanness' hand.

"Maybe I was too hard on him." Johanness stroked the small dog between the ears. He sighed. "It's just you and me again, isn't it?"

Johanness got up, rolled up the awning, put the fold up chairs in the storage area under the RV, and then kicked the chocks loose from the tires.

Telephone Poles

"What can I do in the next five minutes ta move forward?" echoed in his head. *Forward.* The thought and the anger had depth. *Bastard.*

Wham kicked a can down River Road with emphasis and focus, the toe of his boot finding the soft belly of the can. *I'll teach that son of a bitch.* He stomped on the can, walked a few paces and then walked back, stomped on it two more times, picked it up and put it in his overall pocket. He jogged a few steps, then walked with fast paced hatred. The fog was breaking apart. Far off a tractor was tilling the worn out dirt of the valley.

What can I do right now to beat that son of a bitch? Sunlight pierced the fog and mottled the road. I need...I need to. His feet completed the sentence. *Not too fast, work into it. Telephone poles.* It was coming back to him. When he passed the next telephone pole he slowed and walked. *Telephone poles. One today.*

The forsythia bushes were gold. Somehow, he had not seen them bloom. Thousands of bees worked the yellow blossoms. *I needs to transplant em on the hill.* For a moment he could see them and the blueberry bushes and the sunflowers.

Wham approached the low water bridge. Jeb and Sludge fished. *They needs a bench.* Wham waffled on his focus. Happy spotted him and ran to greet him. Wham petted the dog. *Don't sit down. I gots too much ta do.*

"Where's Johanness?" asked Sludge.

"Uh, he made me mad."

Jeb and Sludge waited.

"He said I was gonna lose the farm."

"Why would he say that?" asked Sludge.

"He's got a mean streak in him. I tolt him ta get the hell off'n my property."

"Mebbe he don't like buildin bird houses."

"He might be jealous a ya."

"What the hell are ya talkin bout?"

"Well, ya got a family and friends and a nice farm and ya kids is smart. He ain't got none a that."

Wham closed his eyes and tried to sort it out. *That wern't how it was.*

"Set down afor ya fall down."

"I gots work ta do. I gotta keep a movin."

"Ya needs ta figger out what ya did ta make Johanness mad."

"He mebbe don't like whirligigs."

"He likes whirligigs," said Wham, "likes em a lot."

"He mebbe don't like bat houses," said Jeb.

"Oh yeah," said Sludge, "almost forgot, Pastor Momar wants ya ta build him a ramp so he don't hafta do no stair climbin."

"Yep, Johanness and you'uns could make some good money buildin him a ramp."

Happy woofed at Wham.

Oh hell. Wham turned and walked down the bridge without saying goodbye. *Damn.*

A Rocky Start

"Where's my sweat pants and sweat shirt?" asked Wham.

"They's in the cedar chest. What…"

Wham was in the bedroom before Red could finish.

Red watched as he pulled out old pictures and the white wedding dress. He laid it gently on the bed. "Best day a my life," he said.

"What's a happenin?"

"I gots ta get back in shape." Wham shook out the folded sweat pants and shirt. "I was afraid you'uns threw these out."

Red smiled, "I couldn't throw em out. They meant too much."

Wham stood up and kissed his wife.

Δ

Wham wondered what time it was. And then thoughts of the Great Yam Race took over. He had leaned forward just enough to beat Rascal Rump. He got up and peed but didn't flush the toilet. Wham tip toed into the kitchen. The microwave clock said 5:40. *Electricity.* He put on the sweats and started to the door.

"You'uns needs this," Red handed him his Rocky fisherman's cap. "And this." She gave him the two cans of unopened soup. "If'n ya run inta the giant possum ya can throw the cans at him."

"I's only goin ta the bridge and back."

"Don't overdo it."

Wham smiled, "I won't."

They stepped out onto the porch and looked at the cloudless sky. Red pointed at the remaining star, "Venus."

"Yep, our son did good."

"OK Rocky."

"OK Adrian."

Rocky air punched with the two cans.

Δ

Uncle Seizure took one last drag from the cigarette and flicked it out the truck window. The headlights reflected off the bottom of a can lying in the road and he slammed on the brakes.

Kissin

Uncle Seizure, Red, and Willis carried Wham inside and put him on the bed.

"He's a breathin OK."

Red watched her husband's chest rise and fall.

"What the hell was he a doin out there in the dark?"

"Joggin."

"Joggin? What the hell for? That ain't gonna make him no money."

"He wants ta get back in shape."

"It ain't a workin."

Wham moaned and moved his head slightly.

"I gots ta git or I'll be late for work."

"Thank you so much."

Red and Uncle Seizure stared at each other for a few moments.

"If'n he's a gonna jog he needs ta wait till I go by and cuss atcha."

"Sorry bout hittin ya."

"Well, it ain't all bad. Ya gave me another chapter in my book."

"What's the name of the chapter?"

"Red beats up an old man."

Willis turned away and giggled and then laughed out loud. Red laughed at Willis' laughter. Uncle Seizure smiled broadly. "It's gonna be a good chapter."

Red looked at Uncle Seizure's worn face and could see a crack of softness. "Ya needs ta write a book bout a farmer with no money."

"That ain't much of a story. That's just how farmin is."

"We's gonna make it."

Uncle Seizure said, "Uh, thanks for the bat box. I liked where ya put it and I think the bats like it."

"You'un welcome."

"I gots ta go."

When the screen door slammed Wham opened his eyes. "I saw the giant possum."

"Ya need ta rest."

"He come otta the bushes and scared the bejabbers outta me. It was dark so I dint get a good look but he aint' as big as I thought."

"Might a been a young giant possum," said Willis, "we don't know how many there are."

Wham frowned, pushed his feet over the edge of the bed and Red helped him sit up. "He ain't a bad giant possum."

"There might be a whole tribe a giant possums living in the bog," said Willis.

Wham touched the floor with his left boot and winched. "I's sprained my ankle in a chuckhole."

"Ya might a broke it." Red untied the boot and gingerly pulled it off. "It's swelled up real bad. And ya got a knot on your forehead."

"Yeah, I'uns hit pretty hard."

"Ya gots slobber on ya face."

"The giant possum was a lickin me."

"He might a been kissin ya. Might be matin season," said Willis.

"Nah, he was a lickin on me...like a dog does."

"That might a been possum foreplay."

Wham and Red looked at their daughter. "Wud ya say?"

"Uh, uh, uh."

"That ain't what ya said."

"Now I can do a t-shirt with kissing giant possums."

"No, no, no, no, and no."

"Was it a boy or girl possum?" asked Willis.

"I, I, it was dark."

"I ain't a kissing no man that's been kissed by a giant possum," said Red.

"He dint kiss me."

"So it was a man possum," said Willis.

"Nooo. Quit that."

Willis giggled. "Wait till I tell all the kids on the bus my dad kissed a giant possum."

Red noted the white area on Wham's ring finger. "Where's your wedding band?"

A Glint of Sun

Uncle Seizure was on Wham's mind and the quarter mile walk on the damp road seemed full of self pity. It just seemed far, way too many steps on his crutches. Each step seemed to ignite another negative thought. Thunder rolled into the valley from the valley beyond. Sprinkles melted into his faded blue denim.

Wham stopped in the dirt road and looked at his empty ring finger. *Proof. I ain't got nothin. Why in the hell won't the giant possum leave me alone? I's a good person. It don't seem right. What's next? Did Uncle Seizure see the giant possum? Did he...?* He rubbed his ring finger with his thumb. *Damn. Just oncet I need somethin good ta happen.*

A wink of silver pierced the grey sky and shown on a spot just below the quiet windmill.

Uncle Seizure's truck pulled up alongside Wham. "Ya need a lift?"

"No, I'm fine. Tell me somethin," said Wham, "did ya see the giant possum when ya picked me up the other mornin?"

"I don't know what I saw."

"But ya saw somethin."

"Yeah, I saw somethin."

"Somethin alive?"

"Yeah, it happened real fast like." Uncle Seizure looked at Wham in the eyes. "I saw the can bottom and then you and then somethin big jumped off the road and then I was jammin on the brakes as hard as I can."

"I wants ta thank you'un for not running me over...and takin me home."

"Ya done the same for me when Red hit me."

Wham sighed, "Well, thanks again."

"They still ain't hired nobody for that spot in the factree. Just somethin ta think about."

"I appreciate it and I's sorry bout Red hittin ya."

Uncle Seizure smiled, "I sure as hell dint see that comin."

Wham wanted to brag about Red and then thought better of it. "She's feisty sometimes."

"Feisty's a good word. Not many folks use feisty. I needs ta thank you and Red for givin me another chapter in my book and I's gonna use feisty in there somewhere."

"Is ya sayin good stuff bout Red and me in the book?"

"I dunno yet. Folks likes underdogs. They's always pullin for somebody that's beat down and kicked into ditch. I canst think a nobody that's a better underdog than you'uns."

Wham shook his head, "Ya ain't makin me feel good."

Uncle Seizure's eyes widened, "I just had a great ide'er. I need a photo for my book cover. Let me take ya picture." Uncle Seizure held up his cell phone and steadied it on the window. "Back up a bit sos I can get all a ya."

Wham moved back with his crutches.

"Now, give me a look like you'uns mad at me."

"That ain't hard."

"Now look like ya just had ya dog run over. Good, now grit ya teeth. Good, real good. Now, say I hatecha."

"I hatecha, I hatecha real bad."

"Now, you'un lookin kinda scary. I don't need scary. I needs that broke down farmer look."

"Who in the hell made ya a camera man?"

"Everbody that's gots a cell phone is a camera man. Whist I'd a gotten a picture of the giant possum while ya was a layin in the road. That woulda made a killer book cover."

"So ya did see the giant possum?"

"Well, I ain't a sayin I did and I ain't a sayin I dint." Uncle Seizure glanced at the time on his cell phone, "I gots ta get a goin or I'll be late."

Wham wasn't sure why he said it, "Have a good day."

"You too."

The green truck's wake spun the propellers on some of the whirligigs. Wham pondered, *I don't think he took the ring.* He picked up the pace, reaching with the crutches and vaulting himself forward. *I might be on the cover of a book.* He watched a wall of water advance through the trees and up the river. He was going to get wet. He stopped abruptly and replayed the encounter with Uncle Seizure. *Huh, he wasn't smoking a cigarette.*

Growin

Wham listened through the rain to something coming up the road. *Please be Johanness.*

The large RV slowed, swung wide, drove between two whirligigs, moved up the hill and stopped exactly in the same spot.

Wham stayed beneath the shed roof. *Wonder if'n he can see me?*

Johananess opened the door and let Elliott out and then waved for Wham to join him. "Come have some breakfast."

Wham hurried through the rain on his crutches. Johanness reached down, took the crutches and then grabbed Wham's empty hand as he jumped up the steps on his good leg.

After Wham was seated Johanness started coffee and then asked, "How do you want your eggs this morning."

"How bout some a them Benedict Arnold eggs."

Johanness rubbed the corner of his eye, "Feels good to be back."

"I's glad you'uns back."

Δ

"I's a saw without no wood," said Wham.

"You have wood, a whole pile of slabs."

"I's a chisel without no rock."

"You've got a huge pile of rocks that run down your property line."

"I's a bugger without no nose."

Johananness responded, "You've got a nose. It looks like it's been broke a few times but it looks like a nose."

"I's a windmill without no wind."

"You've got plenty of wind. You just need to put the windmill back together."

Wham frowned, "I's a poor farmer with lots a bills and no money."

"You could grow a few marijuana plants and have plenty of money."

"How much money?"

"Depends, but one marijuana plant can produce a pound of marijuana."

"How much money is that?"

"Somewhere between one and two thousand dollars."

"You mean ta tell me them little plants you got under the grow lights in your camper is worth a thousand dollars a piece?"

"I never said those plants were marijuana."

A few raindrops tapped on the awning.

"How come you know so much about marijuana?"

"I read a lot and watch YouTube videos."

"Ain't nobody dumb enough ta put a video bout marijuana on YouTube."

"There are thousands of videos about growing marijuana on YouTube."

"That ain't right. That's illegal. Ya cants be a showin illegal stuff on YouTube."

Johanness sighed, "We need to get to work."

"Feels cold this mornin."

"You'll warm up once you get to sawing."

"A thousand dollars a plant?"

"Yep."

"How long's it take to get a big plant?"

"Depends on the variety of marijuana, the nutrients, and the amount of light they get."

"Could I get a plant ta grow by the first of June?"

"Not from seed. Let's see...if the plant was already started and had the right conditions it might be possible."

The sky darkened and a far away rumble drifted up the valley. "It's way too early for lightnin."

"I saw it thunder and lightning in a snowstorm in Colorado."

"Mebbe God was tryin ta tell them marijuana addicts somethin."

"Have you ever smoked marijuana?"

"Nope."

"Have you ever been to Colorado?"

"Nope."

"It's a beautiful place." Johanness stopped and looked into the rain. "I need to go see my brother in Denver."

"When ya leavin?"

Johanness hesitated, "Uh, probably the end of July or early August. I want to go backpacking and fly-fishing in the mountains...before my legs won't take me there anymore." Johanness opened his laptop and clicked start. He moved his chair closer to Wham. "Here's some pictures of my trip five years ago."

Wham watched intently as Johanness clicked through the pictures.

"Is that a rainbow trout?"

"No, it's a brook trout. It's, well, it's like an artist painted this fish."

"Ain't very big."

"No, most brook trout are less than ten inches long."

"You'uns id need a whole pile a them fish ta make a meal."

"I release most of the fish I catch."

Wham looked at Johanness, "Ya do what?"

"I let them go."

"Ya climb way up them mountains, then go fishin, and then ya let em go?"

"I don't fish to eat the fish. I fish because it's enjoyable."

"You'uns got dropped on ya head when ya was a kid."

"Why didn't you take the job at the sock factory?"

"That ain't me."

"Well, who are you Wham Wooster?"

Wham took a sip of his cold coffee.

Δ

Wham and Johanness worked on cutting and assembling bat houses beneath the shed until the afternoon sun silvered the hillside. Wham carried one of the saw horses out into the sun, then limped back and got the other one.

"Is your ankle feeling any better?" asked Johanness.

"The swellings a goin down. I can't run on it yet."

"Do they have any 5K or 10K races around here?"

"The only race I knows about is the Great Yam Race in the fall. I won that twice, long time ago. Feels like a hunert years ago."

"You're lucky you didn't break the ankle."

"You'uns got that right."

"When it's better we need to walk up Church Ridge Road. I could get in shape for hiking in Colorado and you could get ready for the Yam Race."

"Thad be a good place ta get in shape."

Johanness changed the subject, "Does anyone in the valley have a greenhouse?"

"Nope."

"We need a greenhouse."

"We? What's this we stuff?"

"Uh, OK, you need a greenhouse."

"Why do I need a greenhouse?"

"Actually, you need a huge greenhouse."

"I don't know nothing bout no greenhouse."

"We could start small and then add more greenhouses."

"Greenhouses. Hold on. We ain't a building no greenhouses."

"OK, we'll start with one greenhouse, but we're going to run out of room real quick."

"What the dickens are you'uns gonna grow; kudzu? Ya ain't planin on growin marijuana?"

"I was doing some tomato math last night."

"Tomato math?"

"Yeah, everybody wants to grow tomatoes."

"I like maters. The ones in the store ain't no account. Ain't got no taste. But maters is hard ta grow. One year they does real good and the next year ya won't get enough for a mater sandwich."

"That's why you need them in a greenhouse, where you can control the environment."

"Willie tried ta get me ta build one. I don't know nothing bout building no greenhouse."

"Building a greenhouse is a lot easier than building a ramp."

"I ain't got no money ta build no greenhouse."

"Some of the greenhouses use cattle fencing and some use PVC pipe for the supports. You've got enough slabs to build the ends. Then all you need is the plastic."

"Where'd we put it?"

Johanness pushed his glasses up his nose, "I don't know. You need a fairly level spot and a place that gets a lot of sun. I could do a video when we build it."

"I ain't gots no money for no greenhouse."

"Hoop houses don't cost a lot. If we do it right we might get by real cheap."

"Real cheap is way too much money."

"Well, after breakfast we'll go up to the thinking bench and work on the numbers."

"What numbers? We ain't got no numbers."

"Maybe, we'll see the eagle again."

"You'uns need ta go ta the doctor. Ya mind ain't right."

"Why's that?"

"One minute we'uns building bat boxes and wood duck houses and zippity do dah, the next we'uns buildin a greenhouse."

"Elliott, do you think we need to build a greenhouse?"

Elliott wagged his tail and nodded his head up and down.

"Somethin bads happnin. When did Elliott start that?"

"About a week ago. He used to just turn his head sideways when I'd ask him questions. But now he nods yes or no. Sometimes he still turns his head sideways, like he's thinking about what I asked him."

"I'll bet Happy's a teachin him," said Wham.

"Or maybe the giant possum is teaching him at night when I let him out."

"I'd be mighty careful bout letting him out at night."

Johanness asked Elliott, "Do I take good care of you?"

Elliott shooke his head no and Wham slapped his knee and laughed.

Δ

Johanness booted up the computer, Elliott ran from bush to bush, and Wham scanned the sky for the eagle. "We should be a workin."

Johanness clicked on the calculator. "We are working. OK, say we started with 40 tomato seedlings. In a few weeks they're growing pretty good and we cut the suckers off and root them. Say we get 10 suckers off each plant every two months."

Wham interrupted, "How many maters we got?"

"None."

"That's bout how many I get."

Johanness scratched his head, "OK, stick with me for a couple of minutes. Alright, in two months we have 400 new plants plus the original 40 plants for 440. Now, in the next two months we cut off 10 more suckers off each plant and root them. That is 440 times 10 or 4,400 plants in four months plus the 440 we started with. That makes 4,840 plants."

"Now, how many maters we got?"

"We don't care. We're giving the tomatoes away."

"Huh? You'uns ain't right."

"Imagine if you had a sign that said, "Free Tomatoes."

"Ever man, woman, and child id be up here gettin free tomatoes."

"It would be like Wall Drug store. Actually, if we play it right, we can give away the tomato plants too."

"You'uns had your brains sucked out by aliens."

Johanness grinned, "Maybe. We wouldn't sell the plants but we'd put out a donation jar."

"Why are we doing this?"

"So you can be a nonprofit business."

"I's already nonprofit."

"But this way you wouldn't pay property taxes."

"We'uns just a dreamin, ain't we?"

"Dammit Wham. Jesus friggin Christ! All you do is piss me off." Johanness slapped the laptop shut and stomped down the hill. "Come on, Elliott." The little dog ran to catch up. When Johanness got to the shed he kicked over one of the sawhorses, took a few steps, turned around and kicked over the other sawhorse. "Dammit." Elliott ran down the road to keep up with Johanness.

Wham looked at the ground and fixated on a blade of sunlit grass. Then he slumped to the wet grass. *What's wrong with me? I done did it again.* Wham looked at his ring-less ring finger. *Damn.* The ground was cold and the wetness seeped through his overalls. His knees began to ache from the cold.

"Here, let me hep ya up," said Red.

"Where'd ya come from?"

"I saw Johanness and Elliott walk past the house and wondered what happened to ya."

"I made him mad again."

"What this time?"

"He was talkin bout buildin a greenhouse and I, well, I donno, I said he was dreamin."

"He's only tryin ta help ya."

"I can'ts go down no more rabbit holes."

"Ya needs ta go down rabbit holes...they's a rabbit in one of em."

"I can'ts."

"Ya gots ta."

Wham lowered his head and sobbed. "Why the hell do ya stay with me?"

Red rubbed Wham's back, "You'un know why. I's after all ya money."

Wham rubbed his eyes and sniffled, "Yep, I knew it. You'uns a gold digger."

Red pulled Wham to his feet and hugged him. "Let me get ya crutches."

"Where we a goin?"

"You'uns gonna tell Johanness we's gonna build a greenhouse, with or without him."

Δ

Wham with his crutches and Red with her man, made their way past the house. Neither one commented on the unpainted wood siding and the green algae or the slight smell from the septic tank. Two curves in the road and the river and Wham stopped "This is where the giant possum run out and rightcher is the chuckhole I stepped in."

Red walked around scanning the gravel in the wet road.

"I's already looked three times. It ain't here."

"Mebbe a truck run over it."

"And mebbe Uncle Seizure took it."

"And mebbe he dint." Red reached over and touched Wham's arm. She pointed to the edge of the woods where a doe and a fawn fed. "Ya member when we was datin and we clumb up the big oak tree and waited for the deer to come out...and we saw the albino deer?"

"I member."

"We was crazy in love."

Wham smiled, "Real crazy."

"I's still crazy in love."

"We needs ta find us a big oak tree."

Red grinned. "Yep."

Δ

"They's a usin the bench ya made," said Red.

Jeb and Sludge, Johanness, and Pastor Momar sat on the bench. "I's glad Pastor Momar ain't a sittin in the middle."

Happy and Elliott ran to meet Wham and Red.

"We'uns needs a longer bench," said Jeb.

Pastor Momar stood up and offered his spot to Red.

"No, I's fine." Red looked at Wham.

"Uh, Red and I was a talkin and we wants ta build a greenhouse."

Johanness pursed his lips and then smiled.

"There ya go," said Sludge, "that's a great ide'er. We could have fresh maters in the winter."

"And peppers and bananas," said Jeb.

Happy woofed and shook his head. "OK, mebbe not bananas."

Sludge's bobber plipped below the surface of the stream. The cane pole bent in a soft arc and he lifted the small bass to his hand. He took the hook out and flipped the bass back in the stream. "Ya place is lookin real good and them forsythia bushes is like clouds a gold on your hill."

"Ya need ta get ya eyes checked. They's forsythia's and that's all they is. They ain't clouds," said Jeb.

Pastor Momar said, "Clouds of gold, I might use that in a sermon."

"Them clouds a gold ain't makin me no money," said Wham.

"They could," said Johanness, "you just need to take cuttings and make bushes to sell."

"I heard tell Jerry Jump grafted a mater to a tater and got taters and maters off'n the same plant," said Jeb.

"Ya ain't talkin bout Jerry Jump from Bump, is ya?"

"Yep, that's him."

Johanness smiled, "I always wanted to try that."

"Wud he call the tater mater plant?" asked Wham.

"Tater mater," said Jeb.

"No, no, no. They'd be mater taters cuz the maters is on top," said Sludge.

"Regardless of what they are called, people id," Johanness caught himself, "would buy them because they're unique. The one's I saw on YouTube were grown in buckets."

"We ain't got no buckets," said Wham.

"Do so," said Sludge, "Jeb and I's been a collectin five gallon buckets from the dumpsters forever, seems like. Must have fifty buckets. Now, we's can'ts be a givin em away. Jeb and I was a talkin a while back that we ought ta get twenty cents a piece for em."

"Did not. I said a quarter."

"That's cuz you'uns greedy. We got em free. God don't like greedy folks, ain't that right Pastor Momar?"

"Um, well uh," Pastor Momar cleared his throat."

"We're waiting," said Johanness.

"Uh, there will always be poor and rich people. Just because a person's successful doesn't mean that..."

Johanness interrupted, "Doesn't it say in the Bible that it is easier for a camel to go through the eye of a needle than for a rich person to go to heaven?"

Pastor Momar cleared his throat again and then sidestepped, "I think what we were discussing is the price of the buckets."

Johanness smiled, "Perhaps, you're right. We were discussing buckets. Are the buckets clean?"

"They's purty clean. We washed em in the river afore we took em up the hill."

Johanness winced, "What did the buckets have in them?"

"Mostly drywall paste, but some had dried up paint. Some's real clean and some ain't so clean."

Wham spoke slow, "Could a man graft a mater plant ta a yam plant?"

"I don't see why not," said Johanness.

"That id make em yamaters," said Red, "we could call em Wham's world famous yamaters."

"Holy spittin spiders," said Sludge, "that's a great ide'er."

"I ain't got no money ta be a buyin buckets," said Wham.

"I'll tell ya what," said Sludge, "half them buckets is mine and I'll trade ya my half for two a them yamaters."

"I'll do the same," said Jeb.

Pastor Momar said, "I'll bring you the buckets later this afternoon."

Wham sniffled. Red smiled, "Well, we better be gettin back. We gots ta git some maters growin from seed and find a spot for the greenhouse." Red looked at Jeb and Sludge for a moment. "Ya can't use bamboo poles to hold up the plastic on the greenhouse, can ya?"

The men all looked at Red. "You'uns a genius," said Sludge. "I wisht I'd a come up with that one."

"Where do you get your bamboo?" asked Johanness.

"From the bog. Lots a bamboo on the backside a the bog. Somes way too long for cane poles but they might be good for a greenhouse."

"I've never worked with bamboo but I'll bet there's a YouTube video on building with bamboo," said Johanness.

"Whoa down," said Pastor Momar, "I need you to build my ramp first."

"We'll order the materials tomorrow," said Johanness.

Red hugged Wham and whispered in his ear, "Toltcha."

Δ

Daylight was fading when Wham and Red reached the spot in the road.

"I still wonder if'n Uncle Seizure took it."

Red reached down in the chuckhole and scooped out some water and gravel. She turned away and then turned back. She got down on one knee and held up the ring, "Will you'uns marry me?'

Distance and time and quiet held still, "I reckon."

Geese

Noisy geese heading north woke Wham. He smiled and threw back the blankets. He placed his feet on the wood floor and applied a small amount of weight. He pressed harder and still no pain. He had slept. It was strange to feel good.

The house was quiet, much too quiet. Was he hearing the last of the geese or a new flock? The "look, look, look" grew to a crescendo and then tapered away.

Today. It was a thought that lingered. He dressed and was soon out the door. The sun was at nine o'clock in the crystal clear blue sky. *How long did I sleep? Where's Red?*

Wham's walk took on more speed. Each step gave him more confidence in the ankle. He shadowboxed, tentatively at first and then with more vigor.

Wham stopped at the first post with a whirligig, spun the propeller, and the giant possum waved his cap. *Man, oh man, he looks good.* The third whirligig was gone, replaced by a rock on top of the post. Wham lifted the rock and put the twenty two dollars deep in his pocket.

Close to the road was a pile of tools, a camera tripod, and the sawhorses.

Johannness called out, "Let's go, let's go." Wham jogged to the RV and Johanness put a plate of eggs and toast in one hand and a cup of coffee in his other. "We need to get going. The truck will be here soon."

"What truck?"

"I called the lumber yard and they said they could pick us up and take us to Pastor Momars."

"Ya ain't gots no phone service."

"I climbed the hill and made the call yesterday evening, about five minutes before they closed."

"Great ide'er. We gots us a job, lumber, and a free ride." Wham sat down in the fold up chair and dove into the eggs. "Lots a geese this mornin."

"Yeah, I heard them too." Johanness watched Wham devour the eggs. "You seem froggy this morning."

"I feel good, best I felt in ages." Between bites Wham asked, "Didja member the hose level?"

"Yep, but I don't think we'll have to use it. The parking area and the deck are close to the same level."

"I got my ring back." Wham held up his left hand. "Red found it in a puddle, then she got down on one knee and asked me ta marry her. I tolt her, I reckon. Then she hit me bout four or five times."

Johanness laughed. "Great story. You need to share that with Uncle Seizure for his book."

"Uncle Seizure said his book was seven hunert pages long and he took my picture for the book cover."

Johanness smiled, "It might need some editing. Let him know I can help him with the book cover."

"Ya know bout book covers?"

"Oh yeah."

"When we gits done for the day can we stop at Miss Chatty's? I needs another readin lesson. I wants ta be able ta read Uncle Seizure's book with me on the cover."

"I hear the truck."

Wham inhaled the last of the eggs and the two pieces of toast.

Walkway to Heaven

Pastor Mormar, Elizabeth, Johanness, and Wham stood on the deck overlooking the small valley and the proposed parking spot while the lumber was being offloaded.

"You have a beautiful spot here," said Johanness, "and we want to keep it as natural as possible."

"It is beautiful," said Elizabeth.

"Uh, may I ask what the fishing pole is for?" said Pastor Momar.

"Fishin," said Johanness.

"He wouldn't tell me either," said Wham.

"It's to help layout the ramp." Johanness opened the bail on the spinning reel. He cast the lead weight to the new parking area. "Now, Wham will just go over and tie the layout string to the end and I'll reel it back."

"Where'd ya learn that?" asked Elizabeth.

"On a bridge they built out in Colorado they used a bow and arrow to send a line across the canyon. Then they attached a rope to the line and pulled it back, then they attached a metal cable to the rope and then they put a cable car on the cable. I didn't have a bow and arrow."

"That musta been before they legalized marijuana," said Wham.

"How long do you think it will take?" asked Pastor Momar.

"If all goes well we will have the footings dug by this evening. The county inspector will check them tomorrow morning and then the construction will take two or three days. We're supposed to get rain Thursday and Friday."

"The sooner the better, I hate climbing those stairs."

"Yeah, this is going to be much better."

"And you're going to include a bat house and the giant possum whirligig?" said Pastor Momar.

"Yep, it's included in the price."

Wham raised one eyebrow and looked at Johanness.

"Glad to see your ankle's doing better," said Elizabeth

"Me too," said Wham, "it had me worried that I wouldn't be able ta hep."

The four watched five squirrels running from tree to tree. Elliott spotted the squirrels, ran down the stairs, and took up the chase. "Elliott, you stay close."

"It's more like a bridge than a ramp. How we's gonna put them joistes out there? We ain't gots no ladders."

"We're going to prefab the sections and then the crane will put them in place."

"Crane? What crane?"

Johanness smiled, "The lumberyard has a small crane they use for lifting trusses."

"Ooowee. This I gots ta see. This is like...real construction...like when they builds them buildins in Myrtle Beach. We's a gonna have the whole valley out here ta see this one."

Pastor Momar said, "I could do a sermon and save some sinners."

"And pass the collection plate?" said Johanness.

"That crossed my mind."

Johanness turned away and shook his head. *YouTube is going to love this one.*

"What day is the crane going to be here?" asked Elizabeth.

"If we don't get rained out, it should be here Friday."

"I'll fix some fried chicken and potato salad."

Johanness put his phone on the selfie stick and introduced everyone. Then he swung the phone out over the rail and narrated the project. "The bridge will terminate at the flat spot over there." Johanness aimed the phone at Elliott on the opposite hill, "Elliott, say something for the camera." Elliott woofed. "Wham, have you got anything to share with our Tubers?"

"I's just glad I's gots a job." Wham hooked his thumbs in his overalls and smiled large for the camera. Johanness gave him a thumbs up and clicked off the phone.

"We'll cover up the wood pile and then we'll get started."

Johanness tore open the box with the roll of plastic. Wham and Johanness unrolled enough plastic to cover the wood and placed rocks on the ends.

"They's a whole lot more plastic than we need ta cover..." Wham stopped and looked at Johanness.

Johanness got a devilish grin, "Yep."

The Plastic

"Are ya awake?" asked Wham.

"I wasn't, but I am now," said Red.

"My conscience is botherin me."

"Wud ya do?"

"I dint do nothin. But mebbe I did. I don't know."

"Well if something is bothering you, then you probly did something."

"Well, when we did the job for Pastor Momar we covered up the lumber with plastic. The roll a plastic was like way, way moren we needed. I think Johanness ordered too much on purpose so we'd have plastic for the greenhouse. I kinda feel like we's stealin the plastic from Pastor Momar."

"Damn," Red sighed, "Why do you wait until two in the mornin ta tell me this stuff?"

"My conscience doesn't bother me much in the day."

"What would Jesus do?"

"He'd a just made more maters."

Red laughed quietly. "I's gonna smother ya when ya go to sleep."

"That's why I sleep on my side."

"Dadgum. Look, ya dint order the plastic and what's done is done. Ya feel bad cuz ya dint say nothin. You'uns part a the crime cuz ya dint speak up."

"So I should give back the plastic?"

"I dunno. We needs the plastic and Pastor Momar don't need the plastic." Red sighed. "Its kinda like ya see somebody shoot somebody. Ya needs ta tell the Sheriff."

"What if ya know the bad guy id kill ya family ifn ya said somethin?"

Red sighed again.

"If I tell Pastor Momar that Johanness ordered too much on purpose then he might have words with Johanness."

"It's a mess. Amazin how it can get so tangled up."

"Mebbe we ain't sposed ta do the greenhouse."

"Are ya a hunert percent sure that Johanness ordered too much?"

"I ain't for sure, but I's purty sure."

"They's another way ta look at it," said Red. "Mebbe God wants us ta have a greenhouse and it's his gift to us."

The house was quiet and soon Wham heard Red breathing softly. "Dear Lord, hep me ta do right. Amen."

What's a Goin On?

Red and Willis noted when Wham put down his fork, pushed back in his chair, and crossed his arms. Wham knew that these two kept secrets, it was the little smiles and giggles and whispers. Some things he didn't want to know, girl stuff. And other things...

"What's a goin on," asked Wham, "why don't nobody want me ta go ta the General Store?"

Red and Willis looked at each other. "Um, well, whatcha need at the General Store? Willis can pick it up if'n ya need something," said Red.

"What day ya a doin them t-shirts? Ya ain't invited me up there. I want's ta see my daughter a makin t-shirts."

"Ya been awful busy with Johanness a making bird houses and bat houses and saw horses and..."

"Benches and whirligigs," added Willis.

"I wants ta see this here spray painter thang and watch ya do a shirt."

"I'm going to be there Saturday, most a the day. We can walk up there together if'n ya want."

"I'd like that. I'd like that a lot. Pass me the sweet taters, please."

"How's the bridge a comin?" asked Red.

"Crazy how we's a doin this one. On Miss Chatty's we just nailed her tagether. On this one we's a makin the bridge parts on the ground and we's a gonna use a crane ta put it tagether. We even put the rails on her. Johanness says it'll only take an hour ta put it tagether with the crane. They's four parts. Elizabeth is gonna make fried chicken and potato salad."

"Can I skip school to watch? It'd be educational."

Red's eyes laughed. Wham scratched in front of his ear. "Tell ya what. If'n ya get permission from the principal ya can come watch."

Willis did a fist pump, "Alright!"

"That reminds me." Wham dug in in his overall pocket and pulled out the twenty two dollars along with a wadded up piece of paper. He handed the money to Red, "We sold another one." Wham looked at the piece of paper. "We's runnin low on slabs and well, Miss Chatty's been a tutorin me on readin but I still cant's make it out what Fred put on this paper. I needs ta know how much I owes him for the slabs." He handed the paper to Willis.

"Thank you so much for taking the slabs. Hope you can use more. Also, if you grow blueberries I can bring you a load of sawdust. Fred."

Wham got up and went into the bedroom and closed the door.

Story Time

The footers were dug, ready for inspection and the first of the four identical bridge sections framed on the ground. Wham found that it bothered Johanness to call out measurements "twenty-two and three a them little marks" and so he continued to do so. Johanness took a chance and cut the 2x4 at 22-3/16" and Wham tapped the board into place with the comment, "Nice fit. You'uns learnin."

It was 4:30 when Johanness and Wham left Pastor Momar's and trekked down Church Ridge Road, down the river, and down the valley. Miss Chatty waved at the men, a come on wave, and they turned in.

"Wham, I've got a bunch of books for you. Ever since the word got out that we were going to build a library folks has been bringing me books." Miss Chatty pointed to a stack of thin books against the wall on the porch, "Those are for you."

"He needs a library card," said Johanness.

Miss Chatty smiled, "You're right. How bout going inside and there's some index cards in the top drawer of the china cabinet. There's some packing tape and the black marking pen in the second drawer."

Johanness opened the screen door and stopped. "What the..."

"I told you."

"There has to be five hundred books in here."

"Pretty good start on the library," said Miss Chatty, "but I'm having a hard time moving around with the walker."

Wham poked his head through the screen door, "I ain't never seed this many books."

"Who died and made you the librarian?" asked Johanness.

"I'm not quite sure, just kind of happened."

"Well, I can't think of a better person to be the first Rump River Valley librarian."

Miss Chatty beamed, "I just hope I live long enough to see the new library."

"You'll probably outlive us all."

"I hope not. I want to go to heaven sometime."

Johanness returned with the index cards, tape, and marker. Miss Chatty wrote a big #1 on one side of the card and handed it to Wham, "Write your name on the other side."

Wham frowned, "What if'n I make a mistake?"

"I've got about 200 more cards." Miss Chatty took the card from Wham and wrote Wham Wooster lightly with a pencil. "Now, just go over the letters with the marker."

Cautiously Wham put the marker to the card and soon finished. Miss Chatty smiled, "See, not a single mistake." Miss Chatty handed the packing tape to Johanness. "Laminate it so it will hold up a while."

"Yes, maam. May I interrupt?" asked Johanness.

"You may."

"Where are you going to put the new library? You can't keep putting stacks of books in your house."

Miss Chatty smiled, "Um, good question and one that I've pondered many a night. I started a list of requirements and Willie and I drew up a plan." She handed Johanness the list, a sketch done on graph paper, and a plat. "The plan is based on the free trusses we can get from the lumber yard."

Johanness looked at the list, "This is rather ambitious."

"Yes, it is. Willie had a lot to do with some of those. He has a vision of where we need to go. He is computers and internet and solar panels. I am...well, I only know the past. I know books and I love teaching people to read and write. I think Willie and I make a good team."

"I'm impressed with the list." Johanness stood and looked at the plat and was silent for a few moments. "Would you mind if I took these and made copies? I'll bring them back tomorrow evening."

"Willie has them on his computer, so you're welcome to take those."

Johanness handed the laminated card to Miss Chatty to make the presentation.

"Wham, you are officially the first library card holder for the new library. Take care of that card and you will always have books."

"Thank you Miss Chatty." Wham put the library card in his right overall pocket and felt the folded up paper. He hesitated and then sat down with his back against the wall facing the sun being cut by the black branches of the trees across the river. "Miss Chatty?"

"Yes."

"Ya ever been scared of a piece a paper?"

"Uh, no, I can't recall being scared of a piece of paper."

Wham took out the folded paper. "I's been scared a this piece a paper for two, mebbe three months. I thought it was a bill from Fred that has the sawmill." Wham handed the paper to Miss Chatty. "Last night I asked Willis what it said."

Miss Chatty put on her glasses and read the note.

"I didn't ask nobody cuz I dint want ta look stupid. I's tired a being afraid a thins I cants read."

Johanness got up and walked out toward the river.

Miss Chatty pulled her handkerchief from her pocket and wiped her eyes. "Well, you came to the right place. I'll have you reading in no time. Now, let's get started. Which book do you want to learn to read first?"

"I kind a like the one with the train on the front."

"That's a great book. Good choice." Miss Chatty's eyes sparkled behind her glasses, "All aboard."

Bamboo for You

Wham stood behind his chair until Red and Willis sat down. "I has announcement ta make. Drum roll please."

Red and Willis picked up their knives and forks and drummed them on the edge of the table.

Wham reached in his pocket and pulled out his library card. "I is now officially the first liberry card holder in the valley."

"Alright Dad! I've got to get me one," said Willis.

"Me too," said Red.

"And," Wham waited for emphasis, "Miss Chatty let me check out three books." Wham pulled the three books from the plastic bag. "They has ta go back in three weeks."

"Oh man, those were my favorites when I was growing up," said Willis.

"Let me remind ya young lady, ya ain't growd up yet."

"Is it OK if I bring my boyfriend home for dinner sometime?"

"Ya ain't gots no boyfriend and ya ain't never gonna have no boyfriend."

Both Red and Willis giggled. "Dad, you are sooo funny."

Wham put on his sour face look and they both laughed.

"Dadgum," said Wham as he sat down.

Red started the Spam, eggs, and beans around the table.

"What'd ya do taday?" asked Wham.

"Jeb and Sludge and I went and got bamboo for the greenhouse."

"What?"

"Yeah, it was a good day to be out at the bog. There was enough breeze to keep the skeeters from carryin us off. We got two truckloads of bamboo. Hope it's enough."

Wham broke the egg yolk and mixed in a bit of Spam, "How'd ya get those two ta go get bamboo?"

"I threatened em."

Wham's left eyebrow rose. *I's created a monster.*

"No, it ain't what you'uns thinkin. I tolt em that Miss Chatty wouldn't make em no more raisin pie if'n they didn't hep get the bamboo."

"Thad make me get bamboo."

"I gots ta get her recipe."

"How bout after dinner we take a walk ta see the bamboo?"

"That's a good ide'er," said Willis, "mebbe we'll run inta my boyfriend."

"I's gonna lock ya in ya bedroom if'n ya keep that up."

"I'll just climb out the window."

"Dadgum."

"Yeah, let's go for a walk after dinner," said Red, "mebbe I'll run inta my boyfriend."

"Ya needs ta have respect for the first liberry card man."

Red winked at Wham. Willis saw the wink, rolled her eyes and smiled.

Crane Day

The fog was burning off. Jeff Sickens stopped the crane truck in the road and picked up Johanness and Elliott. "Are you ready?" asked Jeff.

"As ready as we'll ever be. We need to pick up Wham, Red, and Willis."

"Ain't Willis sposed ta be in school?"

"She got permission to attend an educational event."

"You'uns kiddin."

"Nope."

"These kids got it made."

"We got out of school for harvest and the first day of deer season."

"Yep, those were hard times."

"Yeah, and they were good times too.

"Man, look at all the whirligigs and bird houses."

"There's twenty eight whirligigs, nineteen bird houses, two wood duck houses, and two bat houses."

A school bus appeared behind the truck. "Did they let all the kids out for this edjucational event?"

"I don't know, maybe."

Jeff stopped the truck and Wham and Red got in the cab. Willis ran back and got on the school bus.

A hundred yards from Pastor Momar's mountain chalet, cars were parked along the road. Jeff and Johanness looked at each other. "Surely not," said Johanness.

Pastor Momar was directing traffic at the turnoff. "Thank goodness, you're here. People started showing up at 7:00 this morning."

"I hope you have enough chicken and potato salad for everyone," said Johanness.

A worried look came to Pastor Momar. "I, I, didn't expect this turnout."

Johanness smiled, "I didn't either."

Wham and Johanness directed the crane truck into position. Jeff jumped out and scanned the four bridge sections. "I like it. And you put blocks under the sections so I can get my straps hooked up. You've done this before."

"Nope, but I have built roof sections on the ground and used the crane to put them on houses. Same principle."

"Looks good, real good. So that section gets connected to the deck where the joist hangers are and that end sits on the supports on the post and then the bolts go through the holes."

"Yep."

Jeff marveled at the thought process. "And then the next one butts up to that one. And you left the posts long so you can cut them off later. I like it. I need to take some pictures of this."

Johanness spotted Miss Chatty, Red, and Elizabeth on the deck and made his way through the crowd. "I need some help with filming this. Any volunteers?"

Willis appeared out of nowhere, "I know how to do this. How big is your memory card?"

Wham and Red looked at each other.

Johanness said, "You should have ninety minutes worth of run time."

"How long is it going to take?"

"I'm hoping less than an hour."

"What do you want me to concentrate on?"

"You choose what to film. I can edit it later."

"Gotcha."

"Wham, lets go. Jeff already has it hooked up."

Wham followed Johanness to the first section. "OK, here's what we're going to do. We're going to ride the section and guide it into place. Then we nail that end to the deck and then we line up the bolt holes and bolt them tight."

"Uh, uh, uh…uh, I ain't real good with high places," said Wham.

"You got your hammer and your nail pouch."

"Yeah."

"Just hold onto this strap and when the joists get lined up, nail em off. You know what to do. You did this at Miss Chatty's. You can't fall off; you've got rails on both sides."

Wham took a deep breath, "OK."

Johanness climbed aboard the section and twirled his finger in a upward direction. The straps tightened and the section lifted above the grass.

Wham yelled at Johanness, "Can ya hear my heartbeat?"

Johanness laughed, "Pay attention to the ends of the joists."

The section swung out over the ravine and the crowd tensed. Wham eyed the end of the deck and the joist hangers. Two feet, one foot. Wham could feel the section move as Johanness placed his end over the posts. "How you lookin?"

"I needs ta come down about six inches."

"Get down and line it up." Wham let go of the strap and kneeled at the end of the section. Johanness twirled his finger in a downward direction.

"Couple more inches. Little bit more. OK."

"Are the joists tight in the back of the hangers?"

"This sides tight, the others is loose."

"Nail off the tight one. Just one nail. We can get the rest later."

Wham put a nail through the hanger and nailed it off.

"Come down on this end and help me line up the bolts."

Wham hurried to the other end.

"Take that piece of rebar and shove it through the joists and the post. Good, now leave it in the hole till I get this bolt in place."

In seconds Johanness hammered the bolt through his post and put the washer and nut on it.

"Now hold onto the piece of rebar as I pound this bolt through. Good. OK, now undo the straps and we'll have the crane give a little shove to tighten up the other joists."

Johanness yelled for Jeff to use the boom to give the section a nudge. Wham watched the back of the hanger. "Its tight but the joists is too high."

"How much too high?"

"Two a them little marks."

"Put a sixteen penny nail underneath the joist."

Wham tapped a nail under the joist to act as a shim and nailed it off. "Theys tight now."

"Let's go get another one. Put your foot in the loop of the strap and hold on."

Wham swallowed and put his foot in the loop. Johanness gave the up signal and the crane lifted both men and took them to the next section. "The next two should go easier, all we need to do is line up the bolt holes and tighten them up. The last one might take some jockeying."

"So that's why ya made that jig ta drill the bolt holes," said Wham.

"Yep."

"They's a lot to this."

"Yeah, and when it works, it is beautiful."

"Ya ever have it not work?"

"Oh yeah...but that's the way you learn. You need to take chances to learn."

"Theys a rabbit in one a them rabbit holes."

Johanness nodded, "Oh yeah. Climb aboard."

Wham held onto the strap with one hand as the ramp section lifted clear. He waved at the folks on the deck with his cap.

General Store

Wham and Willis walked the damp road.

"We can get ice cream," said Willis, "my treat."

Wham looked at his daughter, "Oh really?"

"Yeah, business has been pretty good."

"So, how many t-shirts have you sold?"

"I won't know until we get there. Mr. Darwin sells the t-shirts all week when I'm in school. The dancing giant possum t-shirt is selling the best. We sell four of those to every one of the others."

"I don't think you showed me the dancing giant possum."

"It's a new design. I saw a picture of two people dancing in nightshirts and I kind of copied the movement."

"Wud you say you'uns company was?"

"Moxie. It means spunk."

"So Mr. Darwin just lets you use the air compressor and the sprayer?"

"Well no, I designed a business card for the General Store to pay for the airbrush and I reinvested my profits and bought the air compressor. Mr. Darwin supplies the t-shirts and a place to sell them."

"So you own the air compressor and a airbrush?"

"Yep."

The three mile walk went by quickly as Willis explained return on investment and expansion plans for the company. As they approached the General Store Wham stopped in his tracks. "Them, them whirligigs is my whirligigs."

"Uh yeah, don't they look great?"

"So Mr. Darwin's a been a buyin my whirligigs?"

Willis giggled, "I've been buying the whirligigs."

"Huh?"

"I had an ide'er that I could buy your whirligigs, paint them, and then sell them up here to the tourists during the summer."

"Sos you'uns makin money off'n my whirligigs?"

"Well, I haven't sold any yet. It's an investment. I'm investing in your whirligigs and I hope to make a profit this summer."

Wham moved closer to the man sawing wood. "Ya painted these?"

"Yep."

"They's beautiful. How much ya askin for em."

"Thirty two dollars."

"Oooowee."

"That's the test price. We should know by mid-summer if the price is too much or not enough."

"Where didja learn all this?"

"From Mr. Darwin and watching YouTube videos about running a business."

"Are ya going to do a website?"

"Mr. Darwin is working on three avenues of advertising; a Moxie website, an Ebay small business, and doing some YouTube videos." Willis looked at her watch. "We need to get set up. Time is money."

Mr. Darwin opened the large wood doors and greeted them. "Wham, come take a look at the shirts. And we're going to do flags and a new sign for the General Store. And here, take some of the business cards that Willis designed."

Wham stared at the business cards with a picture of the General Store. "It looks great." Wham's eyes focused on the other card. "What's this one?"

"That was Willis' ide'er. She gets ninety percent of the profit from that one. Those are fifty cents a piece."

"Ain't nobody gonna buy a card for fifty cents."

"We've sold eleven of them so far and we're not even close to the summer season. It's like...it's like a souvenir card. And if they buy a t-shirt they get a free Giant Possum Hotline card. If they don't buy a shirt they pay fifty cents a piece for them."

"So how much ya made so far on the cards?"

"Nothing so far, but we're over halfway to the point where we will show a profit. We ordered 500 business cards for ten dollars, so each card cost us five cents a piece."

"And ya sells em for fifty cents?"

"Yep, but you have to remember that we also give out the cards with the t-shirts."

"Ya ain't part Jewish, is ya?"

Mr. Darwin chuckled, then laughed, and then said, "Part Jewish," and then laughed some more. "Part Jewish. Oh my."

"I need me some business cards."

"Willis can design your card and then order them online."

"I'd love to design your business cards," said Willis, "and we can get some Giant Possum Hotline cards."

Mr. Darwin spoke up, "I want to take your family to dinner in Bump, anyplace you want to go."

"We like Waffle House real good. It's been forever since we ate out."

"And the video of you and Johanness putting together the bridge is remarkable, an engineering feat. And look at these shirts." Mr. Darwin took one from the rack and held it up.

Wham stood with his mouth open. The dancing giant possum on the front seemed alive. Mr. Darwin spun the shirt around. "Wow," said Wham. He would ask Willis later what it said.

"Come out here on the back porch."

"Did Willis paint this?"

"Yeah, she is really getting good with the airbrush."

"Do ya need it installed?"

"Yep, let me show you where I want you to put it."

"Do you have the posts?"

"No, you go ahead and order whatever you need. Can we do time and material?"

"No problem." Wham repeated in his head, *Time and material. Time and material.*

The air compressor started up and ran for a few minutes. "Dad, come out front and I'll make you a shirt."

Waffle House Code

Red and Wham headed for a booth.

"Let's set at the counter," said Mr. Darwin, "I have something I want to show you."

Red and Wham looked at each other. "The booth is more comfortable," said Red.

"I don't want you to be comfortable."

Red and Wham and Willis stood for a couple of seconds. "You'uns and Uncle Seizure id get along real good. He likes sufferin."

"I promise you that you will enjoy your meal."

Willis spun one of the seats and then jumped up. Wham and Red followed suit.

"Get whatever you want off the menu."

"Man, I'm hungry," said Wham.

"Me too."

"Me three," said Willis.

Mr. Darwin smiled. "Oh Lord, there goes all my profit for the week,"

Willis asked, "Is this a business meal, where you get to write it off your taxes?"

"It is indeed. You already know more about business than ninety percent of the people out there."

Red said, "I want to thank you so much for heping Willis with her business."

"I didn't do it. Willis did. She has moxie. She came to me with an idea and we ran with it. Most ideas die because no action gets taken."

"But something else is a happenin," said Red, "and I can't put my finger on it."

The waitress interrupted, asking for their orders.

As the waitress walked away Mr. Darwin said, "OK, now pay attention to the waitress." She walked off to one side of the grill and called out the order."

"See where she is standing, there's a different color tile on the floor. Wham, Red, and Willis leaned over the counter to see the tile. "Now, watch what the cook does, watch real close." The cook pulled down four plates and put different condiments on each plate in a different place. Then the cook started adding things to the grill."

Willis studied the cook's movements. "I got it. It's..."

"Don't tell," said Mr. Darwin. "We'll see if everyone can get it."

Another waitress came to the tile and yelled out her order. The cook pulled down some more plates and added some more condiments. Then the cook cracked two eggs against each other and then threw the eggshells over his shoulder into the waste basket.

"Whoa," said Wham, "I ain't never seed that before."

"You've probably never set at the counter before."

Another waitress came to the tile and yelled out two more orders.

Wham said, "Ain't a man alive that can member all them orders."

"He'll get all those orders right," said Mr. Darwin.

Willis squirmed on her seat, "Can I tell, can I tell?"

Mr. Darwin smiled. "No, not yet. Keep watching the cook."

Waffle batter was added to four of the waffle irons and then the cooked flipped the bacon and rolled the sausage. Then the eggs were added to the grill.

"Oh my goodness," said Red, "it's all in order."

Wham frowned, "I'd have the biggest jumbled up mess that ever was."

"Can I tell now?"

"OK."

"The cook doesn't have to remember all the orders. The strawberry jam and the different stuff he puts on the plates tells him what the order was. It's a cheat sheet. The cook can look at the plate and knows what the order was."

"What else?" said Mr. Darwin.

"And I'm not sure how he does it but he knows that the waffles take less time than the bacon, so the bacon goes first, then the waffles, and then the eggs...It's like listening to good music where each part flows into the next part."

There was silence for a few moments and then Mr. Darwin asked Wham, "Do you see it?"

"Yep, the cooks a cheater."

Mr. Darwin and Willis laughed. "You have a great sense of humor." Wham smiled.

Mr. Darwin asked Willis, "Do you see why this counts as a business meal?"

Two more eggshells hit the basket. "I'm looking at a business model, a super efficient way to cook meals, but it can be used for a lot of other things."

"Boomyow," said Mr. Darwin.

Willis corrected him, "I think it's 'booyow,' no m."

Late For Class

Steve stopped at the lunchroom table, "Pretty neat video of your dad."

"What are you talking about?" said Willie.

"The YouTube video of your dad building the bridge."

"That's not my dad. My dad has a hard time building bird houses."

Steve persisted, "I'm pretty sure it was your dad."

Willie opened up his laptop. "What channel was it?"

"I don't remember. I put in wood bridge building."

Willie clicked on YouTube and typed in wood bridge building. In a few seconds videos populated the screen.

Willie scrolled. Steve said, "Right there. That one."

Willie clicked on the Prefabricating a Wood Bridge video. 5028 views. Willie looked at the date. *That was posted last Saturday.*

Johanness narrated the overview of the project using a selfie stick. Twenty-two minutes later his dad waved at the camera from the boom supported section.

"Please subscribe to this channel if you enjoyed it and be with us next week as we build a hoop greenhouse using bamboo." Johanness smiled and Elliott woofed at the camera. Willie hit like and subscribe.

"What are you doing in here?" asked Mr. Shoemaker.

Willie looked up and glanced at the clock. "Oh no."

"Yeah, you're late."

"First time in eleven years."

"Tell the teacher you had a stomach problem."

"I can't do that. That'd be lying."

"I had a student tell me that aliens stole his homework."

Willie laughed and ran for his class.

Δ

After school in the library Willie replayed the video. 5,494 views. *Crazy.*

Willie scrolled down to the comments. The fourth comment caught his attention.

What is that on the hillside behind Wham's left shoulder when he's waving his cap?

There were 35 replies.

Willie backed up the video to 22:04 and rubbed his chin with the back of his hand. He clicked full view. It was too pixilated.

The Road Less....

"I dint want ta make him mad again."

Red said, "At least you could have asked him where he was goin."

"I woulda felt like a penny waitin on change, like I dint trust him."

"Money makes folks do bad things."

"He dint run off with the money," said Wham.

Willis said, "The last time he left he went to Bump ta empty the black tank." Red and Wham looked at Willis. "Sides, he has too much goin on here. He needs the valley for his videos and one last thing," Willis took a breath; "I think he's got eyes for Miss Chatty."

Wham and Red listened to the termites eating the walls.

Willis added, "He built the ramp for Miss Chatty for nothin and he tuned up her piano."

"And he learned me ta build ramps and bridges and bat houses," said Wham. "And we's gonna put up the sign at the General Store and build a greenhouse and we'uns gonna run the Yam race."

Δ

Johanness stopped the RV at the junction of the steel bridge. *No stop sign. Why isn't there a stop sign?* He listened to the quiet and the river. "What do you think, Elliott?"

Elliott cocked his head and wagged his tail.

"Colorado or Bump?"

A pickup approached from the road to Bump, slowed, then turned and stopped next to the RV. Johanness recognized Jeff and rolled down his window. "How's it going?"

"I's fine. Just wanted ta say the folks at the lumber yard was real impressed with the bridge construction. That was the most fun I ever had running the crane."

Johanness smiled, "It sure went together. Usually there's a glitch or two."

"The lumber yard got a couple of calls from folks that want ramps and we tried ta call ya."

"I don't have phone service in the valley."

"That's right, I plumb forgot. I heard tell they's a company that wants ta put a tower up that way."

"Oh really."

"Yeah, they been talkin bout that for the last two, three years. Where ya headed?"

"Uh, we'er headed to the Bump campground ta empty the black water tank."

"Well, stop in at the lumber yard. They wants ta talk to ya."

"I'll do that. Thanks Jeff."

Lots of Ones

"You'uns looked so sexy putting the ramp together," said Red. "I wanted ta run right out there and grab ya.

Wham tipped his cap and then sat down at the kitchen table. "Ya din't tell me Willis was a buyin them whirligigs.

"She never tolt me she was buyin em."

"Where'd she get twenty two dollars?"

"She had some babysittin money or...mebbe she used her t-shirt money." Red wondered if she should say more. "Uh, Willis has a bank account at Bump Bank."

Wham's eyes widened and he shook his head. "And Willie's gots a computer that he bought with his tutorin."

Red came around and hugged Wham from behind, "Our kids are doing real good and that's cuz they has the best dad in the whole world."

There was a Johanness knock on the screen door, rapity, rap, rap, leaving off the last two knocks.

"Come on in."

Red offered, "I got coffee."

"That'd be great."

Johanness sat down and held out a small orange toolbox to Wham. "We never really talked money but I got you cash."

Wham flipped the latches on the toolbox and stared at the money. In a blink, Red snatched the toolbox from the table. Johanness and Wham laughed.

"That's the shortest time I ever had money," said Wham.

"My wife was the same way."

"That looks like collection plate money."

Johanness answered, "Well...he does handle a lot of cash."

"Ya think he cheats the govement?"

"He," Johanness looked north, "is entitled to certain tax advantages, so the short answer is no. However, I would think that he pays almost nothing in taxes."

"I needs ta be a preacherman."

"We all do. There's sixteen hundred dollars in there. The materials were right at eighteen hundred dollars, the crane was a hundred dollars, and I split the labor."

"That's too much," said Wham. "You did way moren I did."

"We both worked hard, you deserve it. And," Johanness smiled, "without you the video wouldn't have been nearly as good. People like Wham Wooster. Over 6,000 people have looked at that video."

"Uh uh."

"Uh huh."

Wham smiled, "We'uns gonna make it."

"I toltcha." Red pulled on the back of Wham's chair, throwing him on the floor, and then jumped on him.

"I'll see myself out."

The Giant

The morning sun shown and the robins bounced about. Bees hummed in the clover.

Johanness left Elliott out of the RV and spotted a quiet Wham under the awning. "Beautiful day."

"We gots a problem."

"You want some coffee?"

"No."

Johanness stepped down and then sat in the other chair.

"We ain't fixed nothing. The property taxes took all that money."

"Well, you're going to keep the farm."

"I worked for that money and now its all gone ta the govement. The govement is keepin us poor. We ain't goin nowhere. We'un's still poor. We'uns ain't a gainin nothin. And then they's next year and the next year and all I's doin it making money for the govement. And it ain't never gonna stop, is it? I ain't never gonna have nothing."

Johanness sighed and scratched the back of his head. "How are the other farmers in the valley getting by?"

"I dunno. Some borrowed a bushel basket of money to keep a goin. Others go ta Bump or Landfill or Prune for jobs. Some move away and don't never come back. The kids all move away. None of em wants ta farm. Some sell their land ta rich folks. Some is growin subcities."

It took a couple of seconds for Johanness to process subcities. *Subsidies.* "They're growing corn for ethanol."

"Yep."

"And I thinks some buys crop insurance so when thins don't grow they gets paid," Wham took a breath, "and somes grows marijuana. And I think Ruckus Rump burned down his house for the insurance money. Everythins..."

Convoluted, but said, "Messed up."

"Real messed up. Seems like everbody's getting a paycheck cept me."

"Things aren't like they used to be."

"Seems like everbody's cheatin ta get ahead."

"You can't help what other people do. You can't control what the government does. You can only control you. Forget other people, forget the government. There is only one person standing in your way and that's you. Wham Wooster is standing in your way. Move on. Quit blaming others. Work on you. Be the best you can be. It's you. Wham Wooster is the problem. Nobody else."

Johanness got up and went into the RV.

In a few seconds "Eye of the Tiger" came from the RV. Johanness turned up the volume. He came out and stood in front of Wham.

"You can choose to die, be controlled by others, and live the life that others want you to live, have the life sucked out of you, work for a little bit of meaningless money and make other people rich, never enriching yourself, or you can wake up your giant.

"You deserve more. Why don't you have more?

"It's because you haven't gotten angry.

"You don't know how to focus and you don't know how to think. You're lazy and weak. Americans are weak. We don't know what it is to be strong. Not just physically strong but mentally strong, the strength to overcome hardships. Americans are whiners. Our education system has failed us. We don't know how to think. Thinking is hard work. Most people would rather turn on the TV and watch Gilligans Island.

"You need to revolt. There's a revolution inside of you. You need to lash out and take control.

"There's a giant inside Wham Wooster and he wants out of his dungeon. He's there. You need to let him out.

"You have a choice. You can wake up tomorrow and be the same old Wham Wooster or you can choose to fight.

"You earned sixteen hundred dollars in four days. That's four hundred dollars a day. You can do that again and again. You have the knowledge and the wherewithal. Wham knows how to build ramps and bridges. You can read a tape and use a water level. Get up off your fucking ass and get to work."

Wham jumped out of the chair, "Get the hell out of my way!" He stomped over to the saw horses, grabbed the saw and started sawing a slab.

"Put two slabs together, face to face, and saw two at a time. And you don't need to be drawing a line to make that first cut. Just cut it. Think dammit!"

Johanness loaded up the sawhorses with doubled up slabs. "Your problem is you don't think. Most people don't think. They don't ask themselves how can I do this better and faster. How can I get stronger? How can I improve? Your mind is lazy." Johanness screamed, "Think, dammit!"

Wham sawed faster.

"Give me that fucking saw."

Wham threw the saw on the ground.

"I told you to think. I didn't tell you to saw faster."

The Rocky theme song came from the RV.

"Are you mad? Real mad."

Whams nostrils flared, "Yeah."

Johanness shoved Wham, "You're not mad." Johanness shoved Wham again.

Wham's teeth clenched and the tendons in his neck tightened. "I's gonna fuck you up."

"No, you're not. You don't have what it takes. You can't think." Johanness shoved him again.

"What the hell ya talkin bout?"

"You're not thinking. You're set up to box."

"I knows how ta fight."

Johanness screamed, "Think! Think Wham Wooster!! Wake up the giant. Throw that punch."

Wham bobbed and weaved out in front of Johanness. "What giant?"

"Your giant." Johanness leaped forward and tackled Wham. The two rolled in the grass. Elliott barked and tried to bite Wham's overalls. Johanness broke free and spun to his feet. Wham was upside down on the hill and he wrestled himself upright.

Johanness short breathed, "You're not thinking."

Between gasps Wham said, "I's tired a hearin it."

"The man highest on the hill has gravity to help him. I have the advantage."

"Ya has ta sleep sometime and then I'll kill ya."

"So you're not going to fight fair, you're going to cheat."

"I'll do what I hafta do."

"I thought you hated cheaters."

Wham lowered his fists slightly.

"You can win; you just need to wake up the giant."

"I ain't gots no giant."

"We all have a giant."

"I ain'ts got no giant."

"I had to get really, really, really, really angry before I woke up my giant. So mad I that I wanted to kill everyone and everything. I broke my hand slamming it into a brick wall."

Wham looked at Johanness, "It don't make no sense."

"The giant is your secret weapon. It's inside you, it's always inside you."

"It ain't good for folks ta get mad."

"It's great to get mad. It's fantastic to get mad. Anger is way underrated. It wakes up your giant."

"What's the giant do?"

"It makes you think, it makes you focus, it makes you motivated to use every breath to move forward."

"Can ya tell Elliott ta let go a my pant leg?"

"Come here Elliott." Elliott let go and then jumped up on Johanness to get petted. "Didn't you tell me you won the Yam race twice, is that right?"

"Yep, my legs were strong back then."

"And you didn't cheat to do it."

"I hates cheaters."

"Did you train hard to win those races?"

"Nah, nobody trained back then. We din't have time ta train. Ya just went out and ran."

"So you won because you were naturally fast?"

"Yeah, guess so."

"What if you wanted to win that race today?"

"Ain't no way. Runners come from everwhere ta run the Yam race."

"What if you wanted to win your age category?"

Wham looked off to a place long ago, a place with a blue ribbon, and a hint of joy came to his face.

"So what are you going to do to win?"

"I's gonna train hard."

"No, you're not."

"I am."

"No you're not. You're going to train smart. You're going to optimize your time and effort. You're going to keep a chart. We're going to train for that race. We're going to build a training program and we're going to win."

"When we'uns gonna start?"

"Right now. We're going to start with LSD and then as we get close to race day we'll do HIIT."

"I ain't a doin drugs."

"I'm not either. LSD is long, slow, distance training and HIIT is high intensity interval training or sprints or hill training."

"You've done this before."

"Yeah."

"Damn, you'uns done a bunch a stuff."

"Yeah, and some of it I'm not proud of."

"So, we's gonna run the race?"

"Yeah and we're going to win."

"I's hungry, lets eat some breakfast."

"Sounds good."

"What's time and material all bout?"

"Uh, contractors do time and material when they figure what to charge clients."

"Mr. Darwin needs a sign put up at the General Store and wants ta do time and material."

"OK, so you keep track of the materials and how much they cost and how many hours the job took you and then you add them together and add like 10%."

"Couldja hep me with the figgerin?"

"Sure. How big's the sign?"

"Purty big, Willis did the paintin. Looks real good."

"You're a lucky man, Wham Wooster."

"Yep."

"After breakfast we'll walk up to the General Store and dig the holes for the posts and then jog back. And then we'll climb the hill and you can order the posts and whatever else we need."

"So we really are startin taday."

"Yep, and I'll show you how to make up a training chart on the computer."

"How much ya gonna charge me for the trainin chart?"

"I'm going throw you on the ground and beat you into next week if you don't quit that shit." Johanness sighed, "I want a giant possum t-shirt."

"It's a deal."

The two men walked towards the RV.

"Ya member the other day when we raced ta the water tank."

"And I won."

"Yeah, well mebbe we both could win. You'uns id be in the really old man catergory and I'd be in the sorta old catergory."

"How old are you Wham?"

"51."

"You look a hell of a lot older than that."

"I's gonna have Red put a knot on ya head."

"Maybe she'd like to run the race."

"She might. Then they'd be two a us beat ya."

"Well, I'll be waiting at the finish line for you two."

A tiny breeze carried the sound from the woods and across the river. Wham closed his eyes and listened, "Ya hear em?"

"Just barely."

"I love hearin the turkeys talk."

"Me too."

Unremorse

"That's a giant possum track maker," said Jeb.

Sludge looked hard at the carved wood with the straps, his jaw and forehead were tight. "You'uns made up a big lie."

"I didn't do nothin wrong. All I did was put footprints out there."

"Ya made people think they was a giant possum."

"Mebbe." Jeb smiled.

Sludge walked back across Church Ridge Road and sat down in his River Chair. Soon Jeb sat down in the other chair. Happy sat down between the men.

Sludge said, "Pretty good track maker."

"Yep."

"We needs ta go hep build the liberry."

"We'd just get in the way."

"You'uns probly right. Don't want ta slow up progress."

"Miss Chatty's gonna be a good liberrian."

"Yep."

"I can'ts wait ta read a book."

"Yep, and someday...I's gonna write a book bout the giant possum."

"I still ain't got it figgered out what Wham and Johanness and Uncle Seizure and some a these here other folks say they saw."

"And what screamed at me and Happy in the bog? said Sludge. "And what makes that scrapin noise in the bog? I say they's somethin out there."

"Mebbe, mebbe not."

"What do you think Happy?"

Happy stood on his hind legs and growled.

The Bench

"I's gots a question," said Wham

Both Red and Willis finished chewing and swallowed, "Uh, yeah?" said Red.

"Some folks believe in the giant possum and some folks don't. I don't blame folks for not believin. But, irregardless, they's a bunch of folks likes the giant possum t-shirts and the giant possum whirligigs and the giant possum Hotline cards. And we's doin good cuz a him."

"Uh, yeah, it's kinda good he's around."

"And I know he probly ate my boots and bent down the fence and I should hate him...but I don't. And he coulda chewed my face off but he dint. And he ain't hurt nobody or ate nobody's chickens or cows. Mebbe deep down he or she's good inside."

Willis's eyes swiveled over to her mom. Red asked, "Where ya goin with this?"

"Well, I got this extra bench, see, and it ain't a doin nothing and I was a thinkin I'd put it down there by the bog. I don't know if'n he'd sit on it but, well, just ta kinda say thank you and mebbe he'd knowd we cared about him."

"Wham Wooster, you gots ta be the best, craziest man in the valley. Willis and I will help you carry the bench down there after dinner."

"And I've got to do a t-shirt with the giant possum sitting on the bench," said Willis.

"Oh, I almost forgot, I gave him some sunglasses with "O"s on em a few weeks ago and the next day they was gone."

Willis tittered, "You gave the giant possum a pair of Oakley sunglasses?"

"Yeah, I guess."

"So the giant possum is wearing a hundred and fifty dollar pair of sunglasses."

"Well, I dint know what they was. Sludge found em in the river last fall and asked me to put em on a limb out by the bog for the giant possum."

"So our giant possum is stylin and profiling."

Red added, "And now we're building and delivering giant possum benches."

Willis said, "It just keeps getting better and better."

"I wants ta write him a short letter and put it on the bench, in case he can read."

Willis put her hand out in the middle of the table, Red smiled and put her hand on top and then Wham put his on top. "Go Possum!!" and flung her hand in the air.

Δ

Evening was falling away beyond the hills when the three crossed the dirt road with the bench.

"How far we gonna carry it?"

"I want it far enough away from the road ta where the possum ill feel safe and nobody's gonna shoot at him. We'll put it just on the other side a that little hill."

When the three put the bench down Wham angled it into place. "That a way he can see the sunrise." Wham reached in his new overalls pocket, laid his letter on the bench, and put a rock on top of it.

Harboring and A Bettin

The paint was still tacky on the new sign, "Rump River Library and Community Farm Education Center." Cars and trucks were scattered up and down the road.

Jeb and Sludge, wearing their new giant possum t-shirts, ate raisin pie off paper plates.

"Lots a folks here."

"That ain't good. I don't like it."

"They ain't gonna steal are fish."

"Ya don't know that. One stick a dynamite and blewee, they's all gone."

"These folks ain't dynamite folks."

"Man, that's good pie."

"Yep."

"Them porta potties ain't half bad," said Jeb.

"Willie said they's gonna be two bathrooms in the liberry."

"Ooowee, that's a bunch a plumbin. They's gonna be pipes runnin ever which way."

"Yep, plumbers gots ta be right smart ta know what goes where."

"Wonder what id happen if'n ya flushed both a them toilets at the same time."

"We'll hafta try er out when the liberry gets open."

Jeb and Sludge watched intently as Rascal Rump approached Wham.

"We'uns takin bets that this thin won't get off the ground."

Wham took a deep breath, "Well, we'll see won't we?"

"And they's talk you'uns gonna run the Yam race."

Wham smiled, "Yep."

Rascal held out his hand, "It'll be good ta see ya there."

Wham shook his hand, "Just like old times."

"Ya place looks real nice. Ya done good."

"In a couple a years we's gonna have blueberries for folks ta pick."

"How much is a bat box?"

"Fifteen for the box and forty dollars if'n I install it."

"Is that the friends and family discount?"

"Friends?"

"Just cuz I ain't talked ta ya in thirty years don't mean we ain't friends."

Wham considered his "friend." "Today we got a liberry raisin special. You get a bat house with installation, a giant possum t-shirt, and a giant possum hotline card for fifty bucks. And, and," he repeated, "a free mater plant. These is Japanese maters. Voted best eatin maters two years in a row."

Rascal pulled his wallet from his overalls.

"Go on over to the t-shirt table and Willis ill help ya. And we'uns doing a raffle for a giant possum whirligig."

Wham motioned for Red, "Find Willie. We needs ta roll up the sides on the greenhouse. It's gettin warm."

Willie, Red, and Wham set to the task of rolling up the plastic and tying it into place. Wham stood for a moment looking at the rolled up plastic.

"What are you thinking?" asked Willie.

"If'n we had boat winches on both ends we could wincher up and wincher down."

"I like it. I'll check on Amazon and see what would work. Down the road we can put electric winches on a thermostat and they could roll up the plastic when it got too hot."

"There ya go again, workin me out of a job."

"The winches were your ide'er."

"Tell ya what. You figger out the electric winch thermostat thin and we'll make it happen."

Willie stood flatfooted, "I'll do some research and see what I can find online."

"You'uns gonna make a hell of a astrophysercist."

"Thanks." Willie's eyes misted, it was the first time he hadn't called him an astrologist.

"This is as big as the Apple Festival. I don't know half these folks."

"Social media is powerful stuff."

"Back in the day, we had smoke signals."

A young lady tapped Willie on the shoulder. "Is this your dad?"

"Yep."

"I thought I recognized him from the greenhouse building video."

Willie said, "This is Stephanie Hoffmeister."

"Ooowee, ya done good. I'm Wham Wooster." They shook hands. "Now make sure ya get ya free mater plant."

Stephanie smiled, "I can see where Willie gets his good looks."

Wham did a bobble head thing and Stephanie and Willie laughed.

Miss Chatty appeared next to Wham with her walker, "Willie, is this the young lady you've been pining after?"

Willie flushed red, "Uh, yes. This is Stephanie Hoffmeister."

"You two look very nice together. Hoffmeister is German, is that correct?"

"Yes, it is."

"The Germans are a very smart people, they made the first atomic bomb."

Willie said, "Uh, we've got to, uh to, go get our giant possum t-shirts."

Stephanie held back a laugh, "We can get giant possum shirts later."

"I wish Johanness was here to see this," said Miss Chatty.

Wham smiled, "He is here."

Miss Chatty paused, "You're right."

"And one day hill come back from Colorado and we's gonna run the Yam race."

Willie said, "He might not come back. If they catch him with that stolen RV he might end up in the big house."

"What?"

"When he first parked the RV it had a Florida license plate and when he left it had a South Carolina license plate."

"So, he went and got a new license plate. Ya sposed ta do that if'n you'uns a local."

"Did he ever mention getting a new license for the RV?"

Wham and Miss Chatty looked at each other. Wham's left eyebrow raised up and his eyes darted from side to side. Miss Chatty cackle laughed. "You've been harboring a fugitive. They're going to lock you up, Wham Wooster."

"It'll give me time ta write some country songs."

They laughed. Red and Willis came over, "What's so funny?"

"Wham's going to jail."

"It's about time," said Red. "Wud he do now?"

"Johanness ain't Johanness. He stole that RV and you've been harboring a fugitive."

Red cocked her head sideways. "I liked him...but then again I always did like the bad boys." She hugged Wham.

"Me too," said Miss Chatty.

"Me too," said Stephanie.

"Me too," said Willis.

"Willis, ya ain't likin no boys, period. Ya hear me."

"Gratty has a nose ring and an eyebrow ring and tattoos."

Wham shuddered visibly. Red said, "Don't do that Willis, he'll pass out."

Wham shook again trying to dislodge the image. "I's gonna have to shoot Gratty."

"You don't have a gun."

"I'll borrow one."

Willis hugged her dad, "You're the best."

Mr. Darwin pushed into the group. "I don't mean to interrupt but we're almost out of t-shirts. Can we plug the air compressor into the temporary box?"

"Sure."

Willis said, "You're telling me that we sold over a hundred t-shirts?"

"Right at a hundred."

Willis did a fist pump, "Cha Ching, Cha Ching!!" Willis ran through the crowd to plug in the compressor.

"So are we still on for Waffle House tonight?" asked Mr. Darwin.

"We'll be ready," said Red.

"What time?" asked Sludge.

Mr. Darwin said, "Uh, uh, six o'clock. I need to get back to the table. See you this evening."

Jeb pointed to the sky, "He's back."

The group watched the one legged eagle soar on the updrafts until he was lost beyond the hills.

"I wonder who Johanness was," said Wham. "Somethin tells me he'll be back for the Yam race."

"And to see the new library," said Miss Chatty.

"And to see you Miss Chatty," said Red.

"We can watch his new videos on YouTube ta see what he's up to," said Wham, "and if'n we don't see any more Traveling with Elliott videos we'll know he's in the hoosegow."

"Hoosegow," said Uncle Seizure, "that's a good word."

"It's in a Louis L'amour book I read a while back," bragged Wham.

"I don't like Louis L'amour. Ain't no way the hero always gets the pretty girl."

"You got the pretty girl," said Aunt Seizure.

"Yes, I did," said Uncle Seizure.

Jeff came over, "We'uns ready ta go. This is excitin. I ain't never done a whole roof that's all put tagether before."

Willie pulled the small camera from his pocket.

"Where'd ya get that?"

"I got it from Sludge. He found it in the river and I cleaned it up."

"Didja..."

Willie cut him off, "Yes, I'm going to pick more blackberries."

"If'n ya wait till next year we might have some blueberries."

Willie clicked the camera and began, "Hey, tubers this is Willie Wooster and this will be my first YouTube video. Today, we are going to put the roof on the new library here in the Rump River Valley, home of the giant possum. And this is my dad, Wham, who donated the property for the library and the farm education center. And this is the lady that made the library a reality, Miss Chatty, a woman of great strength and kindness and she will have the honor of being our first librarian."

Willie picked up a brick and held it for the camera. "To raise money for the library we are selling these bricks with your names etched into the bricks. These will be used for the walkway to the library. The walkway is more than a walkway. It is a walkway to the future for all of us, a place where dreams come alive. A ten dollar donation will put your names on the bricks that will build the path to tomorrow. Thank You." Willie clicked off.

"Ya gots the ten bucks from when Johanness video'd us dumpster diving?"

"Yep." Jeb pulled out his dogeared ten dollar bill. "Ya gots the ten bucks from the bike wheels for the roll around workbench?"

"Yep." Sludge pulled out his neatly folded ten dollar bill. "Willie, sign us up for two bricks."

Aunt Seizure nudged Uncle Seizure, "Sign us up for a brick." Aunt Seizure gave him a dirty look. "Uh, sign us up for two bricks."

Δ

Jeff gunned the diesel engine, the straps tightened up. The roof quivered but stayed in place. Jeff gave the engine more. Slowly, the back end of the crane began to lift. Jeff backed off and the back outrigger pads set down.

Wham ran to the cab.

"It's too heavy. It ain't gonna do it," said Jeff.

Wham closed his eyes and searched for another way. *Think dammit.* "What if'n we add more weight to the back end."

"Might work. I could feel we was close."

Willie commented over Wham's shoulder. "If you move closer to the building you'd get more leverage."

"That might help." Jeff retracted the outriggers. Willie and Wham motioned for the crane to move closer. Jeff inched the crane within six inches of the corner of the building and then put the outriggers back down.

"Lemme giver another try." Wham and Willie backed away. The straps tightened and the roof shuddered and one corner lifted. The back end of the crane rose again and Jeff shut it down. *Damn, we're close.*

Wham turned to the crowd and could see the look of resignation in their eyes. Wham's nostrils flared and his eyes turned to steel. "We's gonna do this!" he screamed. "We need more weight on the back end. Pastor Momar git up there. Jeb, Sludge, Mr. Darwin, let's go.

Rascal Rump yelled, "Let's giter done."

The men climbed on the back end of the crane.

"We need just a little lift ta get it movin," said Jeff.

Wham looked at the crowd, "We need hep liftin ta git it a goin."

Men gathered around the edge of the roof. Wham yelled, "Whatever ya do, don't get underneath it."

A woman's scream came from the crowd. Miss Chatty held onto her walker with one hand and waved her Bible at the sky, "Give me my library. You owe me, dammit."

Wham spun his index finger in an upwards circle. The diesel RPM's climbed, the straps tightened up, the men braced themselves and heaved. The roof groaned and then gently lifted from the ground.

Raisin Pie

1 deep-dish piecrust

Filling:
1 medium box raisins (1 ½ c)
¼ cup brown sugar
juice from 1 lemon
½ cup sugar
¼ t salt
3 T cornstarch
2 cups milk
¾ t vanilla
3 eggs, beaten

Meringue:
3 egg whites
1/4 c sugar

Bake piecrust until light brown. Simmer raisins in brown sugar and lemon juice.

In a large saucepan, combine sugar, salt and cornstarch. Stir in milk and vanilla until smooth. Cook and stir over medium-high heat until thickened and bubbly. Reduce heat to low; cook and stir for 2 minutes longer. Remove from the heat. Stir a small amount of hot filling into eggs; return all to the pan, stirring constantly. Bring to a gentle boil; cook and stir for 2 minutes. Remove from the heat; gently stir in raisins. Pour hot filling into crust.

For meringue, in a small bowl, beat egg whites on medium speed until soft peaks form. Gradually beat in sugar, 1 tablespoon at a time, on high until stiff peaks form. Spread over hot filling, sealing edges to crust. Bake at 350° for 10-15 minutes or until golden brown. Cool on a wire rack for 1 hour; refrigerate for 1-2 hours before serving

Other Books

Gold Beneath the Waves: Treasure Hunting the Surf and Sand   Available on Amazon   4.7 Star Rating
https://www.amazon.com/Gold-Beneath-Waves-Treasure-Hunting/dp/0984889108/ref=sr_1_1?ie=UTF8&qid=1529335901&sr=8-1&keywords=gold+beneath+the+waves&dpID=51P-I-fjHXL&preST=_SY344_BO1,204,203,200_QL70_&dpSrc=srch

Soon to be Published

Jeb and Sludge   Part of the Rump River series

Johanness Returns   Part of the Rump River series

Waves of Gold...